"ZOE, THERE'S [barcode] **BETWEEN US AND AS MUCH AS WE TRY TO FIGHT IT, IT'S GROWING HOTTER AND HOTTER."**

"We're not on some romantic getaway, we're supposed to be finding closure for a family. Why don't you keep focused on what's important? Maybe I should've taken this trip alone."

"Because you can't control yourself? I know what's at stake here, Zoe. I'm not going to do anything to put you in danger."

"Put me in danger?"

"You know what I mean," he said, then quickly looked away from her. "Zoe, trust and believe when the time is right, I'm going to make love to you and you won't forget how I made you feel."

Also by Cheris Hodges

Just Can't Get Enough
Let's Get It On
More Than He Can Handle
Betting on Love
No Other Lover Will Do
His Sexy Bad Habit
Too Hot for TV
Recipe for Desire
Forces of Nature
Love after War
Rumor Has It
I Heard a Rumor

Published by Kensington Publishing Corp.

Deadly Rumors

CHERIS HODGES

Kensington Publishing Corp.
www.kensingtonbooks.com

DAFINA BOOKS are published by

Kensington Publishing Corp.
119 West 40th Street
New York, NY 10018

All Kensington Titles, Imprints, and Distributed Lines are available at special quantity discounts for bulk purchases for sales promotions, premiums, fund-raising, and educational or institutional use. Special book excerpts or customized printings can also be created to fit specific needs. For details, write or phone the office of the Kensington special sales manager: Kensington Publishing Corp., 119 West 40th Street, New York, NY 10018, attn: Special Sales Department, Phone: 1-800-221-2647.

Dafina and the Dafina logo Reg. U.S. Pat. & TM Off.

ISBN-13: 978-1-4967-0928-8
ISBN-10: 1-4967-0928-4
First Kensington Mass Market Edition: November 2017

eISBN-13: 978-1-4967-0929-5
eISBN-10: 1-4967-0929-5
First Kensington Electronic Edition: November 2017

10 9 8 7 6 5 4 3 2 1

Printed in the United States of America

Chapter 1

Zoe Harrington was a marked woman and she didn't have a clue. FBI Agent Carver Banks watched Zoe as she watched a man who, he assumed, was a cheating husband. Over the last two months, Zoe's cases had been simple: catch the cheat, prove a parent was neglectful, or that someone violated a protective order. Carver liked it that way. She was safe. At least for now.

After the alert he'd gotten on Friday, he knew Zoe was anything but safe. The only thing missing was a red target on her back. There was something else he knew, as well: If Zoe knew she was under surveillance, there would be hell to pay.

Guns would be pulled, bad words exchanged, and there's a good chance that he'd be nursing a gunshot wound. Carver chuckled, thinking about Zoe pulling a gun on him and having the nerve to shoot him.

It was a risk he'd have to take. Until the threat against her was neutralized, he had to protect her. And Zoe Harrington wasn't the kind of woman who needed protection—at least not in her mind—and she certainly wouldn't accept his help. She thought he was her enemy, when that was the last thing he was.

Carver smirked to himself. The feisty Zoe had a smart mouth, but she was a hell of a kisser. Too bad she assumed the kisses and passion they'd shared two years earlier hadn't been real.

It had been very real to him. Unforgettable. Carver couldn't get the taste of Zoe out of his system. Not even when he had to arrest her on some trumped-up charges because of her ex-sister-in-law, Natalie.

The moment he snapped those handcuffs on her had probably solidified her hate for him. But he'd been doing his job, setting a trap for Natalie and the sex traffickers she'd been linked to. And as he'd tried to explain this to Zoe, she wasn't trying to hear anything he had to say.

Carver wanted more than Zoe even knew—wanted her lips, hips, and thighs pressed again him. But she wouldn't look at him through eyes that weren't clouded with anger. And she had beautiful eyes, light brown with gold specks dancing in them.

He understood why Zoe was still mad, but something had to change, and the sooner the better.

Zoe had noticed the black sedan following her about three blocks ago. "Time for some action," she exclaimed as she made a quick U-turn and blew past the car that had been following her. She couldn't get a look at the driver because of the dark tint on the windows, but she got a good look at the license plate. She made a mental note to run it through the DMV database when she made it to the office.

This was the only thing she missed about police work. Driving like a maniac, weaving in and out of traffic without worrying about traffic violations. What she didn't miss was the bullshit politics in the department and the stop-and-frisk edicts from superior officers that only seemed to target blacks and Hispanics. What she really didn't miss was the thin blue line of silence that kept bad officers on the job and good ones silent. She'd made it her business in the first year of opening her firm to take all cases that were somehow related to the NYPD. She especially liked it when she worked a case that involved one of those upstanding captains who'd been caught with his pants down. She'd had three of those in the early days of her firm. Zoe was proud that she'd brought down two of the most arrogant captains in the NYPD because of their love of hookers. Seeing their faces splashed across the newspapers after their arrest made her feel as if she'd accomplished something great.

Then, a few years ago, she'd taken the case of a family who wanted to prove police brutality against her old partner. Because of her work, seven officers were fired and one was indicted. Of course, there was no conviction. Zoe knew that case had made her a lot of enemies in the NYPD.

Was that why she was being followed? Zoe thought about the cases she'd worked lately. Nothing stood out in her mind as threatening. And it wasn't Natalie, because that trick was locked up. *Maybe I'm being paranoid*, she thought as she headed toward her office. Zoe kept an eye out for the car that had been following her. Satisfied that she'd shaken her tail, Zoe took the back road to her office. On the quiet two-lane road, if someone was following she would know immediately. Though no one was behind her when she arrived at her office, Zoe was surprised to see *him* standing on her doorstep.

For a split second, she thought about ramming her car into him. But killing an FBI agent would be stupid, and the few hours she'd spent in lockup proved jail was not a place she could ever reside. Sighing, she slowly exited the car and crossed over to Carver Banks. Why did that man have to be so sinfully gorgeous? Even in a pair of nondescript black slacks and white button-up shirt, he made her mouth water. She remembered the feel of that muscular body against hers, the taste of his tongue in her mouth as he kissed her senseless. Too bad it had all been a lie.

"You better have a warrant," she snapped.

"Hello to you, too, Zoe," he said with a smile.

Why did her knees go weak when she looked into his whiskey-brown eyes? She looked away. "Why are you here, Agent?"

"Because I need you."

Zoe's breath caught in her chest. "What?"

"Can we go inside and talk?" He nodded toward the door and smiled.

"Why were you following me?" She folded her arms across her chest. "I've had my fill of dealing with you and the FBI."

"Zoe, I'll tell you everything, but it would be a lot better if we talked inside."

She rolled her eyes and then unlocked her office door. "I don't have all night to talk to you. I just got finished working a case, and there's paperwork that I'd like to get taken care of before I go home and get some rest. Can we make it fast?" She pushed the door open and flipped the overhead lights on. Carver gave her a slow once-over, seemingly drinking in her black leather leggings, black tank top and knee-high boots. Catching his glance, she raised her right eyebrow.

"What? Did you lose something over here, or do you make a habit of ogling people who you claim to need?"

"Nothing, you just look like—"

"I was doing surveillance? Like I said, I don't have all night to banter with you."

"I'm investigating a cold case, and though I'd like to say that the Bureau is making it a priority, they aren't. We have some staffing issues in our office, so my superior gave me the green light to get some help. You were the first person I thought of."

Zoe eyed him quizzically. "Let me get this straight. You expect me to work with you?"

"Of course, you will be paid for your work and—"

"I don't need your money, and working with you isn't good for my business." Zoe rolled her eyes and stroked her hair. Did he think she was going to be stuck in close quarters with him or take orders from him? Please! This man needed to get out of her office now. Just the scent of his masculinity was driving her crazy.

"Zoe, you're one of the best investigators that I know, despite the fact that you spend a lot of time working divorce cases these days."

"Are you judging me?" Zoe crossed over to her desk

and sat down so that her knees would stop quaking. His gaze seemed to penetrate her soul. And as much as she didn't want to think about it, her mind flashed back to the night they'd made love.

"Never that, although you've spent a lot of time judging me for doing my job."

"That's not why I judge you," she said as she leaned back in her seat. "Why me, though? If I recall, the last time we saw each other, you wanted me in jail."

"I wanted to solve a case and your arrest was—"

"The most embarrassing thing to ever happen to me." Zoe slammed her hand on her desk. "And I don't care what you said at that press conference, there are people who still think I had something to do with Natalie's crimes."

"There's a name for those people," he said with a wink. "And that's called *stupid.*" He walked over to her desk and leaned in to her. "So, when you go out and do your thing, you always dress like Catwoman?"

Zoe sucked her teeth and ignored his comment and the way he eyed her breasts. "And why do you think I would take this case? The FBI has the strength of the government behind them. What can I add?"

"A fresh set of eyes, a nice smile that disarms people, and you're good at what you do, Zoe. Everything you do."

Her thighs trembled at the timbre of his voice. Had that night meant more to him than she gave him credit for? No. It was just him using her to solve a case. She would never forgive him for playing her like that.

He took a step closer to her. "If you dress like this, I'm sure that we'll get this case solved quickly."

"Get off it," she snapped as she rose to her feet and went around her desk to stand in front of him. "I haven't even said I'd take the case."

"I think you should," he said.

"Really couldn't care less what you think," she said with a sarcastic wink.

"You know what I really think," he said.

Zoe glared at him. "What did I just say?"

Carver shrugged. "You really look like you should kiss me." Carver stroked her cheek as he smiled at her.

She pushed back against his chest, her heart beating like a steel drum. "Not again, Agent. If I take this case, it is strictly business. Then again, that kiss was all business for you anyway." Zoe rolled her eyes and stepped back from him.

"Are you going to take the case?"

"Haven't decided yet."

"Good." In a swift motion, Carver pulled her into his arms and captured her lips in a smoldering kiss. Zoe wanted to fight the pleasure that flowed through her body. She wanted to pretend his kiss didn't arouse all sorts of wicked desire. Then she felt his hands roam the small of her back and she melted against him. He tasted magical and his heat made her wet. Her body's traitorous reaction to his kiss made her angry. Pulling away, Zoe slapped him.

"What was that for?" he asked, stroking his stinging jaw.

"Keep your lips and hands to yourself!"

"Why, you like it too much?"

"You think too highly of yourself. I didn't like it at all."

Carver pursed his lips as if he wanted to say something, but thought it was better to let Zoe's lie hang in the air. She looked away from him and crossed over to her desk. They needed something between them other than temptation.

"Are you sure you and the FBI can afford me? There will be no discounts," she said, then licked her lips. Damn it. Why could she still taste him and why did she like it?

"What?"

"If I take the case, my rate is one fifty an hour plus expenses. If I have to leave New York, I fly first class."

"That's fine," he said. "My agent in charge gave me a generous budget to work with and—"

"And I work alone. When you hire me, you give me control. I don't want you telling me how I should do my job or hear about any tips that you may have to make my job easier. I'm boss here."

"Hold on. This is an official FBI investigation and I can't just give you carte blanche to run the investigation without me," Carver said.

Zoe furrowed her eyebrows. "What's this case all about, and if it's so important, why is the FBI trying to outsource the work?"

Carver took a deep breath. "It's a missing persons case, and as much as I hate to say it, the media has spurred us to look into the case of Jessica Dolan."

"Who is Jessica Dolan?"

Carver stroked his forehead and frowned. "She was a college student who went missing about three years ago. It was around the same time that a few college-age women were killed by the Bayou Serial Killer."

"I remember that case, but I thought the killer was caught?"

Carver nodded. "He was, but we need closure for this family. The Dolans think that we dropped the ball on finding Jessica because she's African American."

Zoe rolled her eyes. "I don't doubt that. Blond hair and blue eyes sells newspapers and mobilizes search parties. Missing black women barely get a nod in the media or with law enforcement. What's so special about the Dolans?"

Carver stroked his forehead. "They're close friends of the former president," he said. "That's one of the reasons why the FBI has reopened the case and why it's important to find her or her remains."

"Interesting, the only way you can get justice is to be connected? What about all of the other missing black women out there who don't—"

"Look, I wish I could find everyone who went missing, but despite what you and the public think, we don't have an endless supply of resources. We need to get started sooner rather than later. I'll see you in the morning," he said. But Carver made no effort to move, and Zoe focused on his mouth as he stood there.

No kiss this time? she thought. *Stop it! You said this is just business and you need to keep your word.*

Carver stared at Zoe's lips, longing to kiss her again. If he didn't get his hormones under control, he was going to get everybody killed.

"You can go now," Zoe said after a tense silence. She knew that after seeing him, she wasn't going to get any work done for the rest of the night. His masculine scent filled her office and she was sure it would linger and mess with her mind.

"Aren't you leaving as well?"

"I don't need an escort," she replied.

"Humor me."

Zoe rolled her eyes and allowed him to walk her outside. "Carver, I hope you know nothing has changed between us."

"I'm aware of that."

"This is strictly business."

"Zoe, you realize I was doing my job."

She rolled her eyes again. "Sure you were."

He closed the space between them. "You were, as well, so you can stop blaming me for everything."

"Excuse me?"

"You played the same covert game, so don't act as if you didn't do anything."

"I was just following the leader. Can we go now?" Carver nodded and Zoe gripped her car door handle as she watched him cross the parking lot.

Lord, that walk, she thought. Strong like a lion. Graceful like a black panther. Always on guard. She shivered inside, thinking of his hips with her legs wrapped around them. *Stop it!*

"Waiting for someone?" he called out when he noticed she hadn't gotten into her car.

"No, just waiting for you to leave."

"Start your car and I will."

Zoe shook her head. "You think it's going to explode? No one is out to kill me, Carver."

If only you knew, he thought. "You ever wonder if some of those cheating husbands might want revenge?"

"Paranoid much?" she asked as she clicked the automatic start button on her key chain. "See, no explosion. And if those husbands didn't want to get caught, then they would've kept it zipped and tucked away."

"Easier said than done," he shot back.

"Spoken like a no-good man," she said, then opened her driver's side door.

"Good night, Zoe."

She pressed the remote start button to shut the car off, then crossed the lot to stand in his face. "So, among all the things that I think about you, you're adding cheater to the list?"

"For some men, it's hard to resist temptation."

Zoe inched closer to him, then placed her hand on his chest. "How hard is it for you?"

He grabbed her hand. "Stop playing with me, because you know I'm the one who will always get to you."

Carver's words sent her reeling. Zoe hadn't realized she'd stepped back until he touched her elbow. "You should go now," he said. "Wouldn't want you to find yourself unable to resist temptation."

Zoe marched to her car without looking back at him. How could she hate him and yearn for him at the same time? Taking this case was a bad idea.

Chapter 2

Carver knew it was a bad idea to follow Zoe home, but he needed to take a look at her place. Find out if her house had any blind spots where someone could hide. He was surprised that she still lived in the Bronx, but it made sense since her family had such a storied history in the borough. Underneath that independent streak was a girl who didn't want to leave home. That made him smile, until he noticed the bushes in front of her house. They had to go. And while he wanted to set up and watch her house all night, he couldn't risk Ms. Hothead finding him in the morning and blowing a gasket. After she pulled into her garage, Carver drove away. He headed to the FBI satellite office for a briefing on the search for Joseph Singletary—the man who wanted Zoe dead.

Singletary had been the mastermind behind the Harlem Madam—Zoe's ex-sister-in-law. When Zoe and the FBI brought Natalie down, there was a ripple effect in the trafficking organization. The FBI was able to raid trafficking rings in North Carolina, California, and

Maryland. But Singletary was always one step ahead of getting captured.

That's what worried him. Singletary could be any-where and no one had a clue. Natalie wasn't talking, nor were any of the other pimps they'd busted. Pulling into the parking lot, Carver pulled out his cell phone and sent the security text to the receptionist.

He walked to the front door and pressed in the code that he'd received on his cell phone. Once the door opened, he smiled at the receptionist, then showed him his ID.

"Agent Banks, they are waiting for you in the back."

Nodding, he headed for the conference room for the briefing. He hated these tight offices with no windows that reminded him of Afghan bunkers. But it had to be done if he was going to take down Singletary before he harmed a hair on Zoe's head.

"Banks," the agent in charge, Delvin Smallwood, said when he spotted Carver at the door. "Did you find Harrington?"

"Yes."

"Good. Just got some intel that Singletary has placed a bounty on her head."

Carver leaned against the wall. "She agreed to work on the case with me. At least I can get her out of New York for now. How are we going to find this bastard and put him away?"

Agent Wendy Covington pointed to an electronic map on the wall. "Two weeks ago, we traced a cell phone call from him in Nebraska. Didn't make sense that he would be there, so we tried to get a hit on the Internet server used to upload the girls on Backpage and got a hit in New Jersey. By the time we got a physical address, everything was gone." She folded her arms across her chest. "It's like he's freaking Houdini."

"What is he, a fucking ghost?" Carver groaned as he glared at the map.

"We need a crack in his organization," Wendy said. "Have you taken another stab at Natalie?"

He shook his head. "She's not talking, even when I offered immunity."

"You did *what*?" Smallwood boomed. "We don't have the authority to do that. The federal prosecutor wants to get a pound of flesh, and right now all we have is Natalie. She's too afraid to talk, so she's going to be the example."

"It was bait, and she didn't take it," Carver said with an eye roll. "I told Zoe that we're reopening the Jessica Dolan case because the family is friends with the former president and they want closure on where their daughter's body is."

"All right. Make sure you keep Zoe away from her family. Last thing we need is for Zachary Harrington to get caught in the cross fire."

Carver narrowed his eyes and clenched his fists. "It's bad enough that Singletary's hurting all of these girls, but now he's out to kill people."

"Zoe did help cripple a large part of his organization," Wendy said, not hiding her adoration. "I guess she really didn't like her ex-sister-in-law. Because she did everything in her power to get that woman behind bars."

"How are we going to keep her alive, though? All of our efforts to find Singletary have failed. I'm beginning to think that someone is feeding him information about the investigation," Smallwood said. He picked up a flip phone and handed it to Carver. "This is how we communicate, and you need to make sure Zoe loses her smartphone and other devices that can be traced. One thing we know about Singletary is that he knows technology."

Carver nodded as he tucked the old-school phone in his pocket. "I need another car so that I can watch her house tonight. She's already seen the sedan."

Wendy tossed her keys to him. "Take my Challenger," she said.

"That purple monster? I don't want her to see me. How am I going to stay in the background in that thing?"

"No one is going to suspect that it's a government car," she replied, and sucked her teeth. Carver rolled his eyes, but she did have a point. Who would think that an FBI agent would be driving a muscle car? He pocketed the keys.

"All right," he said. "Anything else?"

Smallwood shook his head. "Just make sure that the media doesn't get wind of the Dolan case. Keep in mind that we're just using this to keep Singletary off her back and to keep Zoe alive."

"Isn't Jessica Dolan dead?" Wendy asked. "Why are we using this case?"

"Because," Smallwood began, "it gives us a reason to relocate Harrington and it isn't a priority case."

Carver nodded. When Smallwood told Carver that Zoe was in danger, the men sat down and came up with the cover story to get her out of New York until Singletary was apprehended, because every time they seemed to get close to capturing the pimp, he'd get away. As much as Carver tried to pretend this was just another case, it was personal for him. Zoe wouldn't be harmed, and if he had to put his life on the line to save hers, he would.

"I'm out," Carver said.

Zoe walked into her kitchen and grabbed a box of oat cereal. She didn't pour a bowlful or grab milk to go with it; she just took the box and sat on the sofa—eating it dry. Why had she been foolish enough to take Carver's case, or kiss him? Her body tingled with the thoughts of his hands roaming her body, his tongue licking her sensitive spot.

"Stop it," she muttered, then stuffed a handful of cereal in her mouth. Munching mindlessly, she picked up her cell phone to check that payment for her last case had been received. When she saw it had been, she smiled. "Another satisfied customer," she said, then closed her box of cereal. Rising to her feet, she headed for the kitchen and put the box away. Sighing, she started to call her brother, but he was a newlywed and it was after ten. Hopefully he and Chante were working on making a niece or nephew for her.

Work had consumed her life, and in the still of the night, she was bored. It wasn't that she didn't have offers for dates and dinners, but after seeing all of the cheating and everything else she investigated, trusting was hard. She couldn't even go on a date without running a background check on the guy first. And these days, any little thing, from writing a bad check to having overdue parking tickets, was enough for Zoe to decide he wasn't worth her time.

And then there was Carver.

No one compared to that man or made her body hum like a chamber singer. That one night changed her life, and she couldn't get over it no matter how hard she tried. Instantly, she thought back to the interlude in her office and his words vibrated through her body.

Stop playing with me, because you know I'm the one who will always get to you.

Groaning, Zoe headed up to her bedroom to change into her gym clothes. She had energy to burn off. Late-night trips to the gym were becoming a part of her life. A hard workout always put her in the mood to sleep. Though she knew a much better sleep aid—another night with Carver.

"Ugh!" She tied her sneakers and jogged down the stairs and headed out the door. Maybe Marcus would be there tonight and they could do another burpee challenge. Thinking about her workout partner made her smile. If he was about ten years older and had a real job, he might have a chance. But she had to admit, their "workout dates" were doing wonders for her body. She ran her hand across her toned abs and smiled.

Carver perked up in the front seat of the Challenger as he watched Zoe leave her house. Where in the hell was she going this time of night? Okay, it was eleven thirty, but she'd just gotten off work and she should've been preparing for their meeting in the morning. Not.

Making. A. Booty. Call. Wait? Was that a gym bag on her shoulder? That made sense, because she surely didn't get that ass by watching cheating men all day and eating French fries.

Focus, he thought. *Is this a pattern? Does she go to the same gym every night?* Glancing around as she got into her car, Carver looked for signs of a stalker. He didn't see headlights or hear the roar of another engine. He waited for her to pull out of the garage and go two blocks before taking off after her. What he found interesting was that the purple car didn't draw as much attention as he'd thought it would.

The moment he arrived at the gym, he understood why. Challengers of all colors seemed to be the norm. There were even two more purple ones parked there. Carver pulled into a spot at the end of the parking lot, where he had a direct line of sight on Zoe's car and the entrance. She'd already entered the gym before he parked, and he saw her meet a man at the desk. When they hugged, jealousy washed over him like an ocean wave. Who was this muscle-bound clown, and why were they so close? Carver glared at them as they laughed and talked. When the man ran his index finger down her arm, Carver had to stop himself from hopping out of the car and punching him. Even though he had no claim to Zoe, something about watching another man touch her made his skin crawl. Every inch of that woman had been marked as his, and Carver was never a guy who shared anything. And he wasn't going to share Zoe with anyone.

Maybe he's her trainer, Carver thought as he opened

the car door. He took two steps toward the entrance, then looked down at his attire, black slacks and a button-down shirt. He didn't look like a man coming for a workout, and he'd raise suspicion if he walked in there and started following her around. Worse, if Zoe saw him at the gym, it would lead to questions he couldn't answer.

"Shit," he muttered. "Didn't plan this one out properly. And I'm sure Wendy doesn't have anything in the trunk that would work." He checked anyway and was right. Pulling out his binoculars, he watched Zoe and Mr. Muscles walk upstairs. If she wanted to work out, he had some moves for her that she would never forget.

He decided to walk inside anyway; that way he could get the lay of the land. And if someone, other than him, had been following Zoe, he'd get a chance to see where the person could hide. Carver didn't like the fact that he didn't know who was after Zoe. Singletary could have anyone gunning for her.

Immediately, Carver didn't like the openness of the gym. Anyone with a long gun could take Zoe out and get away without being seen.

"Good evening, sir," the receptionist said. "Do you have your membership card?"

"I'm not a member. I wanted to see if I could talk to someone about joining the gym?"

"Our membership coordinators are here between the hours of nine a.m. and six p.m. I do have an application you can fill out and bring back, or you can visit our website."

Carver nodded, looking around to see if he could

spot Zoe and Mr. Muscles. He saw them upstairs, going stroke for stroke doing burpees. That made him smirk. He was her trainer. *Guess he was touching her to see how his work was going. I should've known that he isn't her type. It's not as if he would have an idea as to how to handle this woman. That's my job.*

"Sir?" the receptionist said. Carver looked down at her outstretched hand holding the application. "I hope to see you tomorrow."

He took the application and nodded. "Thank you," he said. "Nine a.m., right?"

She nodded and Carver headed out the door.

"All right, all right, you win!" Marcus fell to the floor. "You're a beast, woman!"

Zoe bounced up and down and threw a couple of air punches. "I told you, I have energy to burn tonight."

Marcus gave her a sideways glance. "I got a few ideas," he quipped.

"Down, boy," she replied as she knelt beside him. "Guess it's too late for a spin class, huh?"

"Yes. What's going on with you? Win the lottery or something?"

"No. Took a big job," she said.

"And you're not going to tell me what you do," he said, and smacked her calf.

Zoe rolled her eyes. "Nope. But this might be more than I can handle."

"Not you. You're a real-life Wonder Woman. My calves will be crying in the morning and probably for a few days."

"Yeah, right," she said as she pinched his arm. "I'm going to run awhile on the treadmill."

"I'm getting a smoothie and going home disappointed. One day, Zoe, you're going to come with me for some Netflix and chilling."

"Keep waiting for that to happen and you will always be going home disappointed and hard." She hopped on the treadmill and started running. After an hour, she felt worn-out enough to go home and go straight to sleep. Zoe skipped the sauna room because the way she felt, she'd probably go to sleep there and wake up in the morning.

In the morning, she was going to come face-to-face with *him* again. What had she been thinking when she agreed to help him with this cold case? He was temptation personified, and Zoe wasn't sure if she could resist him. Even though she lied to herself often and said that she could.

As she walked downstairs, she saw Marcus chatting it up with another woman getting her late-night workout on. She hoped he would have better luck with her. When their eyes met, she winked at him and headed out the door. It was quiet in the parking lot, and a gentle wind blew across her, cooling the heat burning in her muscles. But that ache, which had driven her to come work out this time of night, was still there.

Carver.

Kissing him was hot. Kissing him was wrong. They needed to find Jessica Dolan sooner rather than later. Did the FBI know for sure that she was dead? She thought about the case from Ohio, where three women had been kidnapped and found a decade later. What if that was the case with Jessica? Deciding that she wanted some answers now and not in the morning, Zoe called Carver.

"Banks," he said when he answered the phone, sounding wide-awake. And that pissed her off. She wanted him to feel as uncomfortable as she did when he'd walked into her office earlier tonight.

"Carver, it's Zoe. I had some questions about Jessica Dolan that I didn't ask earlier."

"So, you were thinking about me?" he quipped.

"Thinking about the case and . . . Just answer my question."

"You have to ask it first."

Smart-ass, she thought. "Did the killer confess to killing Jessica, and if so, where did he say her body was?"

"He never confessed to killing her, but her DNA was found in his van."

"Are we looking for a body, or is it possible that Jessica is still alive?"

Carver sighed. "That's highly unlikely. There's evidence of her murder in with the other murders that we were able to convict him of. He just wouldn't give us any details about where her body is."

"Where are we going to start?"

"In Santa Fe, New Mexico."

"Why Santa Fe?"

"That's where Jessica was when she went missing. And if we're lucky, we might get a lead on where we could find her remains."

"What if she's still alive? Maybe sold into a sex trafficking ring or something like that?" Zoe said.

"That's why we need new eyes. I don't think that's an aspect that we've investigated. Let's meet for breakfast, after you pack your bag for the flight, unless you want me to come over tonight."

Zoe sucked her teeth. Did she want him to come over? Yes. She wanted him to come over, come inside, and make love to her until the whole city knew his name. "Why don't we meet at my office tomorrow at nine. You bring the coffee and bagels," she said, then hung up the phone.

Chapter 3

Carver looked at his phone, then smiled. He waited just a few moments before he followed her out of the parking lot. Driving along the freeway, he knew that he was going to have to agree with every theory Zoe came up with about this case if he was going to keep her out of danger. The problem was, if she started looking into things on her own, she might figure out the truth about what was going on.

He couldn't allow that to happen—not when there was so much at stake. Pulling out his flip phone, he called Smallwood.

"What's going on, Banks?" Delvin said.

"I'm going to need a copy of the Bayou Serial Killer's case file and some more details on Jessica Dolan."

"I can get that to you in the morning. Right now we may have a break in the Singletary case. Wendy got a lead that he's in Los Angeles. I'm sending her and a team there now."

"You're actually sending Wendy out into the field again?"

Smallwood sighed. "She's going for the technical side. If we catch Smallwood, I want to go through his computer systems and all electronics and get details on that organization."

"Good idea, but Wendy in the field isn't a good idea. She lacks training and . . ."

"Really didn't have much of a choice. What she lacks in field experience, she masters in technology," Smallwood said. Carver had to agree, Wendy was a whiz when it came to electronics. However, two years ago, her inexperience nearly cost Carver and three other agents their lives because she froze when the leader of the drug cartel they had been investigating got the drop on her. Were it not for Carver's sharpshooting skills, everyone would've died when the dealer pulled out a hand grenade. He didn't think she needed to be anywhere near the Singletary takedown. But it wasn't his call. Still, for the life of him, he couldn't understand why Smallwood sent her to Los Angeles with the team.

But Carver's military training made it hard for him to question his superior officer. Maybe Smallwood saw something in Wendy that he didn't. Carver knew his focus had to be Zoe and keeping her alive. He couldn't and wouldn't question this operation.

"Maybe Zoe and I should go to LA instead," Carver said. "If we're going to take this bastard down, I want to be there to see it."

"No. We're not sure if Singletary is still there, and

the purpose of all of this is to get Zoe out of the line of fire. How's the surveillance going?"

"So far nothing. Haven't seen anyone following her other than me."

"I'll get you what you need and you get her out of town."

"Yes, sir." Carver hung up the phone and focused on Zoe's car. He thought she was heading home, but she stopped at a doughnut shop, of all places. He shook his head.

"All that working out and she gets a midnight snack," he mumbled as he pulled around the back of the shop. He angled the car so that he had a clear view of the front door but was still hidden from Zoe's sight.

When she stepped out of her car, Zoe looked around to see if she had been followed. She couldn't shake the feeling that someone was behind her. Stopping at the doughnut shop had been her way of making sure. Zoe didn't see another car in the parking lot and she shrugged it off as being paranoid.

"What can I get for you?" the clerk asked when she put her smartphone down.

"Are the apple fritters fresh?"

"Kind of. Like, thirty minutes old."

Zoe nodded. "Let me get three," she said with a smile. The clerk rolled her eyes and walked over to the display counter and bagged up the sweets. Zoe shook her head at the woman's attitude, but paid for her food and rolled on. As she got into the car, she took a huge bite of one of the sinful treats. Her hours in the gym had given her the right to devour it. But she stopped herself from eating the whole thing. No matter how warm and sweet the fritter was, it was not a substitute for what she really wanted.

Carver.

He was so deep underneath her skin that it annoyed her to no end. This was the same man who'd used her to solve a case. Slept with her to pump her for information about a man she'd been investigating, so he could solve a case for the FBI. Granted, it had worked out for the best, for both of them.

He'd arrested the criminal and she was able to uncover the money he'd been hiding from his wife. Zoe still took it personally that Carver would play with her emotions and desire to win. Then, if that wasn't bad enough, when the Harlem Madam turned out to be her ex-sister-in-law, and Carver led the investigation, Zoe had been forced to face him again.

Pulling into her driveway, she parked the car and took another nibble of her fritter, remembering when Zach had gone to South Carolina and she'd gotten a call from his assistant about the FBI executing a warrant at Zach's office in Manhattan.

At the time, she'd been in Brooklyn, and rushed to her brother's office. Zach had proudly taken the reins at their family's real estate company, and until he married that barracuda, he'd done a great job of keeping the family legacy going. And Zoe would've worked by his side if Zach hadn't treated her like a fragile doll. She had done the security outline for the company and worked ad hoc as a security adviser for him.

That's why she had been determined not to allow the

FBI to come in, with or without a warrant. Closing her eyes, she saw that day as if it were happening right now.

Zoe burst into the building and grabbed the shoulder of the FBI agent standing near the door. When he turned around, her knees knocked. Carver Banks.

"What in the hell are you doing here?" she demanded.

"It's in the warrant," he said. "And hello to you, Zoe."

"Don't hello me," she snapped as she took the warrant from his hand. Zoe scanned the paper. "What is this all about?"

"An active investigation that I can't discuss with you."

"Being that I'm the security liaison of Harrington Enterprises, you need to tell me what this is about."

"Natalie Harrington is being investigated for human trafficking, and we have reason to believe that there may be evidence here. And Natalie says that your brother is involved in the trafficking as well."

"That's bullshit. My brother has divorced her and there is no way that he would be involved in something so heinous!"

"Why don't you let us execute this warrant and prove or disprove your theory," Carver said.

Zoe narrowed her eyes at him. "This warrant limits your search to Zach's office and computer." She pointed at one of the agents. "So, why is he harassing the receptionist?"

Carver rolled his eyes, then told the agent to move on. "Is this how we're going to do this today?" he asked.

"Yes. Because I can't believe that you're buying what

this lying-ass bitch is saying." Zoe folded her arms across her breasts and glared at him.

"I'm doing my job," he said.

"You're always doing your job. The last time you did your job, I ended up in your bed."

"Don't pretend you were forced," he said. "And for all I know, you were the one using me to get what you needed to solve your little case."

"My little . . . Carver, you are an arrogant ass! G-men like you are the reason why folks want to overthrow the government."

"That sounds like a threat. Should I handcuff you now, or wait until I finish what I'm doing here?"

"Go to hell. And you're done here, Agent Banks." Zoe pointed to a group of agents leaving Zach's office with his computers in boxes.

"You're right, but we're not finished by a long shot."

Zoe slapped her hands on her hips. "You think you're going to come in here and harass my brother's staff, then think we're going to go off and have drinks?"

"Not at all, but if you are this security liaison that you say you are, then I have questions about the computer setup here and the link—if any—to sex trafficking."

She rolled her eyes. "For the last time, Zach is not involved in his ex-wife's crimes."

Tilting his head to the side, he shot Zoe a questioning look. "And you know this how? That twin connection, or has your brother told you about his involvement in his wife's—"

"Ex-wife!"

"Crime?"

"You know what, you've served your warrant. Now get

*out," she snapped. "Or I will file a complaint with your
superiors and tell them all about how you do business."*

*Carver smirked and shook his head. "Be looking for
my call tomorrow," he said as he followed the other
agents out the door.*

*For all of her bravado, Zoe was actually looking
forward to hearing from Carver. If for no other reason
than to show him that his sexy eyes didn't affect her, nor
his full lips and big hands.*

*She wanted him to know that one night in Washing-
ton hadn't turned her into a vapid woman who wanted
nothing more than to be in his space. She may not be
vapid, but she did want him.*

Zoe stepped out of her car, still feeling vexed by her
desire for Carver. It was clear to her that he was a man
who used people to get what he wanted. Was she being
used again?

No, because I'm getting paid this time, she thought
as she headed inside. Now that she was worn-out and
filled with sugar, Zoe could go to sleep and get ready
to see Carver in the morning. She silently prayed that
he wouldn't star in her dreams again tonight.

Carver circled Zoe's block one more time before he
decided to head back to his hotel. He was impressed
that Zoe had motion-activated lights around the outside
of her house. Now he understood why she had the
shrubbery. "Wouldn't be surprised if she has fire-ant
hills buried underneath those bushes," he muttered.

When he arrived at the hotel, Carver headed to his
room so that he could download the materials he
needed for his meeting with Zoe. He also needed to

make sure his cover story was good, because if Zoe smelled a rat, she would shut everything down.

The last thing he needed was for that hotheaded woman to get an idea that Singletary was after her. He knew she would do just what she did when she went after Natalie. But this time she was in over her head, and he would do whatever he had to do to make sure she was safe. Pulling out his flip phone, Carver sent Wendy a text telling her to call him.

Seconds later, his phone rang. "Carver."

"What's up, Banks? And make it fast, I'm in the middle of something."

"Have you found anything in LA?"

"Nope, and our witness is missing."

"What witness?" Carver wondered how she got close to a witness when she was supposed to be there to analyze the computers and technology that Singletary was using. "Wendy, you're supposed to be—"

"I know what I'm supposed to be doing, but when I went to get the computers from the house, there was a girl there who started talking about what was going on. Would you rather that I had ignored her?"

"Where is she now?"

"I was trying to get a safe location for her, but she disappeared."

"Damn!"

"I know, and Singletary isn't in Los Angeles. This might not have even been his ring. You know how most of his girls usually have a brand or tattoo, right?"

"Yeah," Carver said.

"None of the girls we found have them. Maybe our witness did, but I never got a chance to ask her. The other girls could've been moved after the raid. We did take two pimps into custody."

Carver sighed. "Or killed."

"I try not to think about things like that," she said. "What do you need from me?"

"I need all of the case information on Jessica Dolan that wasn't released to the media, and keep me in the loop about Singletary."

"Aren't you and Smallwood working on that without me?" Wendy snorted. "Banks, I know you don't think I can do my job, so why are you trying to partner with me now?"

"Because you and Smallwood are the only two people who know what's really going on with Zoe and Singletary. I'm trying to keep this woman alive, and I know you're good at the technical part of investigations."

"Just what does that mean?"

"Exactly what I said. Are you going to give me what I need or not?"

"What's in it for me? Banks, I want to get in the field on a full-time basis. Being cooped up in an office is not why I joined the Bureau. And you and I both know that Smallwood listens to you. If you put in a good word for me, I'm sure he'll give me a chance to do some real work."

Carver bit his tongue and didn't tell her that she wasn't ready for fieldwork or that she should never have been hired in the first place. But it wasn't his job to tell her that, nor could he fire her. Carver remembered when Wendy had first started in the field office. She'd had so much promise, then something changed. She got sloppy, and the last time she'd been on an assignment, she froze.

"Wendy, I can't worry about that right now. We have to capture Singletary before he kills again or captures any more girls."

"Typical," she snorted. "Because it's my job, I'll send you the case file." Wendy hung up the phone and Carver shook his head. She would have to get over herself right now, because she wasn't his concern.

Chapter 4

Six a.m. came too quickly for Zoe's taste. Then again, she'd brought it on herself with her late-night workout and that call to Carver. Hearing his voice did the one thing she knew it would: fill her mind with thoughts of him that haunted her dreams.

"Stop it," she told herself as she climbed out of bed. "Working on this case changes nothing between us. He's the same arrogant asshole who arrested me." Zoe headed for the basement and logged on to her computer. She kept her home office in the basement so that she wouldn't be tempted to work all night on cases. Not that her main cases these days took much work. She missed working with her contacts from the NYPD on cases that mattered, but the new captain at her old precinct banned the officers from working with her. Not that she was surprised by that after she'd brought down his golfing buddy for having sex with underage girls. And then there was the case she'd handled about the stop-and-frisk tactics in the NYPD.

Due to Zoe's investigation, three of the six victims' families were able to win multimillion-dollar settlements against the city. Zoe had been hurt and disappointed when her former partner had been named in one of the lawsuits.

He'd also been one of the eight officers to lose his job because of her investigation.

Sitting down at the computer, she pulled up the server that was linked to her main office, and entered Carver's name into her case database. She wondered if she'd have access to the case file the FBI had on Jessica Dolan and the Bayou Serial Killer. She typed the woman's name into her search engine and watched the screen populate with links about Dolan. Each story she read seemed to confirm what Carver thought: The twenty-year-old was dead, and they'd be on a recovery mission. Part of Zoe had hoped for a happy ending, finding Jessica alive and reuniting her with her family. She couldn't imagine the pain her parents must be facing, not knowing their child's final resting place or getting the closure of burying her.

Walking over to her coffeemaker, she started a pot of coffee and wondered if she should talk to the Dolans and find out more about Jessica. In all of her cases, Zoe liked to know who she was investigating. Even when she was spying on a cheating husband, she'd always interview the wife to find out what had attracted her to the man in the first place, what he was like during the good times, and when things changed. Zoe'd had one case where those questions actually reunited the couple because the husband hadn't been cheating, just spending time with his mother at the nursing home. His wife hadn't gotten along with his mother, and to keep the peace, he just went alone to visit her. The wife felt so bad that he'd felt as if he had to sneak around to visit his mother, that she went with him the next time and made peace with her mother-in-law.

Zoe had sent the wife her payment back and told her to take her husband on a nice vacation.

After her coffee brewed, she glanced at the clock on the wall and wondered if she should call Carver now or just wait until their meeting to ask about contacting the Dolans. She hated that she was going into this case blind. Depending on media reports and what was on the Internet wasn't how she did business.

Should've never let him distract me with that kiss, she thought as she dumped sugar in her coffee. Zoe made a silent promise to treat this case just like any other one. She was the one in charge, and no matter what Carver Banks said, she was going to do things her way. He'd just deal with it.

Carver finished his morning workout and stayed on the floor of the gym for a few minutes because he had to get his mind right for his meeting with Zoe. Knowing her, she was going to have a lot of questions about why the FBI was reopening the case, and he couldn't say *because of the president* for much longer.

Wendy had sent him the case file on the Bayou Serial Killer and details about Jessica Dolan. He'd spent half the night reading up on the cold case. It had been three years since the killer was captured, and he had always claimed that he didn't kill Jessica. But that was before the DNA evidence had been discovered that linked her to his killing spree. Granted, she was different from his other victims. She was African American and the other victims had been white. She hadn't been a student at the University of Virginia like the other victims, she'd just been visiting a friend there and they'd taken a trip to Washington. For the first two weeks that Jessica had been missing, local police and the FBI hadn't thought that she was a victim of the killer, but when another girl went missing and her body was found, the investigation turned back to Dolan's disappearance, and her DNA was found in the van that was linked to the killer.

"It's a good plan," he muttered as he stood up. Carver knew he had to get to Zoe's office early to make sure there weren't any threats this morning. And he had to return that garish purple car. Heading for his room, Carver called Smallwood to have him send a sedan over so that Zoe wouldn't be suspicious of seeing Carver showing up in that purple sports car.

"Keeping this woman alive is starting to get on my nerves," Smallwood said. "I'll send someone over with the car."

"Thanks, but keep in mind, this was your idea. What happened in Los Angeles after Wendy found the girl?"

"The girl was dead. One of Singletary's henchmen must have gotten to her when they found out she was talking to us."

"Damn."

"While you're taking Harrington on this wild-goose chase, see if you can find out how she got her information about Singletary's operation and what she didn't tell us after we arrested Natalie. If she knows something that we don't, we might need that information to see if we can crack this case and neutralize the threat against her."

"Yes, sir."

"Give me an update once you two arrive in New Mexico. Chief is not happy about the expense."

"I'm sure she isn't," Carver said. "But we have to get Singletary by any means."

"That's right. So, I'm working every angle to make sure it happens."

After hanging up, Carver hopped in the shower. While the water beat down on him, he thought about seeing Zoe in a few hours. His need for this woman was off the charts and he knew she felt the same way, but acting on those feelings would be a huge mistake with so much on the line.

"Just business," he told himself as he dried his chest. If Carver knew one thing, he knew losing sight of the mission would put everyone in danger. From his days in Marine intelligence and working on the terrorism task force in Iraq, he was well aware of how emotions and danger didn't mix.

That's how he lost Monica Curry, a fellow Marine and his ex-fiancée. After an argument, she'd stormed out of the command center and walked into the very ambush they'd been looking to prevent.

Carver shook the painful memory and forced himself to think about the task at hand—saving Zoe.

* * *

The property was quiet and none of the other businesses had opened when he passed through the parking lot. He hated that her door faced the street and that there were cameras on the light poles facing the door. Doing anything at her office would be documented. *Unless*, he thought, *I can get inside the businesses across the street and disable the surveillance. Those cameras weren't put there by the city. Just need fifteen minutes to rig the door and get out of here.*

He was about to pull into the parking lot of the building when he noticed a black sedan coming his way. That was the kind of car that some sort of law enforcement agent might be driving, he thought as he headed down the street. The last thing he needed was to get caught before his plan was put in motion. One thing he knew for sure, when that building went up in flames with that bitch Zoe Harrington inside, he was going to have a front row seat. Parking across the street, he watched the black sedan park and a man get out of the car. He couldn't tell if the man was a police officer or some other law enforcement agent. Maybe he was one of the people whose lives Zoe had ruined. Hell, getting rid of Zoe would probably make a lot of people in New York happy. Maybe he'd even get his life back.

Watching the man roam the property, he wrote him off as some kind of city inspector. He didn't see a gun or a badge, so he knew he wasn't NYPD. Those guys always showed a gun and shield, especially these days. Glancing at his watch, he knew she'd be here soon, and he couldn't let her see him. Not until it was too late.

Today wasn't the day. But soon, the bitch would get everything that she deserved.

Zoe pulled up to her office and wasn't surprised to see Carver was already there. Easing out of the car, she crossed over to him. "Where's the coffee and bagels? Or at least a few glazed doughnuts."

"You look like you don't let those things touch your lips," he quipped. "And I'm not a cop—I prefer apple fritters."

Zoe gasped. How could he possibly know that was her sugary weakness? "That's a stereotype," she replied. "I didn't eat doughnuts during my tenure with NYPD."

"Only because you weren't there long enough," he said as they walked to the front door. Zoe unlocked her office, then punched in the code to her alarm system.

"I was thinking about the case this morning, and I realized that I have very little information to work with," she said as she flipped the lights on.

"I know that's my fault." He handed her the folder he had concealed under his arm. "Here's the FBI file on Dolan's disappearance and the Bayou Serial Killer. Keep in mind that this is classified information and it's not to be shared."

"What do you think I'm going to do? Run to New York One with the story?" she snapped. "Didn't you come to me? If you don't trust me, then why are you here?"

"Calm down. I know I came to you. Zoe, there may be some things in this case file that offend you, and I know you're known to fly off the handle."

She rolled her eyes as she took the folder from his outstretched hand. Sitting down, Zoe flipped through the file. Carver was right. She was offended about how the FBI had handled the case of the missing black girl.

"So, if Jessica had been the last girl this creep killed, you-all wouldn't have found her DNA or anything. Typical."

Carver cleared his throat. "There is no justification for how things were handled, and that's why we want to—"

"Make things right?" Zoe looked up at Carver's face. The man was so hard to read. "Do you feel guilty about what happened? Is that why you're here?"

"I did my job and followed the evidence. I'm here because the Bureau is trying to give the family closure." As much as he wanted to pretend he wasn't affected by reopening this case, he considered never finding Jessica another professional failure.

Zoe grunted and leaned back in her chair. "Will I be able to talk to the Dolan family?"

"No."

"Why not? I want to get to know who Jessica was, why she was in Santa Fe, and what was the last thing she and her parents talked about."

"What difference does that make?" Carver asked as he furrowed his eyebrows.

"That's how I work, and if you don't like how I do things, then we can end this right now."

"Zoe, I don't want to go to the Dolans until we have some real news to give them about their daughter. How cruel would it be to give them false hope when we don't know if we're going to find anything."

Zoe didn't want to admit it, but Carver had a point. Going to the family to ask them questions about their child, without any answers as to why they had reopened the investigation, would bring up sad memories. "Fine," she said, finally. "We don't have to go to the family. But let me ask you this: Did you-all ever interview the parents?"

"Not on video," he said. "I can see if there are some transcripts from the interviews available."

"Would've been great had you brought all of this with you. Didn't you think it would be important?"

Carver folded his arms across his chest. "Keep one thing in mind—you're still a civilian. We're not going to open up everything to you. I have to get clearance to bring reports to you."

Zoe sucked her teeth. "Why all the bullshit when you-all sought me out?"

"I'll tell you what, when I become the FBI director, I'll open all of the files to the public."

She shook her head. "I don't work like this."

"Can you humor me?"

"Fine," she said. "But if you plan on handcuffing me from doing my investigation, I will quit."

"I won't handcuff you unless you ask me to."

She narrowed her eyes at him as heat rose to her cheeks. Why did every conversation with this man turn sexual? Exhaling, she rose to her feet. "Well, I guess we'd better head for the airport."

"Do you need to stop by your place and pick up anything?" he asked.

Zoe crossed over to a closet in the corner of her office. She quickly filled a bag with the essentials: toothbrush, toothpaste, underwear, and her PI license. "Think I should pack my gun?" she asked over her shoulder.

"Aww, no."

"You're right, I don't want to check a bag," she said. "Let's go."

"Are you licensed in all fifty states?" he asked.

"Will my answer be held against me in the future?" He shook his head.

"No," Zoe said. "But I carry in all states, because you never know when death will be coming around the corner. All of my guns were legally purchased in the state of New York, though. You can put that in your notes."

"I thought you only took safe cases," he said.

"And you said it yourself, husbands don't like to lose money. I didn't always spy on the unfaithful."

"Why did you become a PI?" he asked as they got into the car.

"It's not in the file you and the FBI have on me?"

"There is no file on you at the Bureau," he said with a laugh. "Why would you think that we would?"

"Carver, you were very rude to me during the investigation into the Harlem Madam—after everything else that you'd done to me."

"Here we go."

"It's the elephant in the car, and the sooner we get it out of the way, the more effective I'll be in helping you with this case. You used me."

"We had sex and we enjoyed it. You didn't tell me that you were looking into Alejandro Campos for his future ex-wife. National security was at stake."

"Always on the job, aren't you? I bet you have a family tucked away in Idaho."

Carver tightened his grip on the steering wheel.

"What was your endgame, Zoe? You wanted dirt on that man. What if I had been his real bodyguard? Would your legs have spread so easily?"

"Let's put this to rest for the last time," Zoe began. "Because you seem to forget that I told you why I was at that party and that I was looking for access to Campos's financial records. You played the *he doesn't pay me enough* bodyguard and said you'd help. So, what part of the game was dancing with me and plying me with alcohol?"

"You like rewriting history, because you were the one giving me drink after drink," he said with a chuckle. "Walk away, put a little switch in your hips, then come back with two glasses of champagne."

Zoe rolled her eyes, clearly recalling that night Carver started the car and peeled out of the parking lot.

Sophia Campos had given her a memory stick and the blueprint to Alejandro's house. The computer room was in the basement, but getting there wasn't going to be easy. He had three bodyguards and a security detail that roamed the house like the Secret Service. Zoe had been lucky to get in, but a tight dress and a push-up bra was always a good ticket.

Looking around the room, she caught the eye of what seemed to be Campos's right-hand man. Everywhere Campos went, that sexy brown-skinned man with the sparkling eyes was at his side.

What is this guy? A mob boss? What in the hell have I gotten myself into? Zoe thought as she locked eyes with the bodyguard. Walking toward the kitchen, Zoe figured that she could slip down the back stairs she'd seen on the blueprints and get what she needed. The longer she stayed at the party, the more danger she felt she was putting herself in. Just as she was about to enter the kitchen, she felt a hand on her elbow.

"Excuse me, miss," a deep voice said. "What are you doing?"

Turning around, she saw him standing there with a wicked gleam in his eyes. "Was looking for some more of those amazing canapés. You know, the ones with the, umm, cheese."

"Then why don't you find a waiter? And I haven't had a canapé all night. Who are you?"

"I don't want any trouble," she said.

"You've found it. If I were you, I'd leave, right now."

"But you're not me and I have a job to do."

He raised his right eyebrow and Zoe knew she was about to be tied up and thrown in the trunk of a car. Then Campos walked over.

"X, everything good over here?" he asked as he gave Zoe a slow once-over.

"Yes, sir. I was talking to the young lady about the food. She's looking for something with cheese."

Campos placed his hand on X's shoulder. "Show the lady a good time." He nodded toward two women who Zoe assumed were his whores for the night. "I'm about to do the same thing, so you are officially off duty."

"All right, boss," he said, then turned his attention to Zoe.

"You don't seem real loyal," she said when Campos was out of earshot. "I thought you were going to tell him that I was here doing a job."

"I'm underpaid. And tired."

"His wife feels the same way. I'm just here to help

her. Let me do what I need to do and I'll be out of your hair."

X wrapped his arm around Zoe's waist and brought his lips to her ear. "If I allow you to roam around here doing whatever his wife asked you to do, we're both going to be killed. Follow my lead and my directions, things will work out for both of us."

The heat from his breath sent tingles up and down her spine. And why did his hand feel as if it belonged on her body? "Why should I trust you?"

"Because you don't have another choice." He kissed her on the cheek and Zoe started to elbow him in the stomach until she saw two men in black walk past them.

"I'll go get us some champagne," she said, then sauntered away.

Zoe fingered her hair, then shrugged. "I was simply following your lead. But you know what, get over it."

"I have. You're the one who keeps going back to the best night of your life," Carver said as he took the exit for the airport.

"Harrumph, it wasn't even in the top five," she quipped.

Chapter 5

Zoe stood in the security line looking enviously at Carver as he flashed his FBI credentials and avoided the pat-down while she raised her arms above her head. This was the reason why clients had to fly her first class when she worked a case. TSA was the devil. Though the folks were doing their job to keep everyone safe, the pat-down always made her feel as if she'd been molested. For a while, Zoe even blamed Carver and the FBI every time she got stopped.

"I told them I would've been happy to pat you down," Carver said as they walked to their gate.

"Shut up," she said. "Once we get to New Mexico, we have to take a train to Santa Fe."

"All right," he said. "That will give me some time to check my email."

Zoe gave him a quick glance but didn't say anything. Carver caught her gaze and asked, "What?"

Zoe stopped walking and adjusted her belt. "Carver, of

all the contacts you have in the world of law enforcement, why did you come to me?"

"Because you're good at what you do and you're a woman."

"Sexist much?"

"You always have to take it there. Since you're a woman, I figured you'd have some more insight into how Jessica may have been thinking."

"That's such bull . . ."

"And maybe I wanted to see you again, without the handcuffs and drama."

"You didn't have to take on my brother," she snapped. "You brought the drama on yourself."

"I was following the leads as they unfolded, and it looks like things worked out just fine for Zachary. He's in North Carolina with a beautiful new wife who doesn't run a sex ring," Carver said with a grin. "Is it true what they say about twins?"

"What do *they* say?"

"That there's some kind of cosmic connection. Does he know when you feel pain and vice versa? What would your brother think if he knew you were crazy in love with me?"

Zoe rolled her eyes. "Anyway," she said. "He wouldn't think anything because that is so not the case."

"Does he hold grudges like you do?"

"If you're asking if Zach still hates your guts, the answer is yes," she quipped. "Your investigation nearly ruined my family's company and—"

"For the last time, I was following the evidence and doing my job. How was I to know that he and Natalie weren't the happy couple that she led me to believe they were? And I still find it difficult to believe that she was about to pimp those girls while Zach was totally in the dark."

"They weren't even living together and they were divorced. How was he supposed to know that she married him just to get a list of high-end contacts that she could . . . I'm not doing this with you," she said as she shook her head.

"Let's focus on the present and forget about the past. I wasn't trying to take your family down and be malicious. I wanted to stop the trafficking of those girls, and Natalie was only the tip of the iceberg."

"And you thought my brother was the bottom?" Zoe rolled her eyes. "Zach was horrified by what that woman did."

"I know. And I'm—"

"We're focusing on the present," she said, cutting him off. Every time she thought about the investigation and how Zach had lost so much business, it made her angry. Not just at the FBI but at Natalie. How could a woman be cruel enough to trick girls into something as horrific as a sex ring? She wasn't surprised when she found out that Natalie wasn't working alone. She wasn't smart enough to pull that off, just enough of a liar to trick naïve young women.

"What are you thinking?" Carver asked, breaking into her thoughts.

"Just . . . since we're going to be working together for the foreseeable future, we might as well get to know each other better," she said. "Any siblings?"

"Nope, only child. My parents perfected childbirth and didn't want to chance it again."

Zoe shook her head. "Your ego knows no bounds."

"Don't have an ego at all. I'm just telling the truth." Carver's face grew serious. "My mom had a difficult pregnancy with me, so after I was born, the doctor told her having another baby might be fatal."

"Oh, I'm sorry," she said wistfully. Zoe and Zach lost their mother in childbirth. She always wondered if her brother and father wouldn't have been so overprotective if her mother had been around. "You're close to your parents?"

"When they were living we were close," he said.

"Oh, I . . ."

"They've been gone for ten years now."

"Wow," she whispered, thinking how devastated she'd be if she lost her entire family. This man was all alone in the world. Was that why he took his job so seriously?

"What's that look?" he asked when he caught her pensive glance.

"Nothing." Zoe stretched her arms above her head. "This kind of explains a lot about you."

"Meaning?"

"You're so focused on work and doing things by the book. I guess it makes sense now."

Carver shrugged. "Minored in psychology?"

They rose to their feet as the boarding announcement blared across the speakers. Zoe was happy for the brief distraction because sitting across from Carver and looking into his eyes was getting to her in the most delicate way.

"Whatever. Do you ever think of starting your own family?"

"Haven't in a long time. I always wanted a couple of boys."

"I hope, when the time comes, you have a houseful of girls."

Carver gave her a slow side glance as they boarded the plane and took their seats. "Houseful of girls, huh? With eyes the color of yours?"

She tapped his thigh. "Keep dreaming."

"As long as you do," he replied. Before she could reply, the captain began his announcement about the flight time and weather. Zoe fastened her seat belt and looked out the window. Just as she was about to close her eyes, she felt Carver's fingers close around hers.

A houseful of girls? Why am I letting this woman get inside my head about a fantasy life that will never happen? Carver thought as he held her hand. He needed to keep her safe and had to push his desire away. But Zoe was so damned beautiful. Infuriating, but sexy. And as much as he tried to say that she was the one who couldn't get over their tryst years ago, he obviously couldn't. And being this close to her was making him dizzy with need.

Why am I holding her hand? he thought, but didn't let go. He even brought her hand to his lips and kissed it gently.

Zoe turned and looked at him. "What was that all about?"

"Good luck before the flight," he said.

"You're a mess," she said, then unfurled her hand from his.

Carver reached into his briefcase and pulled out a magazine. While he pretended to read, he thought about what they needed to do once the plane reached New Mexico. Yes, Jessica had been in New Mexico, but he wasn't sure where he and Zoe should begin their investigation.

Once the plane got airborne and Zoe went to sleep, he'd Google some hot spots in Santa Fe and plant the seeds of where they needed to look. He also needed to figure out the next city they should go to. But he needed to talk to Smallwood and see if there had been any more threats against Zoe from Singletary. Hopefully that bastard would be behind bars and Zoe would be safe.

"What are you reading?" Zoe asked, breaking into his thoughts.

"*Sports Illustrated*, just something to pass the time. Thought you were sleeping."

She shrugged. "Usually I would be, but I have questions."

"I'm sure you do."

"What kind of investigator would I be if I didn't have questions?"

"Shoot."

"Who was the last person to talk to Jessica before she disappeared?" she asked as she shifted in her seat.

"Her mother. According to the interview, Jessica came to Santa Fe with some friends, hoping to meet some famous author who lives there. She came with some girls from the University of Virginia."

"How long was she in Santa Fe?"

"At least a week. And during the same time, we think the Bayou Killer was here."

"Do you know anything about her friends? How did they escape the killer and Jessica didn't?"

"That's a question that we haven't been able to answer. Maybe the killer stalked her."

"Do you think he killed her before he went back to Virginia, and buried her body in the desert out there?"

"I'm going to check with my contact in the field office and find out if there have been any bodies uncovered in Santa Fe," Carver said. "As soon as we land, though."

"I know this is a long shot, but what if she ran off with a boyfriend and they've been living off the grid?"

Carver rolled his eyes. "All of these years?"

Zoe ran her fingers through her hair and shrugged. "You've never done anything crazy when you were a college student? This is why I'd like to talk to her family. What was their relationship like? Maybe they didn't like the boyfriend and she didn't want to give him up."

"I was young once. Ran off with a girl for two weeks, and my father was livid," Carver said, telling her the truth for the first time. "I was a sophomore at Howard and she was one of those Woo-Woos from Virginia State."

"Do I want to hear the rest of this story, and what is a *woo-woo*?"

"That's what they call their cheerleaders because when they walk by, everyone says *woo-woo*," he said with a chuckle. "I met her at homecoming and we clicked."

Zoe rolled her eyes. Why in the world was his story making her jealous? She hadn't even known him back then, and she didn't want him now. At least that's the lie she'd been telling herself for the last twenty-four hours. But if Miss Woo-Woo got two weeks with him, then why couldn't she?

What in the hell is wrong with you? Zoe thought as she turned her attention back to Carver's story.

"When my dad got the credit card bill with the charges from Virginia Beach, he drove to DC and packed my stuff while I was gone, withdrew me from school, and gave me a choice: Army or Marines."

"What did you choose?" Zoe asked.

He tilted his head to the side and raised his right eyebrow. "You don't remember that tattoo on my arm?"

Zoe pursed her lips. "Can you stop acting like you're so unforgettable?"

"I'm a Marine. Semper fi, baby."

She eased back in her seat and crossed her legs tightly to ease the thumping between her thighs. Here she'd thought all this time that Carver was a suit with an attitude, and he was a Marine. America's first line of defense. Zoe loved Fleet Week when she was growing up, although her father and Zach made it nearly impossible for her to enjoy herself or meet a young Marine. She almost laughed out loud when she thought about the time that Zach actually locked her in the basement when she'd told him about the date she had with a guy she'd met while she was in Midtown.

"What's funny?" Carver asked when he caught her smile.

"When I was younger, I loved Fleet Week, much to the dismay of my father and brother. Zach even locked me in the basement once to keep me from going out with this Marine I'd met when my friend Lola and I had hung out in Midtown instead of going to school that day."

"It was probably a good thing he did that," Carver said. "I know what I wanted during my first Fleet Week." He gave Zoe a slow and lingering glance. "And I can only imagine what—"

"Everyone wasn't a horny dog like you back then." She giggled.

"Yeah, Zach did the right thing, and if you were my sister, you'd still be in that basement," Carver quipped.

"Sometimes he wishes the same thing. Like I would've ever let that happen."

Carver was about to say something when the plane hit a pocket of turbulence and Zoe gripped his arm like a vise. "You okay?" he asked.

She closed her eyes and took a deep breath. After a beat, she released his arm. "Sorry about that," she said. "I really hate flying."

"I see." Carver pulled her closer and brushed his lips against her forehead. "But I got you."

Zoe rested her head on his chest and went to sleep. She hoped when the plane landed she could recover from her moment of weakness.

Chapter 6

Carver watched Zoe sleep and couldn't help but wonder what else she was hiding under that hardcore exterior other than a fear of flying. Stroking her arm, he thought about that night after he'd helped her get into Campos's basement.

"Watch the door," she whispered as she moved around the basement like she'd been there before. Carver wanted to watch something else: her shapely backside. This woman had some spunk and a body that wouldn't quit. But was she really a private investigator, just looking for lost money for Campos's wife, or was she part of the terrorist organization that Campos was linked to? Maybe she'd been a Mata Hari, here to get information that the heads of the Middle Eastern group could use to keep Campos under control. One thing Carver had learned from being his pretend bodyguard was that the man had very little self-control. And if he was keeping secrets from the terrorists, especially when it came to their money, a divorce lawyer would be the least of his worries.

When she wasn't paying attention, Carver had snapped a picture of the woman and texted it to headquarters for an identification. Just as she booted the computer, he got a text message.

> Zoe Harrington. Former NYPD beat cop in the Bronx. Active PI license in NY, NJ, NC, VA, DC, GA, SC. Pending nationwide application. No warrants, no ties to terrorism groups.

This was good news, Carver surmised as he watched her punch in an access code. Mrs. Campos had armed her like a divorce assassin. What else did she know? Carver wasn't going to let this woman out of his sight until he found out.

"I'm done," she said. "Thanks a lot." Her smile made him hard, and as much as he wanted to blame it on the alcohol, he'd only had one glass of champagne all night.

"So, you're done, and now what?"

"I'm out of here, unless there is a reason for me to stay."

Carver smiled. "I can think of a couple," he said.

"Oh, X. I bet you can, but . . ."

Carver pulled her into his arms and kissed her slow and deep, cupping the ass he'd been ogling all night, and it was soft and tight. Part of him thought she'd slap him, kick him in the family jewels and sprint out of there, but she melted against him. Their tongues danced and her moans were the music that turned his body into a raging inferno.

Pulling back from her, Carver smiled. "Come on, let's go."

"*There's a door to the left that leads to the street. That was going to be my escape route.*"

"*Mrs. Campos was serious about getting her money, huh?*"

"*Why shouldn't she be? That vile man wants to leave her broke and their kids without a pot to piss in. Is that fair?*"

"*What else did she tell you?*"

Zoe raised her eyebrow at him. "*Why are you asking?*"

"*Just curious.*"

She opened the door and took off running. Carver followed her and watched her mount a motorcycle. Before she cranked it up, he hopped on the back.

"*Trying to ditch me?*" he asked as he wrapped his arms around her waist. "*It's not that easy.*"

"*And if you're trying to kill me, it's not going to be easy either,*" she said. She started the engine and took off, then took a sharp turn as if she was trying to toss him off the back of the bike. Carver held on tighter.

"*I don't want to kill you, I'm on the job.*"

She slowed the bike. "*What?*"

"*Campos is under investigation and I want to make sure you don't know something that might get you killed,*" he said.

She turned down an abandoned alleyway and stopped the bike. Hopping off, she looked at him with questions dancing in her dazzling eyes. "*What are you, DEA? Police?*"

"*I can't say, but know that I don't mean you any harm. And I don't think you should be riding this thing, considering the alcohol you had at the party.*" He climbed off the bike and crossed over to her.

"So, I'm supposed to turn it over to you, secret agent man?" She rolled her eyes, but Carver thought that was exactly what she should've done.

"We're going to the same place, so it will be fine," he said as he hopped on the bike as if it were his own. Zoe followed his lead and got on the bike. Carver couldn't help but like the way her arms felt around him.

"Ladies and gentlemen," the captain's voice said over the intercom, breaking into Carver's thoughts. "We're running into a bit more turbulence, and for your safety, please bring your seats to the upright position and buckle your seat belts."

"Zoe," he said as he tapped her shoulder. "Sit up, babe."

Her eyes fluttered open just as the plane jostled through another pocket of turbulence. "Shit," she muttered. "Are we crashing?"

"No, more turbulence. Put your seat up and buckle up."

"How much longer do we have?" she asked as she snapped the buckle in place. "I swear this seems like the longest flight in history."

"Can't tell from your snoring," he quipped.

Zoe's eyebrow shot up in disgust. "I don't snore, thank you very much."

Carver stroked her arm. "We should be landing soon, and you can continue to believe you didn't keep every other passenger within earshot from catching a nap themselves."

Zoe looked around as if she expected to see angry faces staring back at her. When she didn't, she hauled off and punched Carver in the arm. "You really make me sick."

"I'm sure I do," he said as he pinched her cheek. "Buttercup."

Zoe rolled her eyes and then grabbed his hand as the plane passed through another pocket of turbulence. "I hate flying, I hate flying," she muttered.

Carver kissed her forehead. "It's all right."

And a few minutes later, everything was just fine as the captain announced that they'd entered calmer air and would be landing in New Mexico in about forty-five minutes.

"Thank God," Zoe said.

"You need a drink," Carver said.

"I don't drink on the job anymore," she said, then rolled her eyes.

When the flight attendant stopped at their seats, Carver got himself a rum and cola. "I'm not on the job, so I'm drinking."

Glancing at Carver's drink, Zoe opted for cranberry juice, though vodka would've calmed her nerves considerably.

For the next few minutes, Carver tried to log on to the airplane's Wi-Fi to see if there was an update on Singletary. It would've been ideal for him to find out that the son of a bitch had been arrested and he could tell Zoe that the FBI had called off the search for Jessica's body. He hated lying to her, because if the truth came out she wouldn't forgive him at all.

By the time he'd been able to get his tablet connected, the captain made the announcement to turn off electronic equipment, as they were about to make their landing.

"Great," he muttered.

"What's wrong? Can't log on to Facebook and find your Jeffrey Osborne girl?"

"My what?"

"The *woo-woo-woo* girl."

"Seriously? You were dreaming about that, huh? My tastes have changed since then. I need a woman who can handle a gun and motorcycle."

"Good luck with that."

"I don't need luck, I know where to find her," he said. Glancing at her, he saw a smile creep across her lips. She knew who he was talking about, and that's all he wanted.

After the plane landed, Zoe was one of the first people on her feet, stretching and arching her back in Carver's face. It took every ounce of self-control for him not to touch her tantalizing backside.

"So happy to be on the ground," she said as she reached into the overhead compartment to grab her carry-on bag.

"We still have a journey," he said as he rose to his feet. "There's a short flight from here to Santa Fe or we can—"

"Take the Rail Runner, we are definitely taking the Rail Runner."

"Good idea. Though I know you're just being a big baby about flying again."

"And? Let me work and you just follow my lead."

Carver gave her a mock salute. "Yes, ma'am."

They filed off the plane with the other passengers and headed for the shuttle that would take them to the famed train. Carver noticed that Zoe moved through the airport as if she were Usain Bolt. He nearly had to run to keep up with her. The time change, coupled with his overnight surveillance of Zoe, was taking a toll on his body. He couldn't tell her that, though. Finally, they made it to the shuttle.

"You're getting soft, G-man," she said as they took their seats on the bus.

"What are you talking about?" Carver asked after catching his breath.

"All of that huffing and puffing. How are you going to catch a terrorist when I can outrun you?"

"Don't worry, I have my ways. And keep in mind, I caught you before."

Zoe rolled her eyes. "Here we go, reliving the past again. Let's agree to let it go."

"Sure," he said, though he had no intention of doing so. If he had his druthers, they'd relive that night.

Carver's presence and his body heat made it impossible for Zoe to think of anything but getting naked with him as they rode the shuttle to downtown Albuquerque. Since the shuttle was crowded with tourists, they had to sit a little closer than what she was comfortable with. When his thigh touched hers, waves of desire tingled her spine. She inhaled sharply and then pulled out her cell phone, pretending to look for something in order to take her mind off Carver's touch, the thought of his kiss, and seeing him naked.

"Was Jessica ever reported missing to the local police?" Zoe asked, trying to think of something other than Carver's naked body.

"The local police weren't very helpful when we were

investigating her disappearance. The police didn't want or appreciate our help."

Zoe snorted. "I bet you guys came in like the gestapo, like you always do."

"Make up your mind. Do you want us to do our job, or is the beat cop inside of you still mad about jurisdictions and whatnot?"

She rolled her eyes, thinking about the one time she was involved in a case that the Feds were also interested in. The agents who had been working on the case acted as if they were the only people who knew how to investigate a crime.

"Shut up," she said.

"We had to light a fire underneath them to even look for Jessica. They didn't want to alarm people when they found out there was a serial killer in town."

"Sounds like someone didn't want to do their job. Anytime black women go missing, no one cares."

"That's true," he said. "Thank goodness for you."

Zoe rolled her eyes. "The FBI isn't any better. Look at how many black and brown girls went missing before you-all even started an investigation into sex trafficking? And all you got was Natalie. Do you-all even have a clue who the big bad wolf really is?"

"Do you?"

"Yes. Joseph Singletary. He's been trafficking girls for the past ten years," she said. "I know if I have a file on him, the FBI should as well. When I talked to Natalie, she was the one who talked about him and how he forced her into the business. She was one of his first victims. Now, I believe everything she said is bullshit, but it was the promise of a glamorous lifestyle behind the whole thing. Those girls thought they were going to be models or actresses. She married my brother to get access to the powerful people he worked with."

"How did she trick him?"

Zoe raised her right eyebrow. "How do most men get tricked? Big butt and a smile. When she told me that she was working with Singletary, I tried to let one of your agents know, but he waved me off, and then I was arrested."

"Sorry about that, but I arrested you hoping to crack Natalie. But she never opened up to us, and that's why she's doing all that time. What else do you know about Singletary?"

"When I was a cop in the Bronx, I stumbled across a young girl who'd met one of his guys online. He tried to turn her out, but my superiors didn't follow up with her. By the time Singletary got on the radar, I was on my way out the door. I did save that girl, though."

Carver smiled with pride. Of course she saved the girl. "What was her name?"

"Why is this starting to feel like an interrogation?"

"I'm just curious," he said. "We are trying to stop him, and getting inside that organization is like trying to break into Fort Knox."

"I know. Singletary is dangerous and doesn't take betrayal lightly. I think Natalie was genuinely scared when she got caught, not that I care. But something spooked her, because she was going to testify against him before you guys got to her. Who is Smallwood?"

"I know him. What about him?"

"That night I found her, she called him. He met us at the police station and then she changed her story, fell on her sword, and that was supposed to be the end of everything. But when you came to the press conference, you didn't say anything about Singletary."

"No one told me that Smallwood talked to her that night," Carver said.

"Not saying Natalie shouldn't have gone to jail, but why did she go down and Singletary is still out there lurking? Do you think it's possible that there is a leak inside your investigation? Maybe even Smallwood?"

"No," Carver said. "But I'm curious as to what he and Natalie talked about that night."

"Why are we even talking about this? We're supposed to be looking for Jessica Dolan. Do you think she might have been a part of the sex trafficking ring?"

"I'm sorry I even brought it up," he said.

She rolled her eyes, slowly beginning to realize why they could never work out. This man thought he knew everything! "When we get to Santa Fe, I'm going to talk to the police on my own."

"All right," he said.

Zoe opened her bag and pulled out her tablet. She pretended to be looking up information, but she was just doing everything humanly possible to ignore the sexy man sitting beside her.

Chapter 7

When the shuttle arrived downtown at the train station, Carver could tell Zoe was simmering with anger. He just didn't know why. The last thing he needed was for her fake investigation to kick the hornet's nest.

If she strolled into the Santa Fe Police Department and started asking the wrong questions, she could lead the wrong people right to her. Carver was going to let her have her anger and wallow in it for a while, because he had questions for Smallwood.

If his superior officer had talked to Natalie and knew about Singletary's organization, why hadn't they done more to stop him? When Zoe walked to the front of the train and took a seat, Carver stayed behind and called Smallwood.

"Why is this bitch still breathing?" Joseph growled at his men. "When are you motherfuckers going to get the job done?"

"She's slippery, boss," one of the men said. "And she

has a lot of security cameras around her house and office."

"Do you think I give a shit about that?" He rose to his feet and grabbed the man by his collar. "She cost me millions, has the FBI breathing down my fucking back, and she thinks she is just going to skip around with no consequences? No! I want her to suffer, and the bitch has to die." He threw the man to the floor and turned to his other two foot soldiers. "Fuck y'all standing around for? Find her and bring me her head!"

The men scurried out of the room and Singletary picked up his phone to call the one person he knew wouldn't let him down.

"Hello?" she said when she answered the phone.

"Hello, beautiful."

"I really can't talk right now, I'm trying to—"

"I know what you're doing, and I appreciate what you did for me in LA. But I need your help getting—"

"Yeah, about that. I can't really talk at this moment. Call you in about an hour," she said.

He ended the call and glared at the phone. What in the hell was wrong with people? They seemed to forget that he was the man in charge, and they were all breathing at his pleasure.

"What do you mean, Smallwood isn't available?" Carver growled into the phone.

"Agent Banks, he's heading to LA because of intel he and Covington received. That's all I know," the woman said. "I can send a message to him, but I don't know what else you want me to do."

"Sorry, Phoebe. I just have some important questions. I'll call back later," he said when he saw Zoe coming his way.

"Carver," she said as she plopped in the empty seat beside him. "I'm sorry if I was a little harsh earlier."

He placed his hand on her knee and shook it. "That's just your way. I came to you for a reason, so I guess I'm going to have to let you do your thing."

"Thanks," she said. "Have you gotten any information from the Bureau about the interviews with the parents?"

"Nothing yet." He grinned at her, hoping she wouldn't ask him another question. How could he keep lying to her when he had no clue if he could trust the people who were supposed to be protecting her?

Zoe relaxed in her seat and watched the passing landscape. The Southwest was beautiful, and part of her wished she was sitting with Carver on a vacation trip. *He isn't your man and never will be. Good sex doesn't make a good relationship.* She stole a glance at him and realized he'd been staring at her the entire time.

"What's with that look?" she asked.

"What look would that be?"

Rolling her eyes, Zoe sighed. "You love to split hairs, don't you? Carver, what's going on with us?"

"According to you, nothing, but we both know that isn't true." He took her face in his hands. "Zoe, there's a sizzle between us and as much as we try to fight it, it's growing hotter and hotter."

"We're not on some romantic getaway, we're supposed to be finding closure for a family. Why don't you keep focused on what's important? Maybe I should've taken this trip alone."

"Because you can't control yourself? I know what's at stake here, Zoe. I'm not going to do anything to put you in danger."

"Put me in danger?"

"You know what I mean," he said, then quickly looked away from her. "Zoe, trust and believe when the time is right, I'm going to make love to you, and you won't forget how I made you feel."

Shivering, she rose to her feet. Then the train jerked and she fell in Carver's lap. *Right time be damned.* He brought his mouth down on top of hers, kissing her with a hot and deliberate passion that made her weak.

His tongue explored her mouth, staking his claim on his woman. Carver wanted Zoe to realize that no other man could kiss her this way, make her moan with such a melody or heat her body like an oven.

She pressed her hands against his chest, pushing him away. "Carver."

"I'm not going to apologize, if that's what you're looking for." He ran his index finger across her kiss-swollen bottom lip. "You taste delicious."

"You're not making it easy for me to focus. And that's a big problem."

"Zoe, you plopped down in my lap, making things really hard for me. So, you got what you deserved."

"Oh my God, you should take your act to the Apollo so that Sandman can usher you off the stage. I didn't plop. I fell. You took advantage!"

Carver folded his arms across his chest. "Isn't that what you do when opportunity falls in your lap?"

"I can't with you."

"You can, you just keep fighting it." Winking at her,

Carver knew he had to get his hormones under control if he was going to have a chance to be with Zoe. Keeping her alive had to come before anything else.

Zoe was about to move away from Carver when her phone rang. She hoped that it wasn't a client looking to hire her for another case when she saw the 718 area code.

"This is Zoe."

"Zoe, how are you? I bet you will never guess who this is."

"Probably not, and I hate guessing games, so just tell me."

"Lewis Martinez," he said.

"Lew, what's going on? And never in a million years would I have ever expected to hear from you."

"I know. I need to talk to you. Are you in your office today?"

"No. What's going on?" Zoe knew she and Lewis hadn't seen eye to eye in a long time. According to the rumors around town, he thought she was the cause of his career ending.

"I'm thinking about suing the NYPD, and I know that's something you're good at. I want you to help me."

"Are you serious?"

"Very."

"What are you suing for?"

"The loss of my pension. It's tough out here, and I need my money to survive. It wasn't easy for me to get another job with what they have on my record."

She sighed into the phone again. "Don't you think this would be a conflict of interest?"

"Despite what happened, I trust you."

"Let's set up some time next week to get together," she said. Carver glanced in her direction with his eyebrow raised. When she hung up the phone, he asked, "What was that all about?"

"Nothing that involves you."

"It does if it is going to take you away from the case I paid you to solve."

"Probably won't because this is a guy . . . my former partner says he needs my help. I'm just going to meet with him out of professional courtesy."

"Why waste your time?"

"Because it's my business and I will do what I want to do with it."

Carver threw up his hands. "Whatever you say."

She narrowed her eyes at him and forced herself not to curse him out. "You don't dictate how I run my business, and until you drop a million dollars in my lap, you don't own what I do."

"You treat all of your clients like this, or is this just reserved for me?"

"It's my understanding that my client is the FBI and not you. I can treat you any way I choose to."

"Zoe, you have a hell of a mouth," he said as he shook his head.

"I can quit. Because, remember, you came to me."

"Not going to let you do that. Zoe, I need you."

"Start acting like it, because I certainly don't need you."

If only you knew how wrong you are, he thought as he turned toward the window.

* * *

Finally, she had a moment alone and she could call Singlctary back. He wasn't going to like what she had to say, either.

"Yeah?"

"Joe, it's me."

"I know. What was going on earlier when I called you?"

"Trying to explain why our witness ended up dead. That little girl was about to tell everything, and I couldn't have that," she said.

"How did you cover it up?"

"Overdose. If I were you, I'd pull up stakes again. Someone in the Bureau has found your current location and we're waiting on a warrant from a federal judge to come raid you."

"Come on, this place is actually clean. Besides, I'm tired of running and there's something I need from you."

"Anything, baby."

"Zoe Harrington has to die. She's the reason I'm living like a fucking nomad. Where is she?"

"Right now, she has protection from . . . I have to go." The call ended and she stuffed her phone in her pocket.

"Ready, Agent?" Smallwood asked.

Wendy smiled. "Yes, sir."

Chapter 8

Zoe stretched her arms above her head as she stepped off the train. She wanted a nap, but she needed to contact the police and find out if they had uncovered any dead Jane Does who could be Jessica.

"Let's get some food," Carver said, breaking into her thoughts.

"You eat, I'm going to go to the police department. The sooner we get started on finding out information about Jessica, the better."

"You're not going to be worth much if no one can hear your questions over your stomach rumbling."

As if on cue, her stomach did growl. "I guess you're right."

"There's a spot right here." Carver pointed to a beautiful art deco building. "Smell that? We just need to follow that scent."

Zoe inhaled and nodded in agreement. "Fajitas!"

"Excited even though you didn't want to eat." Carver shook his head.

"I hope they have Wi-Fi. That way I can eat and do

a little research on Jessica's disappearance and what happened in Santa Fe with the killer. Where was this guy captured again?"

"In Baton Rouge. He went home, took a couple of bodies with him, and that's when the carnage was discovered. Can we eat, then talk about this later?" he said as he turned her toward the restaurant. When they walked in, Zoe wasn't happy to see there was a twenty-minute wait. She guessed that everyone on the train had been just as hungry as she and Carver were.

"While we're waiting, you can call your field office and find out about getting those transcripts from Jessica's parents' interviews," she said as she plopped down on the wooden bench across from the hostess station.

"You just don't stop, do you?" Carver pulled out his flip phone and Zoe shot him a questioning look.

"Really?"

"Doesn't drop calls," he mouthed. He walked outside and hoped Smallwood would answer the phone. Nothing. He hung up and started to call Wendy, but he decided against it. Since Zoe was under the assumption that he wasn't able to get the transcripts from the office, he could tell her that nothing had changed. Returning inside, he sat beside her and smiled.

"Anything?"

He shook his head. "Still waiting for someone to get the files."

She rolled her eyes. "How are we supposed to get anything done without all of the information we need?"

"There are several things that you need, and I'd be more than happy to give them to you. But keep in mind the time difference and the fact that I'm tired. And I know you are, too, even though you want to pretend you're Superwoman. We can take a little time to get our bearings before jumping into this case headfirst."

"Maybe that's how you work, but I didn't travel across the country just for fajitas."

Before he could reply, his phone buzzed. Checking the message, he frowned at Smallwood's response.

Singletary got away, again.

"What was that all about?" Zoe asked, noting the scowl on his face.

"Another case," he said.

"That bad?"

Before he could reply, a waiter approached them to take them to a table. "Welcome to our dining room," the man said. "Would you-all like a window seat, or first available?"

"First available," Zoe said, causing Carver to laugh. She shot him a silencing look. Throwing up his hands, he shook his head, then followed the waiter and Zoe to a table in the corner of the restaurant.

"I'll be right back with chips and fresh salsa. Would you like to order your drinks now?"

"Just water for me," Zoe said.

"I'll have the same."

When the waiter walked away, Carver leaned across the table and smiled at Zoe. "I thought you weren't hungry," he quipped.

She crossed her legs and forced herself not to think of the wetness pooling in her panties. Why was this man so sexy just doing something regular? "Just hush."

"You're the one who said you weren't hungry, but

you wanted this table in the middle of nowhere when we could've waited and had a view."

"Don't need a view, I just need food," she said, and leaned back in her chair. Turning away from him, she forced herself to focus on the menu and not the man sitting across from her.

His lips made her think of how they felt against hers, how good they felt between her thighs, and how he'd kissed her senseless in her office and on the train. What had she gotten herself into?

"Zoe?" Carver's voice snapped her out of her wanton thoughts.

"What?"

"Where did your mind go?"

"Was thinking about the case," she lied.

He reached across the table and pulled the menu from Zoe's hands.

"Why are you trying to hide from me?" His smile was Zoe's undoing. She turned away from him and shook her head.

"No one is hiding anything," she replied. "And I wish you'd stay on task. It's always something . . ."

Carver leaned in and stroked Zoe's cheek, then pulled her in for a sizzling kiss. Any thoughts of resisting his pillow-soft lips floated away from her the moment his tongue parted her lips. She moaned and shivered as he deepened the kiss. When Carver pulled back, he smiled at her. "You needed that."

"No, you need to keep your lips and hands to yourself."

Leaning back, Carver folded his arms across his chest. "Because you hated it so much."

"No, because I'm on the job and you need to let me do it. Call your office and get those transcripts!"

Carver pulled out his cell phone and dialed Wendy's number. "I'm going outside, where there's less noise," he said as the waiter walked over with the chips and salsa. Zoe narrowed her eyes at him as he walked away.

Outside, Carver called Wendy because he needed to know what was going on with Smallwood and the investigation. He was sure that Wendy probably didn't know much, but he hoped that she might have overheard something.

"Agent Covington."

"It's Carver," he said. "Where is Smallwood?"

"Prepping for the raid on Singletary. He got away in LA, but I traced a signal from one of the computers and we have a lock on his new location."

"Where is he?"

"We're not on a secure line, I don't want to say. Where are you and Zoe?"

"We're safe," he replied.

"How long do you plan to keep her wherever you are? I know the raid is going on at one of Singletary's houses soon. So, maybe you can call this thing off."

"Not until he's arrested and we know who he may have hired to kill her."

"Does she know anything about his organization?"

"Working on that. She did tell me something disturbing. Did you know Smallwood talked to Natalie the night she was arrested?"

"No. What did she say?"

"Don't know. Why don't you do me a favor and see if there is a report or a recording of his interview. The way Singletary wiggles out of charges, I'm beginning to think that he has an insider in the Bureau feeding him information."

"And you think it's Smallwood?" Her voice rose with disbelief.

"Zoe said he talked to Natalie the night she was arrested. And right after he talked to her, she clammed up."

"She did, but I can't see Smallwood working with Singletary. He's by the books."

"I'm sure someone thought the same thing about Robert Hanssen."

"Did you read the *History of the FBI* every night before you went to bed?"

"It's important to know these things and know when you're in the midst of a potential double agent."

"The cold war is over, I doubt Smallwood is some kind of spy." Carver could've sworn he heard her laugh.

"And you don't think stopping Singletary is important? If someone inside that Bureau is funneling information to him, we need to find out who it is."

"So, now we have to investigate while doing an investigation? This is too much," she said. "We have enough to deal with."

And this was why he couldn't trust that Wendy was the right agent he could depend on for information about Singletary. Something about the way she was dealing with the case gave him pause.

"This is important," he said.

"I know that, but getting Singletary is the priority. You're looking for things that aren't there."

"Wendy, how do you know that we don't have a mole

in the agency? Singletary is always a step ahead of us. How do you think that's happening?"

"I have to go."

"Wendy!" Carver said, then looked at his phone, realizing that she'd hung up. Returning to the restaurant, Carver took his seat across from Zoe.

"Everything all right?" She gave him a slow once-over, noting the scowl on his face.

"Yeah, I was talking to one of the agents who should've been sending me some information on Dolan and hasn't done it yet."

"I guess you had to throw your weight around, huh? You like having power and control, don't you?"

"Don't do that," he said. "I'm trying to do my job and I need other people to do what I ask them to do so we can solve this case."

Zoe threw her hands up and shook her head. "Well, I did order you fajitas. Did I do that right?"

"Depends, did you get meat?"

"Yes, I did. But I wasn't sure if you wanted steak or chicken, so I got a combination of steak, chicken, and veggie. Hope that's okay."

"That's awesome, because I'm starving. Though, you can keep the veggies to yourself."

Zoe raised her right eyebrow as she fingered a chip. "So once we're done, I want you to check into the hotel and I'm going to the police department to see if I can make friends with an officer who may have worked on the Dolan case."

"Thought you wanted me to throw my FBI cred around to get you easier access to the information that you wanted."

"Changed my mind. I want to talk down and dirty with the police officers. Don't want to hurt your feelings."

"My feelings won't be hurt, and I'd like to know what's going on."

"You will when you get my report," she snapped. "It's time for you to stop acting like you're my partner, or that I need you, so that I can do my job."

"Whatever. That's not what I'm doing at all. But you were brought on to help me, not to take over and do your own thing."

Zoe tossed her chip in the bowl. "You know what, I can leave. There are plenty of other cases in New York I can be working on. I don't need you. According to you, you need me."

Carver popped a chip in his mouth. After swallowing, he focused his gaze on Zoe. "I do need you. And I'm not trying to be an ogre here, but there are still protocols that I have to follow. So, if I seem a little heavy-handed sometimes, don't take it personal."

Zoe rolled her eyes and held her tongue. She was about to say something when the waiter walked over to the table with a sizzling pan of meat and grilled veggies.

Zoe spooned meat and peppers on her soft tortilla.

"So, I'm going to get the silent treatment now?" Carver asked.

She nodded, then took a bite of her food. Carver grinned and reached across the table for her hand. "This isn't going to work. Zoe, we're in this together and communication is going to be key to solving this case."

"Stop touching me. I'll talk to you when I have something to say."

"Tell me this, what are you going to do at the police station?"

"Work. Do you need me to share every detail with you?" Zoe rolled her eyes and slipped her hand from underneath his.

"I'm going to let you run the point on this; however, I'm going to the police department as well."

Zoe took another bite of her food, reminding herself that Carver had every right to go with her to the police station. But he would cramp her style if he went in there flashing his FBI credentials. "Fine." The rest of her blistering comment had to die on her tongue as the waiter returned to the table to check on them. Forcing a smile, Zoe told him how she was enjoying the food.

"Too bad I can't say the same about the company," she muttered.

"Heard that."

She speared Carver with an icy glare. "Meant for you to."

"Sometimes you act like a big baby, you know that, right?"

"And you always act like a giant asshole."

"You know what's big and giant about me. Whenever you're ready to release that tension, just let me know."

Zoe narrowed her eyes at him and wondered if the grilled peppers or the steak would have a bigger sting if she tossed either at him. Instead, she made another fajita. "You don't know how lucky you are that this food is delicious. Otherwise, you'd be wearing this right now."

Carver knew he needed to get serious, and though it made all the sense in the world for Zoe to visit the police department without him, he wasn't going to let her out of his sight. Not when he didn't know if there was an inside man trying to help Singletary take Zoe out.

What if I tell her the truth? She should know that someone wants her dead and why.

Zoe locked eyes with him. "What?"

"Nothing, I'm just sitting here wondering if you were a mean girl in school or the one who got revenge on the bullies?"

"Why, are you a bully and you think I'm going to kick your ass?" She smiled wickedly at him. "Because I can."

Carver returned her smile with a smirk of his own. "You wish."

"When I find Jessica, we're taking this to the ring."

"You just challenged me to a fight, yet I'm the bully? But you're on, babe. And when I win, what do I get?"

"You know what happens when you assume things, right, Agent Banks?"

Before Carver could reply, the waiter was back at the table. Zoe had no idea what she'd started with her challenge.

Chapter 9

Carver watched Zoe as she walked the few blocks to the Santa Fe Police Department. No one followed her, though a few men took notice of the shapely PI as she hustled along. Maybe no one in the Bureau had leaked their location to anyone. Yet. He still had nagging questions about Smallwood talking to Natalie the night of her arrest. She'd been the only way into the organization, and he let her walk. Even if she'd only walked into a jail cell.

This makes no sense, he thought as he kept a keen eye on the man who'd stopped Zoe in midstroll. When he saw Zoe give the man a hard shove to the chest, then dropped him as if he were a sack of potatoes, he started to rush over to her, but two police officers grabbed the man and put him in handcuffs. Then he watched one of the officers shake hands with Zoe as if she'd done them a favor taking the strange man down.

All right, Betty Badass.

* * *

"Some people are so stupid," Zoe said as she walked into the police department with her new best friend, Officer Tony Carroll. "How do you snatch a purse this close to the police department? And then he called me the last thing a woman ever wants to be called."

"The dreaded B-word, huh?"

Zoe nodded. "Bet he won't do that again."

"Those moves out there—are you a police officer?"

"In another life. Now, I'm a private investigator based out of New York."

"Really? Are you working or vacationing in Santa Fe?"

"Working a case, and I need some help."

He expelled a breath. "Probably going to have to point you in the direction of the chief, because we have a policy about working with outside agencies."

"Do I look like an agency? Now, to be honest, I am working with the FBI on a cold case that I'd love for you to help me with. Let me ask you this, would you rather deal with an arrogant G-man, or me?" She batted her eyelashes for emphasis.

"Okay, what's this case about?"

Zoe gave him the elevator pitch about the disappearance of Jessica Dolan and the Bayou Serial Killer. He nodded as she spoke, telling her that he remembered the case and how many people in Santa Fe were scared when a body was found at the Trailer Ranch RV Resort.

"Just one body was found there?" she asked, hoping that he wouldn't stop talking.

"Yes. It turned out that it was a homeless man who'd died of natural causes, but around that time, there were reports of the killer being in town. People were on edge for months. There was even a local group who started digging up the land behind the resort because they swore the killer had buried bodies there."

"Had he?"

"I don't think anything was found, but I'd have to look at the reports again. That's been several years ago."

Zoe smiled at him and placed her hand on his forearm. "Would you get a copy of the report for me?"

"Only because you're pretty and saving me from having to deal with a prick from the FBI. Come with me and I'll see what I can dig up for you. But if anyone asks what's going on, I'm just taking your statement."

She offered him a bright smile. "Thank you." They walked over to an empty desk and the officer sat down to boot up the computer.

"What's her name again? The dead girl you're looking for?"

"Jessica Dolan."

Typing her name in the computer, he looked over his shoulder and glanced at Zoe with a smile on his lips. "I'm off tomorrow. If you want me to, I can show you some places where you might find a dead body. I'll even bring the water so that we don't get dehydrated."

"Thanks, but I like to work alone. The last partner I had turned out to be on the crooked side."

"Come on, you can't judge us all by the bad behavior of one."

She rolled her eyes, thinking that it was more than one bad apple that'd spoiled the bunch. And she was going to have to go and deal with one in a few minutes.

* * *

Carver dialed Smallwood's number and it went straight to voicemail. The raid on Singletary had been hours ago. Why wasn't he answering the phone? He started to call Wendy back when he saw Zoe walking out of the police department with a smiling officer. Rolling his eyes, he urged himself not to give in to the burning jealousy in the pit of his stomach and deck that man.

How could he resist Zoe? Hell, Carver was having a hard time doing that himself. Just looking at her made him want to make love to her until they were sated and she was branded as his. Part of him wondered how well he could protect her when all he wanted to do was strip her clothes off every time she was next to him. Carver knew one thing for certain. He was not going to lose another woman he loved. Not to violence. Not when he could stop it.

Turning away from Zoe and the cop, he pulled out his smartphone and logged on to the Hotels.com app to book a room. Carver said a silent prayer that no one would trace what he'd just done. Luckily the hotel that was closest to the police department had two adjoining rooms available for the evening. He dashed down the street to get checked in and hoped to have the keys before Zoe called him. He tucked the smartphone in his carrying case with his tablet after turning it off. Then his flip phone rang.

"Agent Banks."

"Carver, it's Wendy. We have a situation. Smallwood was shot during the raid on Singletary's safe house."

"What?"

"It was as if he knew we were coming. I think you

and Zoe need to get out of New Mexico as soon as possible. Singletary is tracing her cell phone."

"How do you know this?"

"We found evidence of it before we got involved in the shooting. Once we started questioning him about Zoe, that's when things got out of control."

"How is Smallwood doing?"

"It's touch and go," she said. "I told him that we shouldn't have gone in before we had a backup team in place, but he was adamant."

Carver furrowed his brows. That didn't sound like Smallwood at all. He knew this man to be by the book. But then again, after the Natalie situation, he didn't know if he could trust what he thought he knew about his boss.

"I have a plan to get us out of here, but how am I going to pry that phone from her hand?"

"Where are you guys going next?"

"I'll let you know when we get there." Carver hung up the phone when he saw Zoe coming his way.

"Please tell me you have a room. I'm about to drop."

He nodded. "I have reservations at this spot right here," he said as he pointed to the quaint inn across the street.

"There had better be two rooms, or you will be the second man I take down today."

Carver grinned. "Don't threaten me with a good time. And yes, there are two rooms."

"Have you gotten those transcripts yet?"

Carver shook his head. "I've been checking my tablet, but it died and I haven't had a chance to charge it. And since I don't have a smartphone, I can't check my email. Let me take a look at your phone. Maybe I can pull up the email there."

"We can do it later, I just need twenty minutes to sleep."

"I can take care of it while you're asleep."

"Carver, you think I'm going to hand my phone over to you and let you install some kind of spyware? I was born at night, but not last night."

Baby girl, you're already being watched. If you want to live, you better give me that phone, he thought as he stared at her. "Zoe, I'm always going to find you, and I don't need spyware for that." He took a step closer to her. "I can smell you when you walk in the room."

She opened her mouth, but no sound came out. Then she turned her back to him and reached into her pocket to retrieve her phone. "Here."

"Thank you." Carver fumbled with the phone for a second, then dropped it, smashing it on the cobblestone walkway. Zoe screamed, causing a few passersby to give them sidelong glances.

"You fucking idiot! You just broke my phone."

"I'm so sorry, Zoe. It was an accident. Why didn't you have it in a case?" He struggled to keep his poker face. Her reaction was priceless.

She narrowed her eyes at him, then punched him as hard as she could on his shoulder. "You are not turning this around on me. Clumsy! So, how am I supposed to get in contact with my other clients? You and the FBI aren't the only people I work for."

Carver would've felt bad if he hadn't taken a step to save her life. "I can replace your phone, Zoe. It's not that serious."

She narrowed her eyes at him. "Go to hell."

This time, Carver did laugh. "Get a temporary phone until we get back to New York. I'm sure you have a service that can route your calls to your new cell."

She pointed to the entrance of the hotel. "Make yourself useful and get the room keys."

Carver pocketed her broken phone. "Yes, ma'am." *Mission accomplished.* After getting the room keys, Carver walked outside and found Zoe pacing like a caged tiger.

"Here you go," he said. She snatched the key card from his hand, still glaring at him as if he'd killed her puppy. "Zoe, it's just a phone."

"And you're just a jackass. Where is the room? I hope we're on separate floors."

"You're right next door to me. So, don't invite your little cop friend over for a booty call," he teased.

"I really don't like you." Zoe sauntered away and Carver was mesmerized by the sway of her shapely hips.

"Damn," he muttered, then rushed to catch up with her. "We're on the third floor."

"I see that." She waved the card in his face. "The number is clearly written on here."

"Are you really that mad about your phone?"

"I will be charging you for it. And I'm talking full retail." She pressed the up button on the elevator. When the doors opened she stepped on and glared at him. "Take the stairs." Zoe pressed the button to close the doors and left him standing on the other side.

Carver didn't head for the stairs immediately; instead he walked over to the front desk clerk. "Hi. I dropped my key card to room three-sixteen. Can you make me another one, please?"

The comely clerk smiled at him. "No problem, sir. Are you and your wife going to be okay? Someone said they saw you arguing in the walkway."

"It's nothing a little blue box from Tiffany's can't fix."

She handed him the key. "Smart man. Good luck."

Zoe plopped down on the queen-size bed and sighed. She was tired but too keyed up to sleep. Rolling over on her back, she stared at the art deco ceiling. "It is just a phone, and accidents happen." A beat passed and Zoe was on her feet. The right thing to do was to go next door and apologize to Carver. Phones could be replaced, and if anyone else had dropped her phone, she would've just shrugged it off, but it was Carver. Something about him just made her angry and filled with want. She still felt the sting of his betrayal two years ago. Waking up in that bed alone had made her feel cheap. And his note.

Sorry to leave you like this, but last night was wonderful.

The next time she'd seen him, he was FBI Agent Carver Banks, not Xavier. And he had the nerve to act as if nothing had happened between them—at least publicly. He'd tried to explain what had happened that night—FBI investigation. Had to take Campos down and keep her out of harm's way.

The last thing Zoe needed was protection. She was good with a gun, she could take a man down in hand-to-hand combat, and if push came to shove, she always kept a knife on her. She had grown tired of people thinking she needed someone to look after her—as if she couldn't do it herself.

Zach and her father wanted her to get into the family business, and for two months after graduating from college, she tried it. But every time she wanted to show a property or set up a meeting with a client, one of them wanted to be there. She could understand her father's hovering. She had been brand-new to the business, but Zach! He was just being annoying and using that five-minutes-older mess as an excuse.

So, she quit and joined the NYPD. She hadn't given them a heads-up until she'd been in her third week of the police academy.

Zoe grabbed her room key and headed next door to do something she rarely did. Eat crow. Knocking on his room door, she braced herself for whatever smart-ass comments Carver would lay on her.

He opened the door, shirtless with a white towel wrapped around his waist. "Zoe. Wasn't expecting you."

She blinked as she drank in the absolute magnificence of his body. And there it was, left shoulder down to his forearm, the Marine tattoo. She was transfixed by the detailed artwork and reached up to run her finger across it. He grabbed her hand. "Really?"

"Sorry. I came to say that I'm sorry about how I reacted about the phone. Maybe I was just tired and . . ."

"Come inside. I have some news about those transcripts that we've been waiting for."

Zoe took a deep breath and followed him into the room. The steam from the shower had filled the room, or maybe she was just that hot for him. She started to sit on the bed, but that would've made temptation too damn easy. Instead, Zoe leaned on the edge of the desk and watched him move across the room as if he was fully dressed.

He knows what he's doing. "So, what's the news?"

"One of the agents in the field office finally sent over the transcripts, and I was reading over them. It seems as if there may be a connection with Jessica and the killer that goes to Vegas. She may not be buried here."

Zoe nodded. "That's what Tony said. He's getting me some more information on what the local investigation uncovered on the serial killer after he was spotted with her."

"Tony, huh? You two got really close in such a short period of time."

"Can we be serious for a minute?" Zoe tried to keep her focus on his eyes, but that muscular thigh peeking from underneath that towel made it hard to focus. She rubbed her throat as he turned toward the bathroom.

"I am being serious," he said, then closed the bathroom door behind him. "I guess it's a good thing he was so helpful. Now we know that we don't have to stick around here much longer."

"Do you know that for sure? There may be some clues in the reports that could help us when we head to our next stop." Zoe's breath caught in her chest when Carver walked out of the bathroom in nothing but black and silver boxer briefs. Simple boxers, she could've handled, but that form-fitting underwear did nothing but highlight every throbbing inch of his tantalizing body. *Jesus.*

Carver smirked, seemingly reading her dirty thoughts as if she'd written them on the mirror in bright red lipstick. "What's wrong with you?"

"What are you talking about, Carver?"

"You keep looking at me like I'm a piece of meat. Have you heard anything that I've said?"

"Every word." She forced herself to look into his eyes. "Are we off to Las Vegas now, or are you going to wait until we get the reports from the police?"

"We can wait another day, I guess. Then you can kiss your new boyfriend goodbye."

"Please stop it. You're acting like a pure jerk." Zoe turned her head toward the window, but Carver's presence filled the room, and no matter how she tried to avoid him, there he was. Sexy. Masculine. Dangerous. She inhaled and her chest was filled with the scent of Carver's manhood. It was familiar to her; she'd gotten drunk on this smell two years ago when he pretended to be X. Pretended that their passion was real.

As if he knew what she was thinking, Carver closed the space between them and wrapped his arms around Zoe's waist.

"I should go," she said in a near moan.

"Stay."

"No. Because if I do, we're going to make the biggest mistake in the world, and I need to call my brother."

Carver smiled. "He doesn't like me much, right?"

"Hates your guts."

"And how does his sister feel?" He pulled her closer,

knowing she felt the effect she had on him. She groaned as he pressed his hardness against her thighs.

Zoe pushed against his chest. "I-I have to go." She dashed out of the room and promised herself that she was not going to fall for Carver Banks!

Chapter 10

Carver watched with a smile as Zoe practically ran out the door. Even though he knew the flirting was wrong, especially if he was going to keep Zoe safe, he couldn't help himself. He wanted that woman as much as he needed his next breath. But the most important thing was to keep her safe, and he couldn't do that if he kept focusing on his hard dick.

Sighing, he thought about his next move and how he was going to keep it secret from the Bureau. Going to Las Vegas wasn't going to help them find Jessica Dolan's body, and as much as he didn't want to keep doing it, he was going to have to build another lie to keep her in the dark about their cross-country movements. Part of him wanted to tell her the truth, but he knew her reaction wouldn't be a good one. All he had to do was look at how she went crazy about a broken phone. Shaking his head, Carver knew he had to nix the idea of being honest with her.

Besides, he had to figure out who he could trust with this assignment. He didn't even want to get Wendy further involved in this either. Was there a mole in the middle of the investigation against Singletary, and how long was he going to be able to keep Zoe in the dark about her life being in danger?

He thought about getting rid of his phone as well. Picking up his phone, he took it apart to see if there was any kind of tracking device inside the phone Small-wood had given him. When he didn't find anything, Carver put the phone back together and tossed it on the bed.

He dressed quickly and headed to the hotel's business center. He didn't want to risk using his tablet and having the signal traced. He'd already messed up when he used his smartphone, which he had turned off and buried in the bottom of his suitcase. Hopping on the computer, he Googled Las Vegas hotels with wedding chapels. The list seemed to be endless, but what did he expect? Besides gambling, people went to Sin City to get married. He decided that he was going to tell Zoe that Dolan and the killer had been seen in Vegas. After booking a room at the Hilton and choosing the option to pay at the location, Carver realized that things had gotten even more serious.

Wendy nestled against Joseph as he slept. She was too wired to sleep. Too excited to close her eyes. Shooting Delvin Smallwood had been the most exciting thing she'd ever done in her career. That idiot shouldn't have been her superior. She'd worked hard for the Bureau, and all she'd gotten was a pat on the head and a job behind a computer. Wendy wanted to be in the field, she wanted to be in the thick of important terrorism investigations, not trying to save fast-ass girls who wanted to sell their bodies.

After all, no one told them to talk to strangers online to begin with. Yes, Joe was a criminal, but these girls were hardly victims. And if that bitch Natalie hadn't gotten caught and been entangled with Zachary Harrington, the FBI wouldn't give a hot damn about missing black and brown girls. Wendy released a frustrated sigh as she thought about the botched search for her missing sister. No one cared about Amber Covington. She'd been a bright college student who'd gone missing from the University of South Carolina, and even with Wendy being an FBI trainee, she couldn't get the help she needed to find her sister.

When the Bureau and the local police actually took the case seriously, Amber's body was found in a shallow grave outside of Sumter, South Carolina, where an airman from the local Air Force base had buried three other women whom he'd raped and murdered. When she'd found out that Smallwood and Carver had been assigned to her sister's case, she knew that she would get her revenge one day.

It had been kismet when she'd been assigned to the field office that Smallwood ran. And then Carver Banks became one of the senior agents there. He never even acknowledged her loss. Cocky bastard. That's why she'd hoped their first time out in the field would've been the end of his life. Instead, he'd made it seem as if she was inept, and she'd gotten the cyber duties.

It wasn't hard for her to start working with Singletary. At first, she'd been chatting with one of his pimps on a social media website; then she'd had the chance to meet the man himself.

Joe wasn't much to look at: average height, a beer belly and a beard, but he made up for his average looks with his confidence and swagger. Somehow he knew she wasn't the typical FBI agent and he fed into her anger. He told her that if she'd help him stay ahead of the investigation into his organization that he would reward her greatly. She needed him to make that reward happen soon. She was tired of playing this game, and with Carver having his suspicions, her double life might be coming to an end. But once Joe paid her, Wendy could disappear to Haiti or some other country where no one would think to look.

With Smallwood out of the way, she could work with Joe without having to look over her shoulder when feeding him information about investigations, keeping him one step ahead of the FBI. All they had to do was get rid of Carver and Zoe. As soon as she found out where they were going after New Mexico, she was going to make that happen.

Joe stirred as Wendy licked his earlobe. "Wake up. We need to celebrate a little more."

Groaning, he opened his eyes and smiled at her. "You're a freak, and I like that."

She mounted his growing erection. "Then go ahead and show me how much you like this."

Zoe woke up from the most delicious dream. Carver's face buried between her thighs, licking her wetness as if it were melting ice cream. Her screams woke her and she prayed he didn't hear it. Zoe figured by the way she called his name, he hadn't. Otherwise, he'd be at her door right now. And when she opened it, she'd be certain to live out every minute of her erotic dream.

"Oh my God, I'm insane." She rose from the bed and headed for the bathroom. An ice-cold shower was in order. Just as she was about to strip out of her clothes, there was a knock at the door. Figuring that it was temptation on the other side, Zoe started to ignore it.

But the knocking continued and she crossed over to the door. When she looked out of the peephole, she didn't see Carver, but a man with a cart who looked to be from room service.

"I didn't order anything," she called through the door.

"Compliments of the hotel."

"I'm good."

The man didn't leave, and Zoe couldn't see what he was doing as he knelt down next to the cart. Backing away from the door, she looked around the room for a weapon and cursed herself for listening to Carver and leaving her gun in New York. She unplugged the heavy lamp from the nightstand and waited to see if the man on the other side of the door was going to try something.

He knocked again. "Room service."

"Go. Away!"

She heard a bang, as if the man was trying to kick the door in. Zoe wrapped the cord around the base of the lamp and got ready to pounce. Then the banging stopped. Holding the lamp, ready to strike if needed, she opened the door and saw Carver on top of the man and a gun at his side.

"What in the hell?" Zoe exclaimed. Carver locked eyes with her as he slammed the man's head into the floor.

"Go inside and lock the door."

"What's going on, Carver?"

"Inside!" His order came out like a bark, and Zoe followed his direction. She slammed the door and locked it.

"Who are you?" Carver growled as he held the fake waiter down on the floor.

"Get off me!"

"Answer me." Glancing over his shoulder, Carver saw two security guards and a police officer coming his way. The officer was about to draw his weapon when Carver lifted his free hand. "FBI, I'm on the job."

"Fine, but you need to let the man go." The officer reached for his handcuffs. "What happened here?"

Carver narrowed his eyes as he let the would-be hit man go. "Can we talk about this at the department?"

The officer groaned and cuffed the man. "Fine. You guys could've given us a heads-up that the FBI was working a case here."

Carver held his tongue because he wanted to tell the young cop where he could stick his snotty attitude. The last thing he needed was for Zoe to hear the truth about why they were in New Mexico.

Arriving at the police department, the officer handcuffed the suspect to a chair and then waved for his sergeant. "Have a seat," the officer said to Carver.

"I'll stand."

"Whatever."

The sergeant, a tall and shapely woman with fire-red hair, approached Carver with a scowl on her pale face. "Agent, what are you doing in my city?"

Carver pulled out his FBI badge and showed it to her. "Can we find a quiet corner where we can talk?"

"Sure, follow me." They walked into an empty office and she sat down behind the metal desk. "So, Agent Banks, what's going on?"

"I'm investigating a sex trafficking ring. There are no ties to New Mexico, but the woman that man was trying to kill is a key part of the investigation."

"Does she live here?"

"No. We came here together. I need to know everything about that guy. He may be involved in a murder for-hire plot the FBI is investigating. I'd like to question him."

She folded her arms across her chest. "You gave me a lot of surface information and I'm just supposed to turn a suspect over to you because you have those capital letters on your badge? Who is your superior? I want to verify that—"

"He was shot last night, and I don't have time to get into a pissing contest with you about a would-be killer. After I question him, he's yours."

"I never said I was going to allow you to question him. I have to clear it with my lieutenant."

Carver folded his arms across his massive chest. "Then why don't you do that?"

Rising to her feet, she rolled her eyes at Carver and slow-walked to the door. Then she turned around and said, "You can catch a massive amount of flies with honey, but you Feds like to come in here and pretend you know everything about law enforcement and we're just rejects."

"I'm trying to keep someone alive, and you can help or get the fuck out of my way." The hardness in Carver's voice must have been the honey she needed to head out the door and get her supervisor. Didn't take long for a bearded man in a pair of slacks and white button-down shirt to walk into the office.

"Agent Banks, what brings the FBI to our fair city?"

"I guess your sergeant didn't tell you?"

"Just want to hear it from you. The US Army always taught me to trust but verify." He extended his hand to Carver. "Lieutenant Dana Shanult."

"Nice to meet you." The men shook hands and Carver felt less combative. "Listen, the woman that man was trying to kill is under my protection. We're here because of an investigation and the fact that there is a hit on her life. I can't go into intimate details with you about it."

"Of course. You boys in the Bureau always have your secrets, but this attempted murder did happen in my jurisdiction."

"I don't care who tries that son of a bitch. I want the motherfucker who hired him. Like I've said before, this isn't about where the crime took place. I have bigger fish that I'm looking to get on the hook."

Shanult rocked back on his heels. "You seem to be taking this case rather personally. Now, if I give you clearance to talk to this man, do I have to worry about hearing that he was abused in Santa Fe?"

"No, and you have my word on that."

Shanult nodded. "Follow me, I'll take you to interrogation."

Zoe banged on the door that separated her room from Carver's. "Open this damned door!" One more knock and she realized he was probably at the police department. She needed answers. Why would an armed man be knocking on her door? Was he looking for her, or was she just a random victim? Did Santa Fe have some kind of hotel serial killer roaming the hallways of the city?

Tony! Zoe rummaged through the pockets of her discarded jeans until she found his card. She was about to reach for her cell phone when she remembered that Carver had broken it.

"Glad hotels haven't taken these landlines out of the rooms yet." Dialing his number, she hoped he would answer.

"This is Officer Carroll."

"Tony, how are you? It's Zoe from earlier."

"Aww, yeah, Ms. Sexy PI Lady."

She rolled her eyes, but realized that she was going to have to be a really great actress to get information from him. "I'm glad you remembered me. Something happened at the hotel where I'm staying, and it's gotten me a little shaken."

"Don't tell me that it was your room the fake room service guy came to."

"Word travels fast around here, huh?"

"Yeah, especially when some FBI agent walks in all huffy about it. Damn, lady, do trouble and federal agents just follow you?"

"No. Do you know if that FBI agent is still at head-quarters?"

"Couldn't tell ya, babe. I'm out on patrol. I just keep hearing chatter about it. If you want, I can come and pick you up."

"And leave the citizens of Santa Fe in danger? I couldn't ask you to do that. Besides, it's a short walk from the hotel."

"I hope I get to see you before you leave town, and remember, tomorrow is my day off, beautiful."

"Goodbye, Tony." Hanging up, Zoe slipped her feet into her shoes and headed for the police station. Some-one was going to give her some answers.

Singletary watched Wendy as she walked out the front door of his Brooklyn apartment. She'd come straight to his place when she returned from Los Angeles and told him what the FBI had been planning, including the raid on his safe house outside of Virginia.

Though she'd been good at getting him that critical information, she still failed him. Zoe Harrington was still alive.

He knew if he wanted Zoe dead, he was going to have to take the lead in getting the bitch. Wendy was a good little mole. But when she became useless to him, she was going to have to die as well. Too many loose ends would unravel his network. He felt bad for the drug dealers these days. People were getting highs from prescription drugs and making shit in their bathrooms, but sex was the moneymaker. Zoe Harrington had cost him too much money. Natalie had had everything he needed: access to millionaires who didn't want a soul to know they liked little girls and boys. Not only did they pay a pretty penny for the sex, when the blackmail attempts came, they paid even more. That bitch cut off his pipeline. Natalie was sitting in prison and had the nerve to try and cut a deal with Smallwood. Well, that motherfucker was dead, and in a few days, Natalie and Zoe would join him.

Picking up his burner cell phone, he called his contact at the Bedford Hills Correction Facility. "Today is the day. I want that bitch dead." He hung up without allowing his contact to say a word. He might be weakened financially, but people still feared him. Joe was pure evil and didn't care about hurting people's loved ones in order to get his way. That's why anyone who challenged him or went against him in any way had to learn a painful lesson.

Zoe would learn that lesson sooner rather than later.

Chapter 11

Zoe walked into the Santa Fe Police Department and realized she didn't have a game plan. She knew how police dealt with victims and how they always made folks feel as if the rights of the accused were more important than the victim's.

Time to play the PI card, she thought as she approached the desk sergeant.

"Can I help you, ma'am?"

Zoe smiled. "Yes. My name is Zoe Harrington and I'm a private investigator."

"Here we go." The man sighed and slammed his hand on the desk. "What's this about? The mess at the hotel?"

"Must be a slow day." She offered him another smile. "I think my client was involved in the attempted murder. I'm just doing my due diligence to keep him safe."

"I thought it was a woman in the room." He stroked his chin. "And what did you say your name was?"

"Zoe Harrington." She reached into her pocket and pulled out her wallet to show him her license.

"Can you even work in this state?"

"Yes, I can. Otherwise it would be stupid for me to be in the police department announcing that I'm here." She offered him a bright smile. The man seemed unfazed by her, unlike Tony.

He rose to his feet. "Wait here."

Zoe missed the days of paper reports. There was no way that she could sneak behind the desk and get into the computer files without getting caught. Tapping her foot on the tile floor, she wondered if Carver was still inside. Was he being questioned or doing the questioning?

"Ma'am," the desk sergeant said, breaking into her thoughts, "I can't help you."

"What?"

"All I can do is refer you to the public information officer once the reports are released. No one has been arrested at this time." He shrugged his massive shoulders. "Nothing I can do."

"Who *can* do something? Is there a supervisor I can speak with? This is kind of important. We're talking life and death."

He wiggled his finger at her so that she'd come closer. "Listen, you seem like a nice person, and from the way you talk, you've been around the block a little bit. The FBI is here, so we're being watched. If I could help you, I would."

"Is the FBI questioning that guy?"

He nodded. "And I can't tell you anything else because I don't know anything else."

Zoe nodded and decided to cut her losses. "You've been very helpful. Thank you."

"No problem, but you didn't get any information from me, right?"

Zoe did a zipping motion across her lips. "Not a word." Winking at him, she headed for the exit. So Carver had pulled out his FBI badge. But why? Zoe turned around and walked over to the desk again.

"Hey," she said. "Can I ask another question?"

"All right, now you're starting to push it."

"This is a general question that you can answer with a yes or no."

The man rolled his eyes. "Go ahead."

"Is there a killer running around Santa Fe with his MO? Fake room service, then bang?"

"We have had an uptick in violent crime, but this is new. Your client might want to watch his back."

"Thanks." Zoe headed out the door, wondering if she really had been the target. But who would want to kill her, and how did anyone know where she was? She hadn't even told Zach that she was in Santa Fe.

Carver has to be the target, she thought as she walked back to the hotel. Now she had to do the thing she hated the most: wait. Instead of heading back to her room, Zoe went to the bar and ordered a glass of Chardonnay, which she planned to nurse until Carver walked through the door.

* * *

"Who hired you?" Carver asked as he locked eyes with the man who'd tried to kill Zoe.

He leaned back and folded his arms across his chest. "Lawyer."

"This is how you want to play this? You're not facing state charges, asshole. We're talking federal time. No parole. You want to go down alone, or do you want to tell me where I can find Singletary?"

"Don't know what you're talking about and I want a lawyer."

Carver leaned in and glared at him. "Look, David, I can help you now. But when that lawyer walks in and Singletary finds out that you didn't get the job done, you're on your own."

David's eyes widened. "Are you the guy?"

"What?"

"Joe got . . . Nah, I'm not saying nothing, but that bitch better watch her back. I'm not the only one after her. And just know this, Joe got people and eyes everywhere. You can't save her, Captain."

Carver wanted to put his fist through that man's face. But his little slip-up gave him the signal he needed to know that someone inside had been working with Singletary. And he thought it was Smallwood. Did this mean that Wendy was in danger, too, because she worked with Smallwood? Was that why Singletary shot him?

Carver was about to grab David by the throat when the door opened and a detective walked in. "Agent Banks, are you done?"

"Nope."

"Well, you are now. I'm Detective Planko, and as far as I know, this guy is facing state charges. We're going to take over from here."

"Federal charges are pending, so it doesn't matter. He's already asked for a lawyer." Carver walked toward Planko and shook his hand. "He's all yours."

As much as he wanted to choke the hell out of David, Carver knew that the best thing he could do right now would be to get Zoe out of New Mexico. But how was he going to explain the attempt on Zoe's life? He knew she was going to have questions, and if he didn't have an answer, that was going to be a problem.

Leaving the interrogation room, Carver knew he had to come up with a good story to convince Zoe to leave without asking too many questions. He headed to the hotel and made a beeline for Zoe's room. Before he made it to her room, Zoe seemed to appear out of nowhere in the lobby and started questioning him.

"What is going on?" She slapped her hands on her hips. "And don't tell me *nothing*, because I know you went over to the police department flashing your FBI badge."

"The MO of this guy looked like a case that the Bureau was working last year. I just wanted to make sure it wasn't the same guy."

She narrowed her eyes at him. "Why do I feel like you just fed me a line of bull?"

"Believe what you want, but we need to go ahead to Vegas. I've talked to one of my contacts with the Las Vegas Police Department and they may have found Jessica's body."

"Really? That's all well and good, but what was that commotion outside of my room all about?"

"I don't know," he lied.

Zoe narrowed her eyes at him. "And in all that time you spent at the police department, you didn't find out anything?"

"Like most cowards do, he lawyered up. I have to respect the Constitution," Carver said.

Zoe shook her head and started for the elevator. Carver followed her and touched her elbow. "Will you calm down?" he said.

"No, I won't calm down! You got me out here un-armed, some crazed man tried to kick my door in, and I'm supposed to be okay with it?"

"Listen," he said as the doors to the elevator opened, "as long as we're out here together, nothing is going to happen to you."

"You're damned right, because I'm not going to Vegas without at least one of my guns."

A tense silence fell over them as the elevator car rose to the third floor.

"Zoe, we need to talk about this gun thing," he said as she stalked off the elevator and headed for her room.

"There's nothing to discuss. I'm not getting caught out here unarmed again," she snapped as she unlocked the door. Zoe walked in her room and plopped down on the bed. Looking at her, Carver wanted nothing more than to take her in his arms and make love to her. He wanted to assure her that she was safe and that no harm would come her way. Carver knew beneath that anger she was scared. And she had reason to be, she just didn't know it.

"Why are you standing there looking at me like that?" she snapped, breaking into his thoughts.

He focused on her face. "What?"

"Do I even want to know where your mind went?"

He sat down beside her on the bed. "Depends on when you want to get back to New York. And why do you need multiple guns again?"

"Because I won't be caught off guard again."

"That wouldn't have happened if we shared a room. I could've protected you."

Zoe pushed him off the bed. "I don't need your protection, Banks. And let's remember that you came to me. I'm not some rose blowing in the wind."

Carver propped up on his elbows on the floor. "Zoe, I know you're quite capable, but you can't carry your firearms on a plane. I can. That's all I meant. So, if you want to go and get your guns, Annie Oakley, we can do that. But as a federal officer, I'm not going to be able to help you break the law if you're not licensed to carry in certain states."

She rolled her eyes. "Get out of my room."

"Let me check under the bed first, make sure there aren't any strangers lurking around." He pulled the edge of the blanket up, then rose to his feet.

She shook her head and crossed the room. Zoe snatched the door open. "Go book my flight."

Carver gave her a fleeting look as he walked to the door. She was so damned beautiful. Why couldn't they just be on vacation together, making love and eating great food?

"Why are you still here?" They locked eyes and Carver could've sworn that he saw her tremble.

"Because I'm waiting for you to take off your clothes and tell me you want me to make love to you."

"Is that so?" Smiling, she placed both hands on his chest and just as he leaned in, expecting a kiss, Zoe pushed him out of the open door.

"Keep waiting." She slammed the door in his face and Carver heard her laughing on the other side. He'd have the last laugh, though. Zoe could have round one because he was going to win this war of hearts.

Zoe leaned against the door and willed her heartbeat to return to its normal pace. Could that man see through her? Did he know she wanted everything he'd said? Was it showing in her eyes as she hungrily drank in his image? Had he heard the thumping of her heart when she pushed him off the bed? Another couple of seconds near his heat-radiating body and she would've taken her clothes off and made love to him. But that was not why they were in New Mexico. They needed to solve this case so that she could leave Carver Banks alone.

It had been easy to pretend she had forgotten about Carver when he was out of sight. She assumed he worked in DC, had a nice townhouse in Georgetown, dated pretty women who liked the strong hero type. They probably went out for tapas and expensive wine. She hated tapas. She tolerated wine, but preferred vodka and cranberry with a side of hot wings and extra blue cheese.

Carver was the kind of man who needed that bougie pretty girl, and that was not Zoe. It was Zach's fault for making her play the role of a tomboy growing up so his friends wouldn't want to date her. If she had her phone, she'd call him and have one of those irrational twin conversations that they hadn't had in a long time. At this point, she would do anything to take her mind off Carver Banks.

Chapter 12

Carver booked the flight to New York as Zoe wanted and sighed. Instead of sitting in the business center of the hotel, he'd rather be making love to Zoe. But lust and longing would have to take a back seat to keeping her safe. He needed to know what Singletary's next move was and who he'd sent after Zoe. He knew that man was smart enough not to post a listing on Craigslist for a hit man. Carver figured that it was someone within the organization that he'd probably put on Zoe's tail.

That made things worse. Singletary's thugs were like ghosts. Just like that fool sitting across the way in jail. Carver wished he could log on to the FBI's secure server and run that guy's face through the facial recognition system. But he didn't want to give anyone direct access to their location, since he didn't know who he could trust anymore.

Wendy was his only contact right now, and he wasn't sure if he could trust her. "Maybe I'm just being paranoid," he muttered as he pulled out his cell phone. Dialing her number, he hoped that she had some information about Singletary's location.

"Agent Covington."

"Wendy, it's Carver."

"I was wondering what was going on with you. Are you and Zoe still in New Mexico?"

"Yeah, for now. I need some help. I'm going to email you a mug shot. Run this guy's background and let me know if he has any ties to Singletary."

"Why don't you use your tablet?"

"It's dead and I don't have my charger," he lied. "Text me what you find out."

"Got it."

"How's Smallwood?"

"I'm sorry, he didn't survive."

Carver muttered under his breath. "We have to take Singletary down."

"I'm working on it. We're building a new team."

"Who's in charge?"

"I don't know yet, but I'll keep you posted."

"All right. Are you back in DC?"

"For now. We're trying to trace Singletary's girls, so I'm back to monitoring Backpage. I want to get back out there in the field and take him down. But it seems as if I'm being punished for the ambush."

Carver sighed. He'd heard this song and dance from Wendy for years. She wanted to be in the field. She wanted more responsibilities, but when she got it, something always happened to undermine cases. Carver often wondered how she'd even gotten a job with the Bureau.

"I doubt that. Everyone knows that Singletary is a

dangerous man, and we're all at risk when we do these jobs. Smallwood was a good man."

"At least we hope he was. There's still the issue of what he said to Natalie the night of her arrest. I've thought about what you said, and the fact that Singletary targeted Smallwood might have been him tying up a loose end."

"Until we uncover evidence of wrongdoing, all we can do is keep tracking Singletary." He couldn't help but find it suspicious that all of a sudden Wendy was ready to believe that Smallwood was corrupt.

"I'm on it."

"Keep me in the loop."

"You do the same. Let me know where you and Zoe are going next."

"Will do." Another lie, because Carver wasn't willing to put his trust in anyone else at the Bureau.

Wendy added Zoe Harrington to the FBI Watch List. She had a feeling that Banks wasn't going to tell her where they were going. Now she would get an alert when she got on an airplane. The bitch had to die so that Wendy could get her money and get from underneath Singletary. Now that Natalie had been taken care of, Wendy had to deliver Zoe. Her career with the FBI had stalled, and she put the blame squarely on Banks's and Smallwood's shoulders.

She might be part of the team, but they treated her as an afterthought, a joke. No one was laughing now. Wendy pulled out her cell phone and called Joe.

"Have you found that bitch?"

"Hello to you, too."

"I don't have time for the niceties. I need to know if Zoe is still breathing."

"Your guy failed. As a matter of fact, he's in jail and Carver is trying to find out who he is. I can stall him, because he's asking me for information on the guy; he doesn't want to use the servers himself, in case he might be traced."

"What the fuck! How did he get arrested? This guy was supposed to be the best. I'm tired of the incompetence!"

"I told you that I would handle this, but you won't let me. I don't know why or how your guy messed things up."

"Since you're supposed to be my inside woman, you should have a damned idea."

"One thing I do know is that Carver knows someone is working with you. He's being really cagey about where he's going next."

"You got seven days; then I'm going to handle it myself. And you can kiss that payoff goodbye."

Before Wendy could protest, Singletary hung up.

"Shit."

Zoe decided to hit the hotel's gym, hoping she'd wear herself out and drift off to sleep. As she stepped off the elevator, she ran directly into Carver. How could a man look so mouthwatering in a white tank top and jeans?

"Where are you going?" he asked.

"Gee, Dad, I'm just going to work out. Is that okay?"

"Funny." He folded his arms across his massive

chest. "I could've joined you. I need to work off that food we had earlier."

Zoe nibbled on her bottom lip as she envisioned a sweat-covered Carver in compression shorts. She'd probably trip on the treadmill and get a concussion. "Well, I wanted some time alone."

"You really can't stop me if I want to come work out. But I'll respect your space."

"If you really want to work out, I can't stop you."

He shrugged his shoulders. "That's the most back-handed invitation I've ever heard, but let me grab some shorts. You want to come with me?"

"No, I'm going to warm up the treadmill." Zoe took off for the workout room and grabbed the free weights. She was hoping to get all of her pent-up desire under control before Carver walked in. She dropped the weights and moved over to the stair stepper. Going up and down, Zoe tried not to think about him. Sweat dripped down her back as she walked faster and faster.

"Whoa," Carver said. Zoe looked over her shoulder at him. His smile made her miss a step and she almost fell from the machine. In a flash, Carver was behind Zoe with his hand on her back. "Slow down, Wonder Woman."

"You shouldn't have distracted me." Zoe slowed the machine down. "This is why I work out alone."

"If you say so."

Zoe stopped the machine and wiped the sweat from her face with the towel she'd taken from her room. She walked over to a clear corner and started doing squats. From the corner of her eye, she noticed Carver standing still and watching her every move.

"Thought you came to work out."

"I was taking everything in."

Zoe stopped mid-squat. "You're a jerk."

"And you know I want you, Zoe." Carver crossed over to her and drew her into his arms.

"People want a lot if things they can't have."

He ran his finger down her cheek. She took a deep breath and closed her eyes as tingles exploded throughout her body. "Please don't do this. We said this was strictly business, and you keep trying to cross the line."

"Can I tell you something? I've haven't been able to get you out of my system. It's been two years and no one can compare to you." Leaning in to her, Zoe knew he was going to kiss her. When he didn't, she was disappointed. "Why don't you stop acting like you don't want me as much as I want you?"

"Because I don't. Carver, you're not that irresistible."

He pulled her even closer to his chest. "But you haven't let me go this whole time. What do you think that makes me think?"

"I'm not doing this with you." Zoe pushed out of his embrace. "When we get back to real life, you're going back to DC to your tapas-loving woman and your dry wine. I'm not your on-the-case booty."

Carver tilted his head to the side. "I don't live in DC full time anymore, and I've never dated a woman who loves tapas. You've been spying on me?"

She rolled her eyes and felt like the biggest fool in the world. "I'm done working out. What time is our flight out of here?"

"Seven."

"Then we should go to bed, separately." Zoe took off out of the workout room and ran up the stairs to her room.

Carver shook his head as he watched Zoe tear out of the room. She was such a sexy coward, though he couldn't blame her for not jumping into his arms. They didn't have the most romantic history, and if she found out that he was lying to her and taking her on a wild-goose chase because Singletary was trying to kill her, they wouldn't have a chance at a future. Knowing that he'd already taken out Smallwood, Carver couldn't let Zoe be next. He headed back to his room and called his college roommate, Steve Mitts. He knew Steve had a private jet and he and Zoe could fly under the radar.

"This is Steve."

Carver laughed, realizing that his friend probably didn't recognize the number. "Man, you can turn off that millionaire boys' club voice. It's Banks."

"Look, brother man, don't call me from new numbers. I thought you were one of the investors I'd been courting."

"Nah. Not this time. I hate to be that dude who only calls when he needs something."

"But you need something?"

"I can't go into detail, but I'm working this case and I need transportation."

"Whatever you need, let me know when and where. You can use my private jet to get where you need to go. I always got your back."

Carver told him that he was going to be flying off to New York in the morning and would need the jet tomorrow afternoon.

"This is like some James Bond shit, huh? All that's missing are a couple of fine girls and some martinis."

Carver started to tell him about the fine girl, but he didn't want to put too many people in the mix when it came to protecting Zoe. "When this thing is over, I will get you as many martinis as you want."

"Yeah, in between saving the world, huh? We need to get together because you have to meet my new wife."

"Damn, is this wife number four?"

"Yes. And she is going to be the last one."

"I think you said that the last time." Carver laughed. "And the time before that one, too."

"Yo, don't remind me of my own words. Anyway, I'm going to get the plane ready. Is it just you?"

"It's going to be me and Brenda Jones."

"Oh, so there is a woman?"

"She's an agent, don't get ahead of yourself. I'm not trying to have a bunch of wives and exes."

"Yeah, yeah. Every man needs two ex-wives. Makes you appreciate it when you find the right one."

"Well, why not make sure you marry the right one the first time?"

"Didn't ask you to be logical, Banks. And as the old saying goes, shit happens."

"Whatever, dude. I'll see you tomorrow." After ending the call, Carver headed to the bathroom to take a long, cold shower. The temptation of having Zoe Harrington next door was too much for him to deal with right now.

* * *

Zoe wished she could trust how clean the bathtub was, because she needed a long, hot bath. Well, that wasn't all she needed, but she would settle for the bath, to ease her aching muscles. What she would have preferred was Carver's big hands on her thighs, stroking and squeezing and rubbing her.

Sighing, she started to get in the shower when she heard the water start next door. Closing her eyes, she imagined Carver's magnificent body stepping into the shower. She felt herself getting wet as she thought about water dripping down his ebony body.

Zoe turned the shower on, stripped down, and stepped in.

This must stop, she thought as she slipped her hand between her thighs. *All about business. The sooner we get closure for the Dolans, the sooner Carver will be out of my life.*

Chapter 13

Morning came too soon for Carver and Zoe. They left their rooms at the same time, meeting in the hallway.

"Good morning, Zoe."

"Not until I've had several cups of coffee."

Carver walked over to her and took her bag. "I know the feeling. But I have good news for you. We don't have to take the train this time. I found a rare direct flight from Santa Fe to New York."

"That is awesome." She yawned and pointed her index finger in his face. "And don't forget that you have to get me a new phone when we get back to the city."

"I'm pretty sure you wouldn't let me forget," he said with a wink. "I'll get you a new phone, maybe even get you an upgrade. Sound like a good plan?"

She smiled. "You say that as if you had a choice." Zoe nudged him with her elbow. "Let's get some coffee and head to the airport."

Shaking his head, Carver followed her to the elevator. How did a woman look this sexy in the early morning with her hair pulled up in a high ponytail, no makeup, and dressed in a simple pink cotton dress? Licking his lips, Carver watched her hips as she stepped into the elevator car. Her time in the gym was definitely showing.

"Carver!"

"What? Huh?"

"I said I have a meeting in New York, so what time are we leaving for Vegas. What were you thinking about?"

"Coffee."

She rolled her eyes. "Sure you were."

Once they arrived downstairs, Zoe made sure she and Carver got two big cups of coffee. He took his black with two sugars, and she needed cream and three sugars. While she gulped her coffee, Carver arranged for them to get seats on an airport shuttle. Carver was glad that they wouldn't be traveling commercial much longer. While Zoe went to her meeting in New York, Carver's plan was to go to the satellite office and see what he could find out about Singletary's movements. He also wanted to see if there was a record somewhere of Smallwood's meeting with Natalie. *Something is off and I can't believe Smallwood was working with his killer.*

"Carver, the shuttle is here."

"Good, now we can put this thing to rest, I hope."

Zoe nodded, keeping her thoughts to herself about how she wanted to solve this case and get back to life without being tempted by Carver Banks every day. She handed him his cup of coffee and they headed out to the shuttle. Carver glanced at her as she sat down. "What kind of meeting do you have today?"

Zoe took another sip of her coffee. "Why are you

being nosy? I told you that you're not my only client. I have more cases."

"I'm just trying to figure out what time we need to be ready for the flight to Las Vegas. Calm down." He kissed her on the cheek. Zoe shivered, and despite herself, she leaned against him. The energy around them sizzled like a thunderstorm on a summer afternoon. Locking eyes, Zoe and Carver leaned into each other and kissed each other slow and deep. His hands roamed her back and she pressed her body closer to his. Shivering and moaning, Zoe wanted to rip her clothes off and make love to him right there. But this was wrong. This was what she said they were not going to do. Pulling back from him, she moved one seat over.

"We have to stop doing this," she whispered.

"Then we need to get the tension out of the air."

"I don't need you distracting me with those lips."

Carver inched closer to her. "Zoe, I want you more than I need my next breath. But I need you to admit the same thing. If you think I'm a distraction, then I'll back off—tomorrow." He captured her lips again, devouring her mouth and slipping his hand underneath her dress.

She gasped and arched her hips into his fingers as he toyed with her wetness through her panties. Pulling her lips from his, Zoe wanted to tell him to stop, but he was making her feel too good. He controlled her body with two fingers. Two. Fingers. Zoe felt an explosion building between her thighs and just as she was about to explode—he stopped.

"Carver," she breathed.

"Not until you admit you want me as much as I want

you. Until then, I'm going to stop distracting you."
Looking into her eyes, Carver licked his finger and
smiled. "Damn, you're sweet, though."

"You. Make. Me. Sick."

Carver winked and leaned back in his seat. Zoe
rolled her eyes and squirmed in her seat. *I hope Jessica
Dolan's body is in Las Vegas. I can't take much more of
this from Carver.* She looked out the window and willed
her body to stop throbbing. But every time she stole a
glance at Carver, it just made her wetter.

Teasing Zoe may have been wrong, but watching her
try to deal with it made Carver laugh on the inside. He
reached out and stroked her arm. "You all right?"

"Don't touch me."

"Sorry."

"You're not. Why do you keep doing this when you
know we have no future?"

"What makes you say that? We can have a future if
you would stop being so damned hardheaded. Zoe,
you're the one woman I've never been able to forget.
There's just something about you that drives me crazy."

"And I'm supposed to jump for joy because you
want me? It doesn't work like that, boo. You've arrested
me, harassed my family, and now every time I turn
around you're trying to get into my pants again. How is
that a future? You feel lust for me, nothing else. You
know what happens when you try to build a relationship
based on lust? You get some good sex, but that's it. I'm
not built to be a bedmate, and I won't be yours. So, this
has to stop!"

"Who said I only want you in my bed? I want everything, Zoe. I want your heart, mind, and soul. But you have to stop punishing me for doing my job."

"Where in the FBI handbook does it say sleep with women to get information on a case?"

"Here we go again! Stop acting like you weren't doing the same damn thing. That night you thought I was just some bodyguard who was going to help you and your client find money. I was doing something to safeguard a nation."

She rolled her eyes and turned back to the window. "I don't know why I took this case. Being that you've been following me around the country, you could've looked for that girl's body without me! As a matter of fact, why don't you go to Vegas alone and let me get back to my work in New York?"

"I'm not doing that, and you're not abandoning me when I need you." Carver touched her shoulder. "Look at me."

She turned around and focused on his face.

"Zoe. I really need you. Please don't doubt that."

What he wanted to tell her was that he needed her alive because he was in love with her and he knew she was in danger. But that would mean owning up to the lie he'd been telling her since that night in New York when he showed up at her office. If he did that right now, she would bolt from him and run straight into danger. Zoe's life was important to him, and if he had to carry on with this lie until Singletary was neutralized, then so be it. But there was no way in hell that he would allow her to die.

"Fine. We're doing this. But the moment the Dolans

get their closure, I'm out of your life with my panties intact."

"Fair enough."

Meanwhile, in New York, Lewis Martinez had found a way to get his revenge on Zoe. There were no security cameras behind her office. Under the cover of darkness, he set his explosive trap. He wired the back door with digital sensors that looked like alarm parts, but they we're filled with C-4. When that door opened, Zoe would get the shock of her life.

Looking around, he made sure he wasn't being watched as he jimmied the door open. Since he'd cut the power supply to the entire complex, he didn't have to worry about the alarm going off, but he needed to be quick. The patrol in this area would begin soon. He might be dressed in a generic uniform that made him look like an alarm installer at a glance, but if anyone took a close look at what he was doing, he'd be on his way to federal prison.

The way Lewis saw it, Zoe probably had so many enemies that his name would be checked off the list in about fifteen seconds. He'd even planned what he was going to say to the investigators. That's why he'd called her to ask her for help.

"Just wish this bitch would come back to New York so that she can die," he muttered as he set the devices in place. Once the work was done, Lewis hopped into the white van he'd stolen from a car lot and headed to the Harlem River to drown the van and evidence of what he'd done.

About an hour later, Lewis looked like any other guy taking the subway before dawn. With his headphones in his ears and a white T-shirt and jeans on, he blended in with the natives. As much as he wanted to smile, he tempered his excitement until he saw news of the explosion.

"Why are flights to New York always overcrowded?" Zoe muttered as she tried to stuff her carry-on bag in the overhead compartment.

"Hold up, Zoe. Let me get that for you." As he reached for the bag, another passenger bumped into Carver, crushing him into Zoe. Gasping, she closed her eyes because his heat was overwhelming.

"Sorry," he said.

"No problem." She turned around and sighed. "Hopefully that's the most turbulence that we're going to experience this morning."

Taking their seats, Carver touched her knee. "My shoulder is here for you if things get choppy in the sky."

She shook her head, but kept silent. She knew that he wanted to offer more than just his shoulder. But as the plane took off, Zoe did take him up on that shoulder offer. She even held his hand.

With his free hand, Carver stroked her knee. "Take-off is always the worst."

Zoe nodded and held her breath until the plane leveled off. Then she exhaled and unfurled herself from Carver. "I'm going to tell you a secret," she said.

"What's that?"

"This is the reason why eighty percent of my cases are local."

"So, your doing this for me means I'm going to be forever in your debt, right?"

She nodded. "Glad you know this."

Carver wanted to kiss her again, but he was going to keep his promise to her and keep his lips to himself. For now, anyway.

She made it real hard for him to keep that promise when she leaned on his shoulder and drifted off to sleep. Her face looked angelic, and those lips. Those lips were temptation personified. He ran his index finger gently across them. She stirred but didn't wake up. A flight attendant walked by their seats and smiled at Carver.

"Sir, would you and your wife like some orange juice or anything?"

"Some juice would be great. And she prefers apple juice."

"And I'm not his wife," Zoe said groggily.

"Oh, okay." The flight attendant poured the drinks and moved over to the next set of passengers.

"I thought you were sleeping."

"I was until someone started playing with my lips." Zoe drank her juice. "Why would you let that woman think we're married?"

Carver shrugged and downed his orange juice. "I'd rather she believe that than that you are my mistress."

"Oh, hush. And don't forget that you need to head to a phone store and get me a new one."

"I know. I'm surprised that it took you this long to remind me—again."

She yawned, then smirked at him. "It came to me in a dream. You were trying to weasel out of getting me a smartphone and wanted to give me a classic flip phone like yours. And just FYI, that's not going to happen."

The flight was smooth and gave Carver a chance to banter back and forth with Zoe. It felt so comfortable talking to each other. He wished they could be like that all the time. No tension, no accusations, no lies. Then he remembered there was nothing but a big lie between them.

Zoe noticed when Carver fell silent. "What's wrong with you?"

"Just thought about something. What happens if we find Jessica's body and pull the scabs off the wounds of her parents when we find her?" he said. The lie caught in his throat and he took another sip of his juice. He hated not being able to tell her everything. But it was the best thing for Zoe. She wouldn't take his advice if he told her a killer was on her heels and she needed to lay low. He could see her strapping on every one of her weapons, like Lara Croft, and daring Singletary to come get her.

"If you feel that way, then why did you take this case?"

"Because when you get an assignment, you take it."

She snorted. "That's why I'm glad I'm my own boss."

"Why do you think you don't need anybody?"

She leaned away from him. "You have a savior complex, don't you? You do realize this isn't a fairy tale and women can take care of themselves. I never said I didn't need anyone. But what I definitely don't need is some man riding in on the proverbial white horse to save me."

"Excuse me for giving a damn about you, Zoe. I

know that you don't need me or anyone else to protect you. You're Superwoman."

Zoe rolled her eyes. "Whatever. I'm not going to argue with you, because it's pointless. And you're right, I don't need you to take care of me." She turned her back to him and eased closer to the edge of her seat.

"Can we not fight?"

"If you stop saying sexist things, then of course we can. Just keep in mind that I made it through the police academy and onto the police force without someone helping me do it. And according to you, I'm one of the best investigators you know, so miss me with your bullshit."

"You think it's bullshit that I care about you?"

"Yes."

He gritted his teeth but didn't say a word to her. Of course she told herself that he didn't care, because it made her feel better. Carver ached for this woman, but he was tired of beating his head against a brick wall to prove himself. Nodding, Carver pressed the button for the flight attendant. "Yes, sir?" she asked, seeming to appear out of nowhere.

"I need a double vodka and orange juice and two pillows, please."

She glanced at her watch, then nodded as she made his drink. Zoe gave him a sidelong glance.

"Why do you need two pillows?"

"Because if you keep talking, I'm going to smother myself."

The flight attendant handed Carver his drink. "Ma'am, would you like anything to drink?"

"Just another apple juice, thank you."

The woman nodded and poured Zoe her juice. As she walked down the aisle, she whispered to another flight attendant, "I think we better watch them. I think they're having a fight."

Carver nudged Zoe. "Now look what you've done. They think we're going to cause a scene."

"Whatever. I'm going to drink my juice and go to sleep. You try to stay sober, lush."

He took a big gulp of his drink. "It's five o'clock somewhere."

Chapter 14

Zoe and Carver had drifted off to sleep, and when the flight attendant came by to wake them up, the plane was making its descent into New York.

"This is probably the best flight I've ever taken," Zoe said as she fastened her seat belt and shifted her seat into the upright position.

"Yeah, and all of the snoring didn't keep the rest of us up at all."

"Too bad you aren't funny, you could have a second career." Zoe hadn't noticed the landing until the plane jerked. Carver pulled her into his arms.

"We're on the ground, it's okay."

"You're loving this, aren't you?"

He shook his head. "We all have our weaknesses. You don't like to fly. I get it."

"And what's your weakness, Superman?"

Smirking at her, Carver nodded toward her. "Zoe Harrington."

She pursed her lips and kept her caustic comment to herself as everyone began to deplane.

"You don't believe me, do you?"

"Nope."

"I guess I'll have to prove it to you."

"You really don't." She grabbed her bag and started for the exit. Carver caught up to her and grabbed her elbow.

"Zoe, when you finally believe in me, it's going to knock your socks off."

She didn't want to tell him that she wanted nothing more than to believe in him. She wanted to believe that they could share real love. But she wasn't going to get wrapped up in a fantasy world. It may have worked out that way for Zach and Chante, but she wasn't under the illusion that she was going to have that kind of future with Carver Banks.

Besides, what would Zach say if she came home with the man who tried to put him in prison? She knew her twin. He held a grudge like a baby held a bottle. And she already knew how he felt about Carver. She wasn't even going to try and explain how she'd fallen for him.

"What?" Carver asked when he looked at Zoe.

"Nothing." She looked down at her watch. "We'd better get moving because I have to get my guns, and you never said what time we're scheduled to leave for Vegas. Have you booked the flight yet?"

"Good thing about this flight is that we're taking a private jet."

Zoe raised her right eyebrow. "Are you on the take or something? How can you afford a private jet?"

"Because I had a roommate in college who became a millionaire. Ever heard of Steve Mitts?"

"You know that creep?" Zoe laughed. "Two of his ex-wives hired me to find out if he was cheating or not. He was."

"Well, he's a good guy deep inside. He just can't keep it in his pants."

Zoe rolled her eyes. "Of course you'd defend him. Typical male. Anyway, I'm going to head home and get my guns, then stop by my office for my meeting. I should be ready about two thirty. Where are we catching this jet?"

"Far Rockaway. It's about an hour from the Bronx."

She frowned at him. "Don't you think I know that? I'm the native New Yorker." Her words were wrapped with sarcasm.

He threw his hands up. "Sorry, I forgot who I was dealing with. I have to stop by the FBI satellite office and check in. But I can meet you at your office in a couple of hours."

"What if my meeting isn't over?"

"Then I'll wait. I know I'm not your only client, but we're going to have to get to Las Vegas sooner rather than later."

"Aye, aye, Captain." She rolled her eyes and headed for the exit.

Carver followed Zoe as she walked down the concourse and blended in with the crowd. He knew he had to keep his distance for a while. He watched the people around her, making sure no one was following her. His heart beat overtime thinking that one of these thousands of people could be the hit man or woman trying to kill her. So far, he hadn't noticed anything suspicious. She headed for the taxi stand and Carver stood a few feet behind her. When he saw her hop into a cab, he pushed through the crowd and got into a waiting cab behind hers.

"Hey, buddy, where ya heading?" the driver asked.

"Just follow that yellow cab that just left," he said. "I'll pay you double the fare." Carver pulled out his FBI badge. "That woman is a witness and I need to make sure she doesn't get away."

"I'm on it! I can't believe I'm part of an FBI sting."

"Yeah, you're really important right now, so don't lose sight of that car."

Wendy had just received an alert that Zoe Harrington had landed in New York. She was about to call Singletary, but she knew if she wanted her money, she was going to have to take care of Zoe herself. Pulling out her burner cell phone, she called her guy.

"She's back in town."

"All right. Where is she?"

"I'd head to her office if I were you. I want her dead."

"What about the man who has been with her?"

"Kill him, too. No witnesses and no mistakes. I'm tired of waiting for something to happen when I need results."

"Yes, ma'am."

Wendy hung up the phone with a smile on her face. She couldn't wait to get the news of Carver's and Zoe's deaths. She would celebrate, get her money from Singletary, and disappear. It would serve that bastard right for underestimating her all these years. Her only

regret was that she wouldn't see the shock in his eyes
like she did when she shot Smallwood. She knew he'd
been the one who'd blocked her promotion two years
ago. She wanted to be a field agent, not chained to a
desk—only going out on occasion. Wendy had been
lucky to get to Los Angeles, and she found that girl
before she talked to the FBI about Singletary's organization. Then there was the little snitch who'd approached
her before the team left LA and Wendy shot her.

So far, her body hadn't been found, and that was a
good thing. She hadn't told Joe, but she'd shot the girl
with her service weapon. If anyone found that out, she
might be the prime suspect. Wendy had tried to hide as
much evidence as she could. Though Zoe and Carver
were in New York, Wendy was in DC, and she hoped
that she could get back to New York before Carver had
a chance to get into the satellite office. She figured that
he was going to continue his surveillance of Zoe.
Though if he did go to the office, there wasn't much
that he'd find. Still, she wasn't sure if there was a video
of Smallwood and Natalie, hidden on a server. She
hadn't been able to find one, but she knew it existed.
Smallwood was a by-the-book kind of guy, and Natalie
had basically spilled her guts to him that night she'd
been arrested. Wendy had deleted the video with the
confession on it and now that Smallwood and Natalie
were dead, no one would know what Natalie said.
That's why Wendy wanted to be sure there wasn't a
copy of that video anywhere.

*Stupid bitch. All she had to do was keep her mouth
shut and she'd still be breathing today.* Wendy rose to
her feet and looked out of the window. She hated her

job. And didn't regret going rogue at all. All she wanted was for Carver to die.

Carver wasn't surprised that Zoe went straight to her office. *Workaholic.*

"Hey, buddy, you want me to wait here? The meter is still running."

"Pull in to the lot across the street."

"Am I waiting or what? And I still get double, right?"

"Not if you don't shut up!"

"No need for the attitude. And you guys wonder why people hate the government. What if I start blowing the horn and—"

"I will arrest you for interfering with an FBI investigation and have you on the no-fly list so fast, you won't even be able to take the subway." Carver watched as Zoe talked to someone who was about to walk into an adjacent office. He tensed up until he saw her and the older man laughing and smiling.

So, that old man is one of the business tenants. Cool.

Zoe was about to open her door; then the old man stopped her again. This time, Zoe frowned and the guy shrugged his shoulder.

Carver didn't like the way this looked. The old man headed to the back of the building and Zoe followed him. Reaching into his bag, Carver grabbed his gun.

"Wait here." He hopped out of the car and ran across the street. When he stepped into the parking lot, he heard a muted explosion. Rushing to the back of the building, he found Zoe on top of the old man. Bits of debris cov-

ered her body; there was a rip in her dress and a few
spots of blood.

"Zoe! You all right?" Fear coursed through his body.
Had he failed? She rose to her feet and reached to help
the old man up.

"Call 9-1-1."

"Damn developers, I know they did this. People act
like the Mafia is gone." The old man snarled and wiped
debris from his pants legs. "Baby girl, you good?"

"Mr. Healy, I'm fine. Carver, have you called 9-1-1?"

A group of people ran out of the building as alarms
blared. "Zoe, Zoe!" a tall woman with fire-red hair
yelled. "I called 9-1-1, are you and Healy okay?"

Zoe waved her hand. "We're fine."

Carver crossed over to her as he pulled out his phone
to call the local ATF office. "What happened?"

"Mr. Healy said someone had been back here tam-
pering with doors and he wanted to show me some of
the marks. We came over and turned the doorknob and
boom." Zoe looked inside and gasped. "Someone was
in there." She ran inside, despite Carver and Mr. Healy
yelling for her to stop. Underneath a toppled bookcase,
she found the cleaning lady lying motionless. Blood
pooled around her head. Kneeling down beside her,
Zoe pushed the case off her broken body and checked
for a pulse.

Carver walked over to the caved-in door and glanced
at what looked like an alarm sensor. But he recognized
the smell of C-4. A chill ran through Carver. This
wasn't a developer trying to run people away. This had
to be Singletary's attempt to kill Zoe. Carver would bet
his life on it.

"Who is this chump?" Mr. Healy threw his thumb in Carver's direction. "You with the developers?"

"No, I'm an FBI agent." Carver headed inside and placed his hand on Zoe's shoulder. "We should leave the scene as it is. There's nothing we can do for her."

Zoe sighed and rose to her feet. "Who would do this?" she bemoaned.

Carver ushered her outside and kept silent. Now would've been the time to tell her the truth. Mr. Healy crossed over to them and folded his arms across his chest.

"How did the FBI get here so quick?" the old man asked.

Zoe shook her head. "Mr. Healy, we're working on a case together." Then she furrowed her brows and turned to Carver. "How did you get here so fast?"

Carver figured there was no need to lie about this. He'd been telling her enough lies as it was. "I followed you."

"Why?"

"Because I wanted to talk to you before we left. I'm going to call the ATF and see if they can come and take a look at this scene."

"That's right! Get the Feds involved since NYPD won't take me seriously."

Zoe motioned for Carver to follow her. Once they were in a quiet corner of the parking lot, she placed her hand on her hip and shook her head. "Please, don't stir Mr. Healy up. There have been a few developers looking to buy this property, but I don't think anyone is stupid enough to try and blow the place up so that they can buy it."

"Then how do you explain this?"

She sighed. "I get threats all the time. Maybe somebody finally decided to try something. I was barely scratched." She looked at the rip in her dress and scrapes on her arms. "That happened getting Mr. Healy out of the way. We need to find the cleaning lady's family. I know that she's new and we hadn't even met yet. I can't believe there is a dead woman in my office."

"I don't like this. And I thought you said you weren't worried about the cheating husbands you investigated. Why didn't you tell me about these threats?"

She shrugged. "Because it wasn't relevant and I'm tired of you hovering around me as if I'm made of crystal." Sirens filled the air as the police, fire, and medics showed up.

"Will you at least get checked out and cleaned up by the medics? We don't have to go to Las Vegas today either."

"Good, I can move my servers and everything to my house. Want to make yourself useful and help?"

Carver smiled. "Are you inviting me to your house? I feel so special."

"Don't get ahead of yourself, cowboy." She winked at him and headed over to the scene.

Zoe kept looking over her shoulder as she spoke to the fire marshal. Carver was inching closer and closer to her. She couldn't tell if he was trying to listen to what they were saying or if his savior complex was showing again. She hid her smile.

"Ms. Harrington, do you normally use your back door?"

She shook her head. "Only when I take the trash out. But I haven't been in town for the past few days. Mr. Healy told me that he saw an alarm guy doing work on the system really late. He thought it was odd because we all use the same alarm company. No one was having any problems either."

Zoe rolled her eyes when she saw Jamie Tegan, a detective she used to work with, coming her way. "Maybe someone is after you, Harrington. You do a lot to ruin people's lives."

"Still trying to learn how to solve cases without planting evidence, Tegan? I can't believe you still have a job. And instead of focusing on insulting me, why don't you check on the dead woman in my office?"

He narrowed his eyes at Zoe. "So many days I've wished you were a man so that I could knock the—"

"Detective! I'm trying to conduct an investigation of a bombing. Can you leave your personal arguments in your squad room?" the fire marshal said.

"A bombing?" Zoe asked. She felt Carver's hand on the small of her back.

"Who are you?" Tegan asked when he looked at Carver. "This is a crime scene."

Do it, please pull out that FBI badge and shut this clown down. Zoe looked at Carver as he reached into his pocket and pulled out his badge.

"Agent Carver Banks, FBI."

Zoe knew the one thing Tegan hated more than her was the FBI. She wanted to scream *bam, in your face*, but Zoe kept her composure. She wouldn't admit it to anyone, but hearing that someone tried to blow up her business and finding a dead woman in her office had her shaken up.

"You guys move fast," the fire marshal said. "I just called the ATF."

Tegan shook his head and walked away. Zoe couldn't have been happier under the circumstances.

"Is it safe to go inside?" she asked.

The fire marshal shook his head. "The police will have to clear the scene before you can go inside."

She tugged at Carver's hand. "I got to get out of here," she said.

"Let's go get some coffee until they turn the scene over to you."

Zoe pointed down the street to a local coffee shop. "They have some great pastries, and I need something sweet right now. And I'm not giving that asshole Tegan a statement right now. I'd rather punch him in his face."

Carver nodded and wrapped his arm around Zoe's waist. He wanted nothing more than to take her away from all of this danger and protect her forever. He knew that to do that, he would have to tell her the truth. Carver could tell that she was scared because she didn't wiggle out of his embrace.

Once they made it to the coffee shop, Carver chose a table away from the windows and headed for the counter to order their drinks and pastries.

"Apple fritters," she called out after him. Carver turned around and flashed her a thumbs-up sign.

For the next two hours, they sat in silence and drank coffee. After eating two apple fritters each, Zoe looked at her watch. "Do you think they're done at the crime scene?" she asked. "I have to get in my office and move my servers. Shit! I hope my guns are still in the safe."

"Let's go check and see," Carver said as he wiped his mouth. "Maybe I can use my influence to get you inside so you can collect the important stuff. For the record, we're not going to Vegas today."

Zoe sighed. "There's nothing I can do here. And that asshole detective isn't going to give me any information. I wouldn't put it past him that he did it."

"Wow. You didn't leave a lot of friends at the NYPD, huh?"

She rolled her eyes. "Whatever. Let's go."

Walking back to the office, Zoe wondered who was behind the bombing and why someone would target her. The only person she could think of with the means and a grudge would be Campos. But he was in federal prison, and as far as she knew, he'd been financially handicapped by the divorce and the Feds seizing his property and money. She didn't have any other cases where someone could or would do this to her.

When she saw the fire marshal and the police leaving the scene, Zoe released a sigh of relief. The crime scene tape had come down and she couldn't have been happier. No more dealing with Detective Dickwad today.

"Let's get my stuff, and I'm going to call the landlord so that he can get this place boarded up."

Carver brought his lips to her ear. "Just tell the truth, you want me alone in your place so that you can take advantage of me."

"You have such a one-track mind." She nudged him in the stomach with her elbow. She pointed him toward her portable servers while she walked over to her desktop.

She was happy to see there was no major damage to anything in her office. A few files had been knocked off her desk; the bookshelf on the back wall had been completely destroyed. She walked over to the pile of books and binders. Zoe picked up her file on Singletary and Natalie. Stuffing it in her carry on bag, Zoe headed for her wall safe, and she was happy to see that it lived up to the manufacturer's claims. Opening it and grabbing her two favorite handguns, she heard Carver say, "Damn. You have a license for all of those?"

"Four. I have four guns, and yes, Agent Banks, I own them legally."

"You should probably take them home, since you don't know when the door will be fixed."

"You see this safe withstood a C-4 blast, but you might be right." She handed him the other two guns. "Now you know if you get out of hand tonight, I can shoot you."

He took the weapons apart and put them in a backpack he'd found in the corner of her office. "I'm not worried about that."

Chapter 15

After the most expensive cab ride in the history of taxi rides, Zoe and Carver arrived at her home. She pointed him toward her dining room so that he could put her servers down. She told the cab driver to leave the computers on the stoop, since he and Carver wanted to act as if she couldn't lift anything.

She wanted to punch them both. "Is that all?" the driver asked. He looked right past her and addressed Carver. Zoe threw her hands up and walked into the kitchen to grab a bottle of water.

She heard the front door close, then she looked up and saw Carver heading her way. "You should've let a medic check you out."

"Please don't start that. I have some cotton balls and peroxide. I'll be fine."

"Mind if I take a look around? And what happened to your meeting?"

Zoe folded her arms across her chest. "I have no way

to communicate with folks, thanks to you. So, I'm going to shower and we're going to get my phone."

"Sounds like a plan. And I'm going to look around to see if there's anything here we should be worried about." Carver leaned in and kissed her on the forehead. "And don't say a word about that. You almost died today."

Zoe shivered. She hadn't wanted to think about that. Didn't want to process the fact that someone was out there trying to get her. "But I didn't, and that's what's important. I'm glad you were there." She turned and headed upstairs to shower. Only when the warm water hit her face did Zoe allow herself to have a moment. Backing against the wall of the shower, she closed her eyes and tossed her head back. She'd been threatened before—from ex-police officers to husbands who had to pay out millions—but no one had ever come after her. And an innocent woman was dead. A family didn't have a sister, a mother, or a friend anymore.

This was what Zach had been afraid of when she'd told him that she was opening her own private investigation firm. She'd fought him tooth and nail because she'd wanted to do her own thing. She had never been afraid—until today.

"Zoe. You all right in there?"

She shut off the water. "Yes, I'll be out in a minute."

"Are you sure that you're okay? You've been in there for an hour."

Zoe stepped out of the shower, wrapped a towel around her wet body, and opened the door. "Please don't do this, okay?"

"Do what? Be concerned about you? This isn't about me trying to . . . Zoe, I almost lost you, and I don't like how that felt."

Her knees went weak when she looked into his eyes. For the first time ever, she really believed that Carver felt something deeper than the lust she'd always accused him of having for her. Now, she was really scared.

"Excuse me, I have to get dressed."

He placed his hands on her shoulders and she felt as if her body was on fire. "Zoe."

"Carver, please."

"You don't have to be tough all the time. You can lean on me."

"I don't need to lean on you. I'm fine." She forced a smile. "Just let me get dressed."

"Fine." He let her go and watched her walk into her bedroom. Zoe slammed the door and sighed as she leaned against it. She wished that she could accept his concern at face value. Maybe what he was saying was real.

Carver knew that he should've told her the truth right in the bathroom. He should've let her know the real danger that she was in. But he couldn't. He didn't want to open his mouth and say those words to her. Zoe tried to act as if she was fine and what had happened earlier today didn't affect her, but he saw in her eyes that she was scared. What would she do if she knew the truth?

Carver pulled out his phone and called Steve.

"Hey, man, have you made it to the hangar yet?"

"No. Looks like we won't be flying out until tomorrow. Is that going to be a problem?"

"Nope. I'm taking the missus out on a cruise in a few days, so I won't be needing the jet or my pilot. It's at your disposal."

"Thanks." After hanging up with Steve, Carver headed into the den and took a seat on the love seat. He started to turn the television on when Zoe walked downstairs. He had to give it to her; she looked as if nothing had happened to her at all.

"Ready to go?"

"And I was getting ready to log on to your Netflix and chill."

She rolled her eyes and headed for the door. "You know you're too old to be talking about Netflix and chill. As a matter of fact, any man over the age of thirty who wants to Netflix and chill should spend the night in jail."

"That's harsh."

"I don't care."

Carver rose to his feet and caught up with Zoe as she walked out the door. "Are we heading to the phone store first?"

"Yes, and since you helped me bring my things in from the office, I'm going to buy you dinner. Where are you staying tonight?"

"I haven't booked a room yet, but I need to check in at the field office before it gets too late."

She nodded. "All right. Well, after I get my phone and we eat, you can call me and let me know where you're going to be and what time we're flying out tomorrow. I'll pull the car around." Zoe bounced down the stairs and Carver called Steve again. He decided that he and Zoe would leave around ten a.m. tomorrow.

"Well, I'll re-file the flight plan."

"Thanks, man. This means a lot."

"You know how many times you saved my life in college? I wish you would reconsider my offer and come head my security division. You're going to make more money working for me than you will for the FBI. And it's a lot safer."

"I just need a few more months of service before I can get my full retirement. Maybe I'll think about it."

When Zoe pulled up, Carver told Steve he had to go. "I'll call you in the morning."

Zoe didn't like what she felt when she saw Carver on the phone, hanging up as soon as she pulled up. He could've very well been talking to a woman. *And it is none of my business.*

"Ready?"

"Yeah." Carver eased into the car and smiled at Zoe.

They drove in silence for a couple of miles, and then Carver glanced at Zoe.

"Are you sure you're all right?" he asked as he stretched his legs.

"If you're going to ask me every five minutes if I'm all right, we're going to have a problem."

"You can't fault me for being concerned."

"It's misplaced and misguided." Her voice quivered a bit, but Carver pretended not to notice.

"You think your brother feels that you're in trouble? That twin connection thing?"

"Really? Do me a favor, let it go. If Zach knew I was in the car with you, he'd think that's the most troubling thing in my life."

"So, what's he going to do when you take me home for our first family dinner?" Carver quipped.

"That's never going to happen. Once we end this case, we're going back to our respective corners and pretend that we don't know each other anymore."

"Not doing that. I'm telling you right now, I'm going to make you mine, Zoe."

"Do I get a say in this? What if I don't want to belong to a man?"

"What are you afraid of? Why can't you open your heart and let me in?"

Zoe nearly slammed into the car in front of her. "Carver, I'm not doing this with you because there's no need to play the fantasy game."

"Who said it's just a fantasy? Zoe, I—"

"Stop. Please stop." She couldn't listen to him say he cared or even loved her without getting scared.

"Okay, I'm done—for now."

They pulled up at the wireless store and walked in silently. When Zoe walked over to the iPhones, Carver cringed. She could easily be tracked with that phone, and he wanted to stop her.

"I think you should buy me the new one—the big one."

"So, I'm your upgrade, huh?"

She nodded as the sales consultant headed their way.

"Good afternoon. Do you two need help with the phones?"

Zoe shook her head. "I want the 128-gigabyte rose gold one."

"Do you currently have a phone you want to trade in?"

Zoe glanced at Carver. "Actually, I don't. Someone dropped my phone and destroyed it."

"Like, cracked the screen?"

"It was an accident in New Mexico," Carver said. "The phone is beyond repair."

"Did you even bring it with you?" Zoe asked.

"You know I didn't. Since I knew I had to replace your phone, I just tossed it in Santa Fe. You did back it up to the cloud, didn't you?"

Zoe rolled her eyes. "Of course I did."

"All right, then. Let me check and see if we have the phone in stock." The sales clerk headed to the back of the store.

"Have you thought about getting a new number?" Carver asked.

"Why would I do that?" Zoe ran her fingers through her hair. "I can't imagine the number of clients I've missed the past few days. I probably need a second line."

"That's on you."

She smiled. "I know. Not going to bilk you out of all of your money." She walked over to some simple cell phones and picked up a flip phone. "This will be my travel phone. Good and sturdy."

Carver nodded. "Good idea."

When the sales consultant came back with the new iPhone, Zoe told her she wanted to add a second line to her plan and held up the flip phone. "Do you have any more of these in stock?"

"I'll check."

Carver eased closer to Zoe, and when he wrapped his arm around her waist, she didn't move. She actually leaned against him. *I could get used to this,* she thought as she inhaled his masculine scent. *But this isn't going to happen. I don't know why I'm pretending that it will.*

"You're in luck," the sales consultant said. "We have the phone in stock."

"Great."

They followed her to the register and Carver held her hand. Zoe rubbed her thumb against his palm. He glanced at her and then released her hand. She didn't say anything as the clerk rang up the purchases and activated the phones. Because she'd been a customer so long, Zoe got her second line and phone for free.

Carver handed the clerk his credit card and paid for her iPhone.

"Sweet," she said as she turned on her phone. The first thing she needed to do was call Zach. "I'm going to call my brother. I'll be outside."

"I'm going to the bodega to get something to drink. You want something?"

"Orange juice."

"Got it."

Zoe stood next to the entrance of the phone store and dialed Zach's number. He picked up on the first ring.

"I was about to book a flight for New York. Where have you been?"

"Hello to you, too," she said with a laugh.

"Don't do that. Chante and I have been out of our minds with worry. Where have you been?"

"I've been working on a case and I was in New Mexico."

"And you couldn't pick up the phone and call me?"

"Actually, no. My phone was broken."

"Really? What kind of case are you working on? Are you in danger, sis? I don't like this, and I told you a long time ago that you should stop putting your life on the line because you want to prove a point to me and Dad."

"Can you stop? I'm working a case with the FBI, looking for the remains of a murder victim. And I'm fine. Just wanted to check in on you and my sister-in-law."

"Well, we're doing very well. You're going to be an auntie."

"What?!" she exclaimed. "This is awesome. When is she due?"

"Around December first. And it's not twins."

"Maybe next time."

"When are you going to take some time off and come to Charlotte? We've actually expanded down here and have a huge contract with the city for reviving one of the historic neighborhoods on the south side."

"That sounds great."

"Zoe, are you really safe?"

"Didn't I just tell you that I was?"

"I just feel like something is going on and you're not telling me everything."

"Zach, don't start this. I can take care of myself and I'm fine." There was no way that she was going to tell him about the explosion at her office. She knew her brother, and he would be in New York before she could blink.

"Well, you need to get your butt to North Carolina, sooner rather than later, so you can have some of this barbecue that I've become a master at making. I'm almost a real Southerner."

"Ooh, that doesn't even sound right coming out of your mouth!"

"Don't knock it until you try it. Charlotte is an amazing city. Clean streets, craft beer, and the second-largest banking center in the world. I don't even have to fly back and forth to New York for funding."

"Are you ever coming back to New York?"

"Yeah, if my sister stays in one place long enough for me to come visit."

"Well, just so you know, I'm heading to Las Vegas in the morning."

"Damn, Zoe! Let some grass grow under your feet for a minute."

"Still working my case." She sighed and decided she needed to tell him who her client was. "Zach, Carver Banks is my FBI liaison."

"Are you freaking kidding me? Why are you helping that prick do anything after the hell he put us through?"

"Zach, he was doing his job, and we wouldn't have gone through any hell had you not brought that—"

"Don't remind me. Why would you take this job?"

"Because he needed my help, Zach. That's why I do this, to help people." Zoe could feel him rolling his eyes through the phone. "And don't give me that look."

"Whatever. This guy is bad news, and I know this is about more than helping him. You and Agent Banks have something going on, don't you?"

"Absolutely not."

"You know I'm the last person you can lie to. Be careful, because I've already told him if he hurts you that he's going to have to deal with me."

Zoe shook her head. "And this is why I don't tell you who I'm dating."

"I have to take care of my little sister."

"Five minutes. You are five minutes older than me! Get over it."

"Nope. Five minutes makes me the older brother, now you deal with it."

Zoe looked up. Carver was coming her way with a small bottle of orange juice. "Zach, give Chante my love and I'll talk to you soon." Hanging up the phone, she crossed over to Carver. "Thank you for this."

"No problem. I guess I should greet you with orange juice all the time." Carver smiled and sipped his coffee. "So, how's your brother?"

"Still thinks you're a piece of—"

"Got it." Carver laughed.

Zoe opened her orange juice and took a swig. "Have you made your hotel reservation?"

"Not yet. I'm going to head to the FBI office first, then book the room."

"Want me to drop you off?"

Carver shook his head. "I can take a cab. I'll meet you later for that dinner you owe me."

"Sounds good. I'm going to head back to my office

and see if the landlord has gotten a cleaning crew out there yet."

"Why don't you wait for me and we'll go together?"

"No. I can handle it. Thanks for the offer, though. See you later." Part of her wanted to give him a hug and a goodbye kiss, but Zoe headed for her car. She couldn't get too cozy with him, especially since Vegas was going to be the end of all of this.

Chapter 16

When Carver arrived at the satellite office, he wasn't surprised to find it empty, no staff there. But all of the equipment was, and that was all he needed. Sitting at one of the computers, he logged on and looked for all references to Smallwood.

He found a file marked HARRINGTON and figured it was about Natalie. When he opened it up and saw the references to Zoe and her "interference" in the Singletary investigation, he was confused. Why hadn't anyone told him about this? He saw the author of the report was W.C.

"Wendy," he muttered. Carver printed a copy of the report, then kept searching. He needed to find out what happened when Smallwood talked to Natalie after her arrest. There had to be some kind of clue as to where Singletary was. How was he always one step ahead of the FBI? What had been Wendy's role in all of this? Because from what he was seeing here, Smallwood and Zoe had been working with each other. Why didn't she tell him about this?

Maybe that was why Smallwood had wanted to keep her alive and authorized the operation. But Wendy, who'd been his right hand, seemed to be against Zoe's *interference*.

Why is she pretending to help if she's undermining the investigation and ignoring what Zoe has to offer?

"Wendy, you're starting to disappoint me. Why is that bitch still breathing?" Singletary huffed.

"She and Carver must have a four-leaf clover glued to their feet. I've been trying to track where they're going, but she hasn't shown up on any flight lists since she got back to New York . . ."

"All I hear are excuses. I'm tired of excuses!"

Wendy pulled the phone from her ear and groaned. She wanted her money and she was tired of Joe and his demands. What was he doing other than waiting on her to feed him information about the FBI's investigation into his organization? Part of her wanted to just turn him in. Maybe if she did that, her career would get an uptick. If she was the one who brought down the country's most notorious sex trafficker, there was no way she wouldn't get the promotion she deserved.

But Joe would have no problem killing her. Maybe she needed to do the job he wanted her to do. Still, Zoe Harrington seemed to have nine lives. No matter what Wendy threw at her, she dodged it. Carver was her lucky charm and she was going to have to kill two birds with one stone. She could get her revenge on Carver for tanking her career and get paid for it.

She placed the phone back to her ear. "Joe, I'm going to handle it."

"Six days."

"I got this."

"You'd better." The line went dead and Wendy tossed her phone across the room. She needed to get back to New York, but how was she going to make that happen? Wendy was stuck in DC working on cyber-crimes, and she didn't have a legitimate reason to go to New York since the office had already been cleared out.

Maybe Carver could. Wendy picked up her FBI-issued cell phone and called him.

"Agent Banks."

"Hey, Carver, it's Wendy. I just wanted to check in on you and Zoe. How's everything going?"

"We're still alive. Do you have a lead on Singletary?"

"Not yet."

"Let me ask you a question," he began. "Do you think Singletary has someone else on the inside? Now, if Smallwood was working with him, who would be doing it now?"

Wendy sighed. "That's a good question."

"I need to interview Natalie Harrington."

"Natalie was killed two days ago. There was a fight at the prison and she got stabbed in the chest."

"What? Why didn't you tell me?"

"She was in prison, what was the point? You're flying all over the country trying to keep this woman alive. I didn't think it mattered."

"Wendy, Natalie was our only link to Singletary. Why wasn't she in protective custody?"

"That's something you have to ask the Department of Corrections. I don't know, and that wasn't our job." She blew into the phone and Carver gritted his teeth. He was pissed off and he couldn't deal with her any longer.

"I have to go." Carver hung up and wondered if Singletary had ordered Natalie's murder because she'd spoken to the FBI. And if that was the case, why hadn't Smallwood put her in protective custody?

This isn't adding up at all.

Carver rose from the computer and headed for the file room. He needed answers, and it was starting to seem as if Wendy was a part of the problem and not the solution. Carver didn't find anything pointing to a connection between Smallwood and Natalie or her cooperation in the investigation.

There were no interview transcripts or anything. But as he dug deeper, he found something strange —a picture of Wendy and Singletary.

"It's been her all along! How in the hell did we miss this?" He had no clue who he could trust right now. One thing Carver knew for sure, he had to get to Zoe right now, because there was no telling who was after her.

Zoe pulled up at her office and watched the crews cleaning the debris from the explosion. As she got out of the car, she heard someone call her name. When she turned and saw Lewis, she forced a fake smile.

"What happened here?" he asked.

"I have no idea. Sorry I haven't had a chance to get in contact with you. I've had some issues with my phone, and as you can see, I don't have an office to work in."

"Things aren't looking good for you." Lewis smiled and Zoe rolled her eyes.

"Why are you here, Lewis?"

"Well, we did have a meeting. Guess that's not going to happen."

Zoe bit down on her bottom lip to keep from snapping at him. "Lewis, I have some work to do. Unless you want to help with cleanup, we can reschedule once I get the office reopened."

"Can I ask you a question?"

Zoe started for the door and nodded. Lewis stood close to her and brought his lips to her ear.

"Did you think you were going to get away with ruining people's lives and no one would come after you, bitch?"

Zoe shoved her elbow in his stomach and Lewis crumpled to the ground. "That's what this is about? Payback? You sorry son of a bitch! Had you done your job, there wouldn't have been a reason for me to investigate you guys."

Slowly rising to his feet, Lewis spit at Zoe. "But I was your partner. We were supposed to be different. You could've had my back!"

Lewis lunged at Zoe and she quickly sidestepped him. Sticking her foot out, she tripped him. Lewis fell on his face and Zoe drew her gun.

"I'm giving you five seconds to get out of here." Zoe cocked her gun. "Five."

"This ain't over."

"Four."

Lewis rose to his feet and took off. Zoe took a deep

breath. No mystery who set the bomb now. Holstering her gun, Zoe unlocked the front door to her office. She was happy to see that the back door had been boarded up. When she heard a knock at the door, Zoe grabbed her gun—just in case Lewis had come back—and crossed over to the door.

"Who is it?" She pointed the barrel of the gun at the doorjamb, then opened it with her other hand.

"Whoa!" Carver exclaimed, holding his hands up. "Why are you pulling guns on people?"

"I had a run-in with my old partner earlier. I'm sure he's the one who set the bomb."

"Why do you say that?" Carver stepped inside and glanced around the office.

Zoe sighed and leaned on her desk. "Well, he threatened me. We got into a fight and it all fell into place."

"You were a great detective, huh? Do you think we need to look into this threat that you think Lewis is?"

She folded her arms across her chest and shook her head. "No one would really give a shit about Lewis and I'm pretty sure he would have enough people cheering him on. Anyway, I never made detective. That was part of the reason why the NYPD and me didn't work out. Sometimes I felt as if that job was another failed relationship. I loved it, but the job didn't like me much."

"Why? I think you were a hell of cop."

"You've met me and you know I don't hold my tongue for anyone. That's where the problems began." Zoe smiled. "Have you thought about what you want for dinner?" She glanced at her watch. "And what time are we leaving for Vegas in the morning? Finding your

Jessica Dolan is pretty much the highlight of my life right now. You have my full attention."

Carver licked his lips and Zoe's thighs shivered. Even at a time like this, that man still touched part of her that had his name written all over it.

"If I tell you what I really want, I might get shot or punched, so I'm going to say let's get some Chinese."

"Really? I'm buying you dinner and you just want Chinese? You better take advantage of this moment. You never know when it is going to happen again." She winked at him. Though she wasn't going to tell him, if he wanted to have her for dinner, she'd be happy to serve it up.

"All right, what do you suggest?"

"I don't know. Neptune Diner?"

"I love that place. Haven't been there in years."

Zoe smiled. "We have something in common. Getting out to Queens can be hell sometimes."

"Since we're flying out of Queens in the morning, why don't you stay with me tonight?"

Zoe raised her right eyebrow. Was he serious? "I don't think that's a good idea."

"It's going to cut down time on driving to Far Rockaway in the morning, and we can cover more ground in Vegas."

"If you as much as put one finger on me . . ."

"I will be a perfect gentleman, tonight."

"Tonight, huh?" Zoe shook her head. "Okay, fine. I just have to go home and pack."

"I left my bags at your place, so do you mind if I catch a ride?"

She shook her head. "Let's go."

* * *

Carver's plan was to stick to Zoe like white on rice until he got in touch with the Shadow Team. It had been six years since he needed his brothers and sister of intelligence. Though they worked for different agencies, ranging from the CIA to the Department of Justice, they had one thing in common: They were all ex-Marines. The four of them— Carver, Kenneth Long, Sarah Greene, and Raymond Tyler—enlisted at the same time.

As their careers took off, they'd made a vow to have each other's backs, no matter what. He sent Sarah a text telling her to call him on a secure line. He gave her his cell phone number and waited.

By the time Zoe pulled into her driveway, Carver's phone rang. "I have to take this," he said. "I'll be in shortly."

Zoe nodded and got out of the car.

"Sarah?"

"What's up, Carver?"

"I've got problems and I need help."

"The whole team?"

"Yep. Have you ever heard of Joseph Singletary?"

"Yes, I've been tailing that slimy son of a bitch for three years. He's real active these days, and I think I have a line on his inside link with the Bureau."

"Delvin Smallwood, right?"

"No. Smallwood was on our side. He believed someone on his team was feeding information to Singletary. You were even on that list for half a second. Agent

Covington, though, we're trying to tie her to Singletary, and Smallwood's murder."

"She was there and she said that—"

"I know the story she told, but the bullets that were fished out of Smallwood were government issued. And from the angle he was shot, it wasn't friendly fire."

"She's been playing us all along. I found a photo in the satellite office of Covington and Singletary. But I don't get how she can help him."

"Wendy needs help, like mental help. Her sister was kidnapped a year before she joined the Bureau. The girl was fifteen and treated like a runaway. She was found sexually assaulted and strangled in a creek out in South Carolina."

"I worked that case."

"Yes. Her death was linked to the airman who'd raped and killed three women. Amber, Wendy's sister, was the last victim. Wendy never really got over it. It really affected her work in the Bureau, at least that's what Smallwood told me when he asked us to do a parallel investigation into Singletary."

"Damn. Why didn't he let her go?"

"Smallwood wanted to fire her. But the girl has skills with the computer, and that saved her job. Can you get me that picture?"

"Yeah. One more thing—Zoe Harrington."

"I wonder why she never applied here? She's good. The night she was arrested, she gave Smallwood more intel on Singletary's investigation than we'd gotten over the previous twelve months. She told him that when she set out to clear her name, that's when she found out about Natalie's link to Singletary. She had a file that she refused to share with anyone, and Singletary wanted to get that file badly."

"I'm not surprised, she was pretty pissed with us back then."

"What's changed?"

"I'm keeping her alive. That's the main thing." He didn't want to tell Sarah everything about his relationship with Zoe. In the Corps, she and Monica had been best friends, and Sarah warned Carver about mixing business and pleasure. He'd thought for a long time that Sarah blamed him for Monica's death, but she hadn't. Her response had been that they were at war and death was around every corner. She'd thought of Carver as a brother and respected the fact that he trusted her to be a member of the Shadow Team.

She and Monica had been two of the few women who worked in Marine intelligence, and not many of their male counterparts respected the fact that they could do their jobs. When Monica was killed, Carver went to bat for Sarah when a faction of the squad wanted to kick Sarah out of the group.

"Well, now I've got to keep both of you alive. I'm going to get in touch with the boys and we're going to track what's going on."

"Thanks, Sarah." Carver looked up and saw Zoe coming his way. "I have to go."

Zoe raised her eyebrow at him. "Must have been an important phone call." She handed him his bag.

"It was. Thanks for this."

"No problem." She popped the trunk and dropped her bag inside. Carver followed suit, then reached out and grabbed Zoe's hand.

"Have you called the authorities about your former partner?" He wanted to get her talking about anything but the phone call she'd walked up on.

"No. What's the point? There's no evidence, and I can't say that anyone in the Bronx would care if he did it or not."

"Not many friends here, huh?"

"You could say that. Let's get out of here. I'm starving."

Carver nodded and got into the car. Zoe turned on the radio and the sounds of Jodeci filled the car.

"I love this song," Carver said, then did an off-key imitation of K-Ci. "'Forever my lady.'"

"Don't quit your day job. I think my ears are bleeding."

"Girl, you know you like that. You want to throw your panties at me right now."

"No, just stuff them in your mouth to shut you up."

Carver and Zoe laughed as they sang off-key to more '90s R & B. "Yeah, you should keep your day job, too," he said as a Mary J. Blige song played.

"Whatever. I could sing backup for Ms. Mary. Ooh, that's my girl. *What's the 411?* is a classic."

"No, ma'am. You need to sing solo."

"Solo?"

"So low that no one can hear you."

"You aren't funny, and I ought to kick you out of this car." She rolled her eyes as she merged onto the highway.

"Can I ask you a question?"

"Yeah."

"What do you know about Singletary's organization?"

She gave him a quick glance, then turned back to the road ahead. "Why do you ask?"

"Because when I was at the field office, your name came up in a file. I know after your arrest—"

"On bogus charges. Don't forget that part."

Carver sighed. "Here we go again."

"Listen, you were the one who took the word of a madam over me. I'm still a little salty about it."

"A little?"

"Anyway. When I found out what Natalie was into, I started looking into her background and who she was working for. I mean, she wasn't that smart and she acted more like a hooker than a real madam."

"And what did you find out?"

"Found out that Joseph Singletary used to be drug kingpin, but after it got harder to traffic drugs, he turned to women. It was much easier for him to make money doing that and easier to skirt the authorities. Since he was dealing with black and brown girls, it took a long time for the FBI and local police to take notice."

"That's harsh."

"But that's the truth. And don't act like the FBI hasn't dropped the ball on this. If little girls from the suburbs with blond hair were being taken and sold by a big black man, Singletary would be dead or in jail."

"I can't change the system by myself."

"I know. But if someone would've paid attention earlier, maybe more girls would've been saved. Have you seen those ads on Backpage?"

"Yes."

"They're horrific. Some of those girls don't look as

if they've gone through puberty. Social media is their hunting ground."

"And the technology keeps outpacing our investigations."

"You guys should hire some hackers."

"Why have you never applied with the Bureau?"

Zoe sucked her teeth. "Are you serious?" She started laughing. "Women don't have a fair shot at having a great career there. I did some research a long time ago, and realized the FBI wasn't for me."

"That's bullshit. If you work hard—"

"Harder than the men."

Carver rolled his eyes. "So, would you burn your bra or your badge first?"

"Are you happy with your work at the Bureau? All jokes aside, do you miss the Marines?"

"I do. When I see my brothers and sisters out there fighting the good fight, I want to go back. Then I think about the losses and the mistakes I made."

"Mistakes?"

Carver nodded. "I don't want to talk about it."

"All right." Zoe slowed down as she took the exit for Astoria. "I remember when Dad used to bring us out here when we made good grades or he closed a big deal. Zach always wanted the juice. If he could've drank his dinner, he would've."

"What was your favorite thing here?"

Zoe turned into the restaurant's parking lot. "Silver-dollar pancakes with powdered sugar."

"You have a hell of a sweet tooth. Must be why your mouth is so delicious."

"There you go, thinking with the wrong head again. And who eats pancakes without powdered sugar?"

"Most adults." He laughed, then leaned over and squeezed her cheek. "If you order that tonight, I won't hold it against you."

"Don't make me regret this. I should've let you suffer with greasy Chinese food."

"And that would've been horrible. This is much better, now I know that you think you can be a backup singer for Mary J. Blige and we can do a duet at the Apollo one day."

"Yeah, right. You know once this case is over and you return to DC, you're not going to give me a second thought."

Carver ran his index finger down her cheek. "Zoe, you know I will never forget you. And trust me, I've tried."

She reached up and grabbed his wrist. "What is it about me that makes me unforgettable?"

He leaned into her, brushing his lips against hers. "These." Carver devoured her lips and Zoe melted against him. A blaring horn stopped them from taking the kiss one step further. Looking at each other through lust-filled eyes, Zoe opened her mouth, but the driver leaned in on the horn.

"We better move," she said.

"Yes. Because another minute and I can't be held responsible for what happens next."

Zoe's mouth fell open as she pulled into a parking spot. "Let's go eat."

Chapter 17

Once Zoe and Carver entered the restaurant, she couldn't stop thinking about that brief kiss in the car. His lips were magical, and if she spent much more time with him, she was going to be in trouble.

"Silver dollar pancakes," Carver said as he pulled out a chair for Zoe. The heat from his breath made her shiver.

Zoe couldn't understand what happened in the last few hours that had changed everything. It made sense, though. As much as she tried to be angry about that night two years ago, she'd never felt such passion and heat since. As much as Carver thought she was unforgettable, she knew he was as well. And now that the memories were back, she didn't know how to handle it.

"With powdered sugar," she quipped.

Carver licked his lips and smiled while Zoe's panties dripped with desire. "I'm going to try that. Maybe add a little whipped cream."

"Now you're doing too much." She crossed her legs

and squeezed her thighs together, hoping to subdue the throbbing.

He leaned across the table. "Maybe I'm not doing enough." Capturing her face in his hands, Carver brushed his lips against hers.

"Stop, we have an audience." She nodded toward two giggling kids who were watching them.

"All right, I'm done for now."

Wendy sent a text to her guy in New York, and when she didn't hear anything from him after an hour, she felt as if she'd been played again. She needed this money from Singletary because she was tired of risking her freedom for this man. *Ungrateful bastard. He doesn't even care how much I've risked to keep him out of prison, and I know someone is going to make the connection between us, if Zoe Harrington and Carver haven't already.*

She stood up and walked over to the window. Playtime was over. She had to get back to New York and track Zoe and Carver down herself. Just as she was about to leave the office, the door opened and three men in suits walked in.

"Agent Covington?"

"And you are?"

"You need to come with us. Be quiet about it and act normal," the other man said.

"What is this about?"

"You can ask all the questions you want when we get to a secured location."

She gritted her teeth and rose to her feet. "Fine." Her

mind was working overtime to find a way out, but the men flanked her as if she was a threat to homeland security.

Once they were on the parking deck, Wendy turned to the man who'd been doing all the talking. "I need to see some identification before I get in a car with you two."

"We're not getting in the car," he said. "We're here to deliver a message. Find Banks and Zoe or you're going to come up missing. Your delay has just cost you a million dollars."

"You tell Joe that I want my full bounty, and the next time he sends fuck boys to threaten me, I'm sending you back in boxes."

The other man turned to Wendy. "Bitch, who do you think you're talking to?"

Wendy squared up with him and then kicked him in his chest. Before the other man could react, she'd given him a roundhouse kick to the head. The third man stepped back and threw his hands up in surrender.

She felt powerful and ready to do something she should've done a long time ago. Wendy was going to confront Singletary and get her money now. She'd done enough for his organization to deserve the money he'd promised her. And with the investigation into Smallwood's death heating up, Wendy knew she had to disappear sooner rather than later. Clearly she'd given him everything he needed to take care of Carver and Zoe. She'd done everything that she could and it was time for Joe to pay her for her sacrifice.

* * *

Carver leaned back in his seat after finishing his meal. He was stuffed. "That was good. Even the powdered sugar on the pancakes."

"I told you so. How do you feel about dessert?"

He shook his head, then smirked at her. "Unless it's you, I can't eat another bite."

She sucked in her bottom lip. "What am I going to do with you?"

"Give me what I want so we can both be happy." He placed his hand on top of hers. "I'm going to give it a rest because we have work to do and a plane to catch."

Zoe slid her hand from underneath his. "Part of me is hoping to find Jessica alive with memory loss or something. Maybe this could be a miracle case, like those girls in Cleveland," she said wistfully. "Or maybe I'm just overreacting because of what happened earlier today. I'm tired of death." Zoe reached into her purse and pulled out her tablet.

"Are you using Wi-Fi?" he asked.

"Why does that matter?"

"Because I don't want to pay for your data charges." What he really meant was that he didn't want them traced.

"You're so damned cheap. I knew you couldn't afford me."

"But who's flying you in style, baby?"

Zoe rolled her eyes. "We're probably riding in a crop duster."

Carver wiped his mouth. "So cynical. You would've been a great FBI agent."

"Whatever. Me and other people's rules don't always work out, you know."

Carver rose to his feet and held his hand out to Zoe. "Can't say that I'm surprised."

She took his hand, and when he pulled her against his chest, he could feel her tremble. Quickly, she pulled out of his embrace. "Where are we staying?"

"I haven't booked a room yet because I wanted to give you the option to help me choose."

Zoe rolled her eyes. "You haven't booked two rooms yet, you mean."

"Of course, because I know you can't control yourself."

"You wish I couldn't control myself. But you wouldn't be able to handle it if I did lose control."

"Handled it just fine last time. Maybe you're the one who can't handle it." Carver smiled at her as he watched her cheeks heat and turn red.

"There's a Crawford motel on the beach. We can stay there."

"I've noticed something about you. When a conversation isn't going your way, you will change the subject."

"I don't do that."

He raised his right eyebrow as if to say *really*. "If that's what gets you through the night, then I'll let you believe that. Or, am I the only one you give this kind of treatment to?"

Zoe wanted to run. Zoe wanted to kiss Carver. Zoe wanted to punch him in the face. But she wasn't going to admit to him that he was the only man who'd gotten under her skin like a virus. The only man who'd branded her body and made her quiver with just a look.

"You really have an ego problem, you know."

"I don't have an ego problem, I have a Zoe problem."

"A Zoe problem?"

"I want you so bad that it hurts."

She started to say something about feeling the same way, but she needed to focus. *I'm supposed to be finding Jessica Dolan, not his erogenous zones.*

"It seems as if we've gotten off track. We're here together because Jessica Dolan is missing. Don't pretend that we're reconnecting and rekindling some lost romance. So, answer this question: If you want me so bad that it hurts, how did you dull the pain all this time?"

"You know how the old adage goes, out of sight, out of mind. But I can say this, one day I was walking down K Street and I thought I saw you. When I chased that poor woman for about two blocks, that's when I knew this problem of mine wasn't going to go away."

Zoe laughed, imagining him following that poor woman. Then a heat wave of jealousy washed over her. "What happened when you caught her?"

"I had to talk her out of calling the cops. Then I bought her a drink, took her home, and pretended she was you."

"Pig."

"The look on your face said you thought that's what I did. Zoe, no other woman will ever compare to you, so I haven't wasted time with, what did you say—tapas, wine, and lobbyists."

"I never said anything about a lobbyist, so you just

told on yourself. Let's get out of here so that we can go to sleep."

"For the record, I'm more into women who can run sting operations and take down a suspect with one hand," he said with a wink. "Lobbyists talk too much."

"That wasn't a suspect takedown, that was me grabbing a tramp that I couldn't stand."

"Well, you looked damned good doing it."

She folded her arms across her chest. "So, that's why you kissed me that night? In front of my brother, I might add."

"I kissed you because I missed you and you made me hot when you got all Foxy Brown out there with Natalie. If you had an afro, I would've made love to you on the sidewalk in front of your brother."

A heated blush colored her cheeks. "Whatever. Let's go."

Zoe knew the sooner they got to Vegas and found out the final resting place of Jessica Dolan, the sooner she could get back to a normal life. A life where she didn't have to change her panties every time that man looked at her. A life where she might be bored as hell, but her heart was safe.

They walked out of the restaurant and headed to the Crawford SeaSide Motel. It may have said motel, but this small, one-story seaside place was luxurious. And when Carver went inside to book their rooms, she felt as though she could breathe freely now.

Moments later, Carver returned to the car. "Got the last two rooms." He handed Zoe her key card. "They aren't even side by side, so you can't sneak in my room if you wanted to."

"I don't have to sneak, when, according to you, I have a standing invitation."

"All you have to do is knock and I'm yours." Carver winked at her, and once again, Zoe knew she was going to have to change her panties.

She pulled the car into an empty spot and looked down at her room key number. "Well, I guess I'd better go to bed. What time are we leaving in the morning?"

"You let me know. We're not constrained by the schedules of commercial airlines this time. We can leave as early or as late as you'd like, Just give me a heads up so that I can alert the pilot."

Zoe nodded. "The sooner we leave, the better. No later than six. Then I can cover more ground in Vegas."

"And I can hit the slot machines."

They stepped out of the car and Zoe headed to her room. She looked over her shoulder. "Good night, Carver. Dream about me."

Zoe's last words turned out to be exactly how Carver spent his sleepless night, dreaming of her in his arms. Fantasizing about her on top of him, her lips pressed against his and their bodies becoming one.

So many times he woke up expecting to see Zoe's naked body next to him. When he just found empty sheets, he was pissed. Then he thought about the real reason he and Zoe were together. He was supposed to be keeping her alive. Couldn't do that if he was trying to get in her pants every time he saw her.

Sitting up in the bed, he swung his legs over the side and reached for his cell phone. He needed to talk to the

Shadow Team and find out if there was a mole on the Singletary investigation. He wasn't surprised about what Sarah had told him about Wendy.

He called Raymond because he knew this man woke up every morning at five.

"Tyler."

"Ray, it's Carver."

"My dude. What's going on? I heard we're getting back together to kick some ass."

"Still ready to fight all the time."

"That's never going to change, and that's why y'all still love me. I've been looking into your official team with the FBI. I think your girl Covington is dirty as a swamp rat. Singletary was tracked down to Los Angeles and she went out there, right?"

"Yeah."

"Well, she might have been the one who killed those little girls who were ready to testify against Singletary. Two victims of trafficking were found that night, one died of an overdose and the other was shot. From what my inside guy says, the one thing they have in common is Wendy. She was seen talking to both of them. "

"Wendy? Kill somebody? I just can't see it."

"That's why things have worked so well with her and Singletary. She's just under the radar. We take her down and we'll be able to get to Singletary. 'Cause I know why you're doing this."

"What do you mean? I'm here to take a—"

"Fool, I have not forgotten about Zoe Harrington, and I know you're trying to keep her alive and get her fine ass back in your bed. Shit, I'd do it, too."

Carver smiled despite himself. "It's more than about sleeping with her. I really   "

"Don't say it! Player, down. You're in love with her, aren't you? You can't make this personal. Have you learned anything from me or nah?"

"This is different."

"You're distracted and you're going to make mistakes."

"I've learned my lesson from that, trust me. My mission is to protect Zoe."

"Where does loving her fit into this?"

"Just get me some information on Wendy Covington and Joe Singletary. I can handle the rest."

"I'm not giving you shit for no reason. I know if something happens to that woman like—"

"I'm hanging up. Call me when you have something I can use." Carver tossed his phone on the bed. Of course Ray was right. Zoe was a distraction. Could that be why he'd missed what was really going on with Wendy?

Losing Zoe would be the straw that broke Carver's back. She could hate him, if and when she found out about his subterfuge, but he was not going to let anyone harm her. Finding Singletary and putting him away had to happen immediately.

Checking his watch, he wondered if Zoe was awake and if it was time to tell her the truth.

Down the corridor, Zoe rolled over on her back and stared up at the ceiling. Another flight with Carver, and this time they would be alone. Was she ready for this?

"I can do this," she muttered as she sat up in the bed. Zoe reached for her cell phone and called her brother—despite how early it was.

"Are you bleeding? Have you been shot?" Zach's greeting was as groggy as it was sarcastic.

"You're supposed to be my big brother. You're always playing that card, so here's your chance to live up to it."

"Aww shit, this is serious, huh?"

"Zach, how did you know Chante was the one?"

"The moment I laid eyes on her. She was different. I could tell she wasn't interested and I knew I had my work cut out for me."

"That's all it took? No wonder you and Natalie linked up."

"I made a mistake with her, but as you can see, I've made up for it. Just tell me that you're not asking me these questions because of Banks."

"And if I am?"

"What in the hell is wrong with you? How can you trust the man who arrested you on the word of a pimp?"

"It's complicated."

"No, being around him has you confused. That man isn't worthy of you."

"Funny, when I told you that about a certain ex-wife of yours, you didn't listen."

"And I've learned my lesson. Don't make my mistakes, just finish this job for him and run in the other direction."

"Yeah, this was very helpful. You suck as a big brother."

"I'm trying to stop you from making a mistake. He's just an arrogant FBI agent with his ass on his shoulder. That mother . . . Look, he was part of the reason why our family business suffered during the investigation into Natalie. I'm not ready to see him in my sister's life. I already warned him."

"I know, one of your brightest ideas, threatening an FBI agent. I wonder about you sometimes."

"You're my little sister. I had to let him know that I wasn't about to let him hurt you."

"And I can take care of myself, just not my heart. I don't want to be hurt," she admitted.

"That's a part of life. Sometimes you have to risk a little hurt to find the right one. But trust me when I say, it ain't Agent Banks."

Zoe sighed. "And you know this because you can see into the future?"

"I just don't trust him. And you obviously have reservations yourself."

She regretted this phone call. Her reservations about Carver were slowly melting away. "Goodbye, Zach." She hung up before her brother could say anything else.

Zoe pulled herself out of bed and headed for the shower. It didn't matter what Zach said about not trusting Carver, Zoe knew something was there. It thrilled her as much as it scared her. She wanted to eat tapas with him and walk along the Potomac.

"Why do I keep thinking about tapas? I don't even like tapas," she muttered as the hot water washed over her.

After about twenty minutes in the shower, Zoe hopped out and wrapped a towel around her body. As she smoothed lotion on her body, her mind went back to the night she and Carver spent together.

"Thank you for your help and the ride out of there."

She smiled at X, thinking if a man's bodyguard hates him, he was in trouble.

He stroked her cheek. "Does the night have to end? That was pretty exciting back there."

Zoe shivered and tried to blame her reaction on the champagne she'd had at the party. But the truth was, X was fine, and it had been a while since a man turned her on like a light switch.

Her phone vibrated, informing her that her client had paid her fee. She had a reason to celebrate and she knew she'd never see this man again. She wrapped her arms around his neck and kissed him—slow, deep, and wet.

His gasp told her that she'd caught him off guard. He quickly recovered and pulled her against his hard body. She felt his arousal and was instantly wet. Zoe wrapped her leg around his waist and ground against him.

"Damn, baby," he moaned.

"Let's go inside, now."

X nodded as if he had the same lusty thoughts as Zoe. At that moment, she'd been seconds away from ripping his clothes off, stripping him naked, and making love to him on the side of the building. But there were way too many cameras around to even risk it. He lifted her into his arms. "I know a shortcut."

"Lead the way." She buried her nose in his neck and inhaled his distinctive scent. There was nothing like a man who smelled good, and X smelled as divine as he looked. Heading into the hotel using the back staircase, she was amazed at how strong he was as he took the stairs while holding her as if she were a five-pound bag of sugar. He leaned her against the wall as he *fished his room key from his pants. Zoe's mouth watered as she saw the imprint of his arousal. Then she had a sobering thought—what if this was a part of a scheme to eliminate her and keep her client from getting what she needed to divorce her drug-dealing husband?*

"You having second thoughts?" he asked when he noticed her pause.

"I just want you to know I'm not the kind of woman who does this on a regular basis, and if you try to hurt me, I'm going to fight back and possibly kill you."

He laughed, a full belly laugh. "Baby, I don't want to hurt a hair on your pretty little head, I just want you to look me in the eye when I make you come."

Her breath caught in her chest as he captured her lips in a hungry kiss. She couldn't help but wonder if he'd just gotten out of prison. X fell backward on the bed with Zoe in his arms. She mounted him and ripped his shirt open. His chest was as amazing as she imagined it would be, rippling and mouthwatering. Licking her lips, she leaned back and lifted her dress over her head.

"Damn, you're beautiful."

"You're not so bad yourself." She buried her lips in his neck, kissing and licking the column of his neck. She felt him shiver and felt emboldened to reach into his pants and feel his throbbing erection. X moaned as she moved her hand up and down.

"Yes, yes," he moaned. She unzipped his pants and slid them down his narrow waist. X kicked out of the pants and Zoe's eyes widened at the sight of his erection—long, thick, and ready.

"Protection?" she asked as she cupped his hardness.

"Shit," he muttered, and lifted her off him. "Give me a second." X crossed the room and pulled out an overnight bag. Zoe impatiently waited for him to find his condoms. She should've known that a handsome man like him would be stocked up for passion. Zoe watched as he rolled the condom in place and returned to the bed. His naked body was a work of art, sculpted and delicious. As he climbed into bed, she reached for him and wrapped her legs around his waist.

"Give it to me." Her wanton actions and words shocked her. But she wanted this man and she was going to have him. It wasn't as if she'd ever see him again. He would probably end up in jail as soon as her client got her money and then turned her ex in. Part of her wanted to warn him, but as X thrust into her, thoughts of police and clients were the last thing on her mind.

Rocking back and forth on the bed, Zoe gripped him with her thighs, pulling him closer. He filled her wetness and palmed her breasts, making her nipples rock hard beneath his touch.

"You feel so good," he groaned. "So good."

Zoe could only moan as he ground against her, touching her most sensitive spots, making her explode. He took her face in his hands. "You're coming, aren't you?"

"Ye-yes," she stuttered.

"Look into my eyes and let me feel you come." He thrust harder and deeper until Zoe melted against his chest.

He lifted her chin. "I'm coming with you."

Zoe blinked, trying to get the memory out of her mind. The last thing she needed was to get on the plane with all of these lustful thoughts in her mind.

She dressed quickly and decided to head to the lobby for breakfast. A good doughnut and cup of coffee would take her mind off Carver.

Who was she fooling?

Chapter 18

As soon as she walked in the lobby, she locked eyes with Carver. She took a deep breath. It should be a sin for a man to look that good while drinking a cup of coffee. Carver waved her over to the table where he was sitting.

"You can do this," she whispered as she walked over to the coffee station and filled a cup for herself. When she saw apple fritters mixed in with the doughnuts, she knew she could focus on her favorite pastry and not Carver's lips.

"Good morning," she said as she sat down.

"It is now." He winked at her and Zoe sighed. She took a bite of her apple fritter.

"Is the plane ready?"

"I called Steve and didn't get an answer. I'm going to try him again in an hour. Looks like we're the only people up right now."

Zoe took a sip of her coffee. "Glad to see that you're up, though."

"Coffee's fresher and I can think better in the quiet."

She shook her head and took a bite of the apple fritter.

"Is that good?" he asked.

Zoe nodded. "Want a bite?" She held her pastry out to him. Carver took a bite and licked the tip of her finger. Shivers ran up and down her spine.

"It is good. Very sweet, like you."

She shook her head. "Here you go."

"I think I've made it really clear to you, Zoe. I want you. And I'm going to have you—as soon as you can admit you want me, too."

Rolling her eyes, she took a sip of her coffee. "I don't want you."

"You're so pretty when you lie."

"So arrogant."

"My fatal flaw." He offered her a piece of his dough-nut. "It's cinnamon."

She accepted the treat, and when she took it into her mouth, Carver wiped her lips with his thumb. "They don't need added sugar."

Zoe's face burned and her thighs trembled with desire. She was definitely in trouble.

Wendy sat outside of Joe's safe house, waiting for him to come outside to walk his annoying pit bulls. She had his schedule memorized, and he should've known better than to try her like this. It was going to end this morning. Right on cue, the front door opened and Joe walked out with the rowdy dogs. Gripping the handle of her gun, Wendy opened the car door.

"Was wondering how long you were going to sit

there," Joe said as he bit down on his cigar. "You better be here with good news."

"I'm here for my money. I'm tired of dealing with your bullshit."

He shook his head and laughed. And hate bubbled in her stomach. "Your job is not complete. What the hell do I look like, paying you for services that weren't rendered?"

"Joe, you crossed the line! Why did you send your thugs after me? I've risked everything for you, and you don't give a shit."

"You haven't done the one thing I needed you to do, and that's kill Zoe Harrington. She can still bring me down, even with Smallwood out of the picture. So, your job is not complete."

Wendy drew her gun and pointed it in Joe's face. "I'm not asking again. Wire the money to my account right now, or I will blow your head off."

He laughed again as her finger grazed the trigger. "This is the part where I'm supposed to be scared and give you what you want? Bitch, please. You're not pulling that trigger and I'm not giving you anything."

"Oh, really? Then I guess I have proved you wrong." Just as she was about to pull the trigger, Joe let his dogs off the leash. Instantly, they attacked Wendy, knocking her backwards. Her shot went off in the air. Joe watched as the dogs mauled her to death.

"Crazy bitch," he muttered, then called the dogs back to him. "Good boys. That'll teach people not to fuck with me." He was thankful that this house was in a secluded area where no one was around to hear the chaos.

Joe stepped over Wendy as if she were a piece of trash and continued on his walk with the dogs.

Carver watched Zoe as she ate another apple fritter. "Where does it go?"

She wiped her mouth. "What?"

"You ate half of my doughnut and two apple fritters. But looking at that body, I'm trying to figure out where the calories go."

"I burn them off, trust me."

"I could help you with that."

"I'm sure you think you can. What are you going to do when I call your bluff?"

"Why don't you just do it and . . ." The ringing of his cell phone broke into their conversation. "I have to take this." Carver headed outside. "This is Banks."

"Your girl left DC," Sarah said.

"Where did she go?"

"Richmond, Virginia. And according to my intel, Singletary has a so-called safe house there. The FBI hasn't been able to obtain a warrant for the place because he doesn't have anything going on there."

"But he's wanted, so why haven't we just gone there and snatched him up?"

"It's complicated. Every time we get close and we send a surveillance team, he's never there. Wendy has to be his inside woman. I just don't know why she's getting so sloppy all of sudden."

"Maybe they're planning something and she thinks we're not on to her. Maybe I should call her so that you can trace her cell phone signal?"

"And she can do the same to you. Too dangerous. You need to get out of New York and keep Zoe off the radar for as long as you can."

"I wish I was there to put the cuffs on that son of a bitch."

"You can be if you want to leave Ms. Zoe exposed or turn her over to one of your boys."

"Hell no. I got this, but I want to see this bastard go down."

"You will," Sarah said. "Ray said you two talked about your feelings for Zoe. I think I'm a little jealous."

"Aww, Sarah, don't do that."

"Boy, I'm just playing. But I haven't seen you this tied up over a woman since—"

"This is different and we're not talking about the past, we're dealing with the future."

"Whatever, man. I'm going to see what I can find out about Wendy. Stay by your phone."

"Will do." Glancing at his watch, Carver decided that he and Zoe needed to get up in the air as soon as possible. Walking back into the lobby, his heart thumped with fear when he didn't see her.

"Boo."

"Don't do that, Zoe," he said as he turned around with a relieved smile on his face.

"Do what?"

"Sneak up on me. You might get kissed." He wrapped his arms around her waist. She was about to wiggle out of his embrace when Carver brought his mouth down on hers. He kissed her slow, deep, and hard. And speaking of hard, having her pressed against his body made him harder than a brick. Zoe gasped as if she felt his arousal. He wasn't finished assaulting her mouth, savoring the taste of her tongue, and reveling in the feel of her heat against him.

Zoe finally pushed away from him, her lips swollen from his kiss. Carver couldn't help but smile. "I'm going to get my bags. We should get going," she said. "And keep your lips to yourself."

"I told you not to sneak up on me." Winking at her, Carver told Zoe he'd meet her in the lobby and they could head to the airstrip.

He headed back to his room and grabbed his bag. As he walked to the lobby, he called Steve to make sure the plane was ready.

"Why are you up so early?"

"Because I don't pay other people to make money for me." Carver laughed. "Zoe and I are ready to take off and I was making sure all the proper documents were in place."

"You guys are good to go. Are you sure you're not just using my plane to take this woman to Las Vegas so you can marry her?"

"Funny. I'm not even trying to start an ex-wives' club like you."

"I hear that. Well, you can't make an omelet without cracking some eggs or marrying a couple of chicken-heads."

"Anyway, thanks again for helping us out."

"No problem. Now I'm going back to bed."

"Later." When Carver walked into the lobby, he saw Zoe standing at the coffee bar stirring sugar and cream into her cup.

"Are you ready for takeoff?" he asked as he crossed over to her. Zoe's head snapped up and she smiled.

"As I'll ever be. I did talk to a friend of mine with the Clark County Sheriff's Office. He said I could go out on patrol with him."

"Oh, really?" Carver burned with jealousy. Who was this friend, and how friendly were they? It wasn't as if he'd expected Zoe to be a nun, and he certainly hadn't taken a vow of chastity after their night together. But something about the thought of another man touching what he'd deemed his made him angry.

Zoe must have seen something on his face. "What?"

"Huh?"

"That look."

"What look?"

"Like you want to punch something or somebody. Where did you go?"

"Nowhere. Let's get going. You think you have enough coffee?"

"You can never have enough coffee." She handed him a cup. "And for hotel coffee, this swill is pretty good."

"That's a ringing endorsement. They should hire you as a spokeswoman."

She elbowed him in the side. "Whatever." They laughed and headed to Zoe's car. "How far is it to the airfield?"

"I have the address. This is your neck of the woods, you should know where everything is."

"Sweetie, I'm from the Bronx. Get it right."

"Excuse me."

As they got into the car, Zoe tilted her head and

looked at Carver. "Where are you from? I can't believe I never asked you that."

"My family is originally from Washington State. I was about ten when we moved to Chicago. So, I claim Chicago mostly."

"Interesting. I just thought you were from DC."

"You judge me too harshly. Just because I work for the FBI, it doesn't mean that I'm all about the District."

"But you are. *The District*. No one outside of the beltway says that."

"You said *beltway*; you're just as dialed in as I am."

She shook her head as she started the car. "I have to know what's going on around me. Your boy Smallwood tried to recruit me after I gave him my overview on Singletary and Natalie. I don't know why you-all think I want to be—"

"What did you tell Smallwood?" Carver tried to keep his voice even, but things were starting to make sense. Zoe must have some explosive information if Joe was going to all this trouble to eliminate her.

"The truth. Why do you keep asking me about what me and Smallwood talked about?"

He knew he could've and should've told her the truth right then. But he couldn't. "Just curious."

"I'm not buying it. You're still investigating Singletary, and you want to know what I know. Why didn't you just ask?"

"Because I didn't want to cross the line, nor did I want to get cursed out."

"Is that so? I mean, trying to sleep with me every five minutes is okay, but asking for my help to stop a sex trafficker is wrong?"

Carver fell silent as she drove. He hadn't asked her about her knowledge of Singletary because he hadn't wanted to slip up and tell her that she was in danger. But with Singletary on the loose and Smallwood dead, he didn't know how much longer he could keep the ruse going.

"Hello?"

"We can go over notes on the plane," he said.

"Why is he so hard to stop?"

"Because he's like a ghost. And since most of what he does is online, by the time we catch up with him or the girls he's trafficking, we can't prove anything. It's frustrating as hell."

"Natalie was ready to spill her guts for a deal when she got arrested. What happened with that? I imagine that she's suffering in prison. Not that she doesn't deserve to suffer."

"How did she get her hooks into your twin without you stopping it?"

"Zach doesn't listen to me." Zoe laughed. "But he made a much better choice of a wife this time. Chante is brilliant, beautiful, and not a pimp."

"You ran a background check on her, didn't you?"

"As if I had a choice not to, after the last Mrs. Harrington."

"Do you and Chante get along?"

Zoe shrugged. "I haven't spent a lot of time with them since the wedding, but she makes my brother happy and I'm excited for them."

"That's good. I wish I had a better relationship with . . ." Carver stopped talking as his cell phone chimed, indicating that he had a text message.

Agent Covington's body was just found in a creek in Damascus. Looks as if dogs attacked her. Waiting on official word from the coroner.

Carver shoved his phone back in his pocket, wondering if he'd been wrong about Wendy. He pulled his phone out and texted Sarah back.

Think we were wrong about her? Maybe she wasn't working with Singletary.

She responded immediately.

We were right. Something went wrong with her and Singletary, obviously. He left Richmond and we've lost sight of him.

"Shit," he mumbled as he shoved his phone back in his pocket.

"What's wrong?" Zoe asked.

"Information about a case I'm working. My fugitive is in the wind."

"If you need to get back to work, I can handle this case alone."

He shook his head. "I'm where I need to be. When it's time for me to get him, I'll be ready."

"All right, G-man. And I guess you can't talk about the case, right? Maybe I can help."

Carver smirked. If only she knew. "You know I can't talk about my case."

"Didn't hurt to try and pry."

"I see that you're really good at your job. No wonder people open up to you."

"And I'm cute, too. You don't know how many cases

I've solved for people because some man or woman thought I was cute."

Carver gave her a slow once-over. "Yeah, I can believe that. You're like Wonder Woman without the lasso. But you can tie me up anytime if you want me to tell you the truth."

She sucked her teeth as she pulled into the private landing strip. "You always take things too far."

"When it comes to you, yes I do."

Zoe knew getting on this flight with Carver was going to be pure torture. She knew that they needed to focus on the Dolan case, but how could she, when all she could think about was lying in his arms? Zoe knew Carver wanted her as much as she wanted him. And the more she tried to deny it, the more her desire grew. Maybe talking about sex trafficking would get her mind off of sexual pleasure.

Joseph was pissed and tired of people failing him. Wendy was an especially huge disappointment. She'd had access to Zoe Harrington and couldn't get the job done. Then she'd had the nerve to make demands of him. Who did she think she was? Didn't matter now because she wasn't a problem anymore. Although that did leave him with a gaping hole in his surveillance of Zoe Harrington. Now he would have to go to New York and find out how to hurt her the most.

Thanks to Wendy, he knew she still lived in the Bronx. And thanks to his snitch inside the NYPD, he knew Zoe had plenty of enemies in the department, including her former partner. He should've known that people didn't like that bitch. Zoe was the kind of woman who got in the way and didn't learn her lesson. Much like all of the women in his life. Joseph grew up watching his mother use men for everything. He never knew his father, because she had a revolving door of men in and out of their home. He thought that was how men and women interacted. Until she met Clark Simmons. That man had changed everything in the eyes of ten-year-old Joseph. Clark would slap his mother when she got loud with him, would force her to cook his dinner—even after she'd brought takeout home for dinner. And Clark taught him the game when he was older.

"Never trust a woman, not even ya mama," he'd said to a fifteen-year-old Joseph. "They're always plotting and you have to stay one step ahead of these bitches."

Clark had been like a father figure to Joseph, and when his mother shot Clark, he knew that everything Clark taught him was right. These bitches couldn't be trusted.

Zoe Harrington was the last bitch he needed to get out of his way, and this time, he wouldn't put his trust in a woman to handle this job.

Singletary hated taking the train, but getting to New York undetected was his mission, and Amtrak was the way to go. There wasn't as much security at the train stations as there was at an airport. And he'd been able to get one of his men to purchase his ticket. All he had to do was keep his head down and not get caught. Since he had several warrants for his arrest, a beat cop looking to make a name for himself would love to slap handcuffs on him.

Joe didn't look anything like the man on the FBI Most Wanted poster anymore. His thick beard gave him a trendy look, and no one gave him a passing glance.

Zoe kicked her shoes off and smiled. "This is definitely the way to fly." The plush carpet of the jet made her feel as if she'd stuck her feet in a cotton pool. Leaning back in the chair, she smiled.

"I told you I was going to keep you riding in style," Carver said.

"You're making it really hard for my next client."

"That's a good thing. Now I'm totally unforgettable."

You already were. She smiled and took a sip of her ice-cold juice. "Whatever happened to those transcripts?"

"Good question. I have to check and see what the holdup is in the field office. There's been some upheaval this week."

"All right."

Carver crossed over to Zoe and sat on the arm of her seat. "More juice?"

"No, thank you. I'm actually going to have an adult beverage. Maybe it will put me to sleep." Zoe took a deep breath, and when her nostrils filled with the scent of Carver's essence she was nearly ready to strip out of her clothes. She rose to her feet so fast, she nearly knocked him over.

"Where's the fire?"

"I just need to stretch." Zoe raised her arms over her head, causing her shirt to rise. Carver ran his fingers across her exposed skin and Zoe shivered.

"Stop," she whispered.

"Zoe, let's stop acting like this isn't what we both want. I need you so bad that it hurts."

She sighed, "I want you, too." Carver lifted her shirt over her head. He ran his fingers across her skin and she quivered with desire. Then he unbuttoned her shorts and slid them down her hips. Carver smiled when he saw she didn't have any underwear on.

"Nice."

She reached out to him and unbuttoned his shirt. "Carver," she moaned as she ran her fingers across his tattoo.

"Zoe, you're so beautiful." He leaned in and captured her lips in a hungry kiss. Their tongues danced a slow and sensuous tango. Zoe's body heated like a campfire as his hands stroked her hips, then slipped between her thighs. Still kissing her, he skillfully toyed with her throbbing bud. She squirmed underneath his touch, her yearning for him becoming nearly unbearable.

"Carver!"

"Yes, baby. I want you to come for me."

"Carver." Zoe's legs quivered as her passion poured down like warm honey. When he removed his finger and licked her wetness, Zoe moaned in anticipation.

"You're so sweet. I need another taste." He planted her on the leather sofa near the windows. Then Carver spread her legs apart and dove into her wetness. He licked, sucked, and nibbled at her throbbing bud until she screamed his name as she came over and over again.

"Need. You. In. Me!"

Carver seemed to ignore her request as he continued to nibble, lick, and suck her pearl as if it were the most delectable piece of candy ever made. Zoe's knees quivered and shook as if she were on the San Andreas Fault in the middle of an earthquake.

Peeling his mouth from her, Carver licked his lips. "Delicious."

"You have to stop torturing me," she moaned.

"What if I don't want to?"

"Then I have some torture of my own," she replied as she reached out and stroked his hardness. Carver's moans filled the cabin.

"Don't stop, Zoe," he groaned as her hand moved up and down his shaft fast, then slow, then fast again.

As much as she wanted to guide him directly to her wet spot, she wanted to give him some of the pleasurable torture he'd given her as well. Easing down his body, she brought her lips to the tip of his penis and licked him slow. Carver gasped as she took the length of him deep down her throat. He fell backward onto the floor and Zoe climbed on top of him. Allowing her tongue to be her guide, she toured his body. She swirled her tongue around his nipples, licked each pack of his abs, and then she licked his hardness again. Carver could barely contain his climax as she ran her tongue up and down his erection.

"Stop, stop!" he cried as he pulled back from her. "I get the point."

"Now, get a condom!"

Carver crossed the cabin and reached into his overnight bag and pulled out a condom. He rolled the sheath in place and returned to Zoe. She rose to her feet and wrapped her arms around his neck.

"This is what you wanted." She wrapped her leg around his waist, giving him direct access to her sensitive spot. Carver thrust deep inside her and Zoe matched him stroke for stroke. Their deep, guttural groans filled the quiet cabin, and as she felt the wave of an orgasm attack her system, she slowed down—wanting to savor the moment with Carver.

The rational side of her knew this had to be the last time she gave in to lust. She had an itch and Carver scratched it. Now, it was done. Right?

"Carver!" she exclaimed, unable to hold back her orgasm any longer.

"Let me come with you, baby!"

They both exploded and fell backward on the leather sofa as the aftershocks of their climax rippled through their bodies. Zoe leaned her head on his chest and sighed. Carver pushed her sweat-dampened hair off her forehead.

"Are you all right?"

"Yes, Carver. I'm fine." She pressed her hand against his chest and propped herself up. "Now that we've gotten that out of the way, do you think we can get back to business now?"

Chapter 19

Two hours after making love to Zoe, Carver was hungry for more. But looking at her sleeping figure, he still couldn't get what she'd said out of his mind. *Can we get back to business now?*

What the hell did she mean by that? Glancing at her, he hoped she didn't think that what they shared was a one-time thing. There was no way that he could let her go again.

She was beautiful when she slept. This was probably the only time he'd ever seen Zoe relax. She looked like an angel, and it took everything in him not to stroke her cheek and kiss her. Somehow, he was going to have to make her understand this wild-goose chase once Singletary was in custody. How would she feel about it? he wondered.

At least she will be alive, mad or not.

Joe headed for the boarding area of the train and pulled out his cell phone to Google Lewis, Zoe's former partner.

"Damn," he muttered as news links about the officer

and Zoe popped up. "She is a traitor. That guy was her partner. These bitches have no loyalty." He took his seat on the back of the train. Leaning back, he closed his eyes, satisfied that his partnership with this ex-cop would give him just what he needed to snuff Zoe Harrington out. She would learn the lesson of a lifetime. He couldn't wait.

The train ride was uneventful and Joe loved that. Arriving in New York, he headed for the Bronx so that he could check out Zoe's office and house. If he had to kill her himself, he would catch her by surprise. He was surprised that she was so easy to find. Then again, it made sense for her to be so visible. She was a private investigator and people needed to find her so she could be nosy and get into their personal business.

"Perfect job for that bitch," he said as he looked at her office building. Joe smiled as he took note of the yellow tape around her office. He wasn't surprised that she had enemies. A woman like that deserved everything that came her way. Too bad they hadn't gotten the job done and killed that bitch. Maybe Wendy had been doing her job and Zoe Harrington was just like a cat with nine lives. This was going to end now. A woman walked by Zoe's office, and Joe reached out to touch her shoulder.

"Excuse me, beautiful."

"Yes?"

"Have you seen Zoe Harrington? The PI?"

She shook her head. "Not since the explosion. This place has been a ghost town. A lot of the businesses are closed until the investigation into the explosion is over. A lady died in there. It was so sad."

"Oh, man. I really needed her to work a case for me. You have any idea how to reach her?"

She shook her head and pointed to a number in the window. "Maybe you can call her."

He smiled at her, thinking that she'd catch a pretty penny in his squad. But that's not why he was here. He had to find Zoe. Needed to make her hurt. Then an idea hit him like a lightning bolt. If he wanted to flush her out of hiding, then he had to attack something that was important to her. Family.

Zachary Harrington.

Zoe woke up with a start, her hand on her chest. It took about thirty seconds for her to realize that she was in an airplane. Then she locked eyes with Carver.

"Hello, sleeping beauty."

"Guess I was a lot more tired than I thought," she said.

"What woke you up? You looked as if you were having a nightmare."

Sitting up, Zoe stretched her arms above her head. "It was nothing." She didn't like telling people that she had dreams about her twin and it usually meant trouble. Zoe didn't understand what the dream meant. Zach was sinking in a pit of mud, and as she reached for him, she couldn't grip his hand.

"Are you sure everything is all right?"

"Yeah." She rose to her feet and crossed over to the bar and poured herself a glass of cranberry juice.

Carver walked up behind her and wrapped his arms around her waist. "Can we talk about earlier?"

She wiggled out of his embrace. "What's there to

talk about? The sexual tension between us has been intense since the moment you showed up and asked me to take this case. We've finally gotten our carnal needs out of the way, and now we can focus on solving this case for the Dolan family."

"You think that's all it was?"

She looked at her watch. They had about an hour left before the plane landed. "Listen, we know that's what it was. You and I don't have a future and you know it as much as I do."

"Why don't we have a future? What are you afraid of, Zoe?"

"Nothing. Carver. You have this life in DC that I know nothing about. And I'm a New York girl who doesn't believe in long distance relationships."

"It's Maryland, actually. We can make this work, Zoe. And every excuse you throw at me just shows me one thing."

"And what's that?"

"You're afraid, and you feel the same way that I do." He stroked her cheek. "You're the one I want in my life, and I'm not going to stop until you're mine."

She shivered as he brought his lips close to hers. "And, Zoe, you will be mine."

"I'm not a possession for you to capture, Carver. And who said that I wanted to belong to you or any other man?"

"I know what you want, but until you admit it to yourself, you're going to continue to pretend that you don't want or need me. It's getting tired, but I'm not the kind of man to force a woman into something she's not ready for."

Before Zoe could respond, the pilot's voice came through the speakers. "Guys, we're going to encounter some rough air. I need you to return to your seats and fasten your seat belts."

"Great," Zoe muttered. "Even these jets have turbulence."

"I got you," Carver said as he placed his hand on her knee. She closed her eyes and didn't respond. When the plane hit the first pocket of turbulence, Zoe was all right. But the second pocket made the plane shake violently, and she gripped Carver's arm like a vise.

He stroked her hair and wrapped his other arm around her shoulder. "We're good. We're good."

"I should've just stayed asleep," she muttered. "You like this, don't you?"

"No. I get no joy from you being this upset."

Zoe smiled and held on to him a little tighter. "Carver, I have a confession."

"What's that?"

"I do care a lot about you, and yes, it scares me. You're in a dangerous profession, and I don't deal with loss well. I'm scared to love you and lose you."

He took her face into his hands. "You're not going to lose me."

"You can't say that with certainty."

"Yes, I can." He brushed his lips across hers. "Zoe, I waited a long time to hear you say that you feel this way about me, because I've felt like this about you for a long time."

"Before or after you arrested me?"

Carver rolled his eyes. "Are you ever going to let that go?"

She laughed and shook her head. "Nope."

"Then maybe I need to allow you to slap some handcuffs on me so that we're even."

"If I put handcuffs on you, you're either going to be really happy or really excited." She winked at him as the pilot announced that they would be landing in Las Vegas in about thirty minutes and the air was clear. Carver unhooked his seat belt and fixed two cups of juice for him and Zoe.

"Should I give you the handcuffs now?" He winked at her as he handed her the juice.

"How about we solve this case first?"

Carver sipped his juice and nodded. "Zoe."

"What?"

"Thank you for this."

She grinned at him. "Just because I love you, that doesn't mean you're not getting a bill."

"Wouldn't expect anything less."

"I'm glad you know this."

Charlotte, North Carolina

Chante Harrington smiled as her husband walked into her law office carrying a dozen roses.

"Zach," she said.

"Hello, beautiful. I missed you this morning."

"You were really restless last night, Zach. Is everything all right?"

He set the roses on her desk and took a seat across from her. "I think so. I just had a bad dream about Zoe. I think something is going on with my sister that she's not telling me about."

"So that twin connection thing is real?" Chante rubbed her barely there baby bump.

Zach nodded, then rose to his feet and kneeled in front of Chante. "How's my son doing in there? Are you feeling all right?"

She took his hand and placed it on her belly. "You feel that?"

"He's moving."

"Yes, *she* is." Chante leaned forward and kissed Zach on the forehead.

"I hope God doesn't give us a daughter who looks like you. I don't know if I want to spend that much money in ammunition."

"That's not sexist at all."

"Speaking of sexist. How did the case go this morning?"

She took his face in her hands. "Who am I? Of course I won."

"I married a superstar." Zach leaned in and kissed her, slow and deep. As they broke the kiss, he looked into her eyes. "But you're going to have to slow down."

"Here we go again. Zach, I'm not doing anything to put our baby in danger."

"That's why this baby has to be a boy. Between you and Zoe, I need backup." He laughed and stroked her stomach.

"Well, you should be happy to know that I only have one more big case that I'm taking. A couple of victims of human trafficking are suing the state."

Zach shivered. "This can be dangerous."

"I know, and it puts me at odds with my best friend,

who just happens to be married to a state senator. But Liza is classy enough not to say anything about it."

"Can't you hand it off to one of your associates?" Zach rose to his feet and spun Chante's chair around.

She grabbed his wrists. "I could. But I won't. Why don't we go get something to eat? Your son and I are hungry."

"I see how this works. He's my son when you want something." He winked at her. "Do you know how much I love you?"

"I do, but that doesn't mean you have to stop telling me."

Zoe wanted to kiss the ground when the plane landed. Private jet, commercial flight, she still hated to fly. Carver grabbed their bags and pulled out his cell phone to call a car service. This was probably the only thing she liked about the private jet. No waiting for baggage and hailing a taxi. But it was a little warm outside. She pulled out her cell phone and Googled missing girls in Las Vegas. No African American women. She sighed, knowing that a missing black woman just didn't make headlines.

"You all right?" Carver asked when he locked eyes with Zoe.

"Yeah. Just ready to get off this tarmac. I hope this is the last stop. Do you know if anyone from the FBI has contacted the Dolans to let them know what's going on?"

Carver rubbed his forehead. "I don't know."

"Do you have a source at the Bureau that you can press to help us?" Zoe ran her fingers though her hair.

"No. I mean, I do have a friend I might be able to

reach out to, but this was something that I was trying to avoid. We don't want the public to know what's going on, in case we don't find Jessica's body. The fewer people we talk to about this case the less chance we have of leaks making it out to the media."

"Why? We're at a dead end, a roadblock. We have to do something, Carver. And maybe there is someone out there who knows something. It wouldn't hurt to get the public involved."

"Zoe, I'm still following your lead, so whatever you think we should do, I'm with it."

She glanced at her watch. "Well, after a nap and some food, I'm going to head out with my buddy from the sheriff's department and see what we can find out. Have you booked our rooms yet?"

"We still need two?" Carver winked at her.

"Yes. Because I can't be distracted by you." Zoe stroked his cheek and smiled. "The sooner we find Jessica's body, the sooner we can head back to New York and figure out how we're going to make this thing work."

"I'm looking forward to that." Zach leaned in and kissed Zoe, slow and deep. Quivering in his arms, Zoe was sure that she and Carver had the future that she'd been dreaming about.

Chapter 20

Lewis Martinez had been in hiding since the bombing at Zoe's office. He wished she'd been in there. When he walked into the bodega on the corner, he noticed a man following him.

He wasn't going down like this. Turning around, he was ready to push a rack of chips into the man's chest. "Martinez, right?" the man said.

"Who are you?"

"Someone who wants Zoe Harrington dead, and I'm willing to pay you to make it happen."

Lewis shook his head and backed away from the man. "This is a setup."

The man pulled out a wad of money and handed it to Lewis. "There's more where this came from. And this is not a setup."

"Who are you?"

"Let's get out of here and talk. We have a common goal."

Lewis narrowed his eyes as he counted the money. Three thousand dollars. "You wearing a wire?"

"No." The man headed for the door and Lewis followed him.

"All right," he said once they were outside. "What's this common goal?"

"Dancing on Zoe's grave. I know what she did to you, and you guys were partners. Police officers are supposed to be closer than that."

"And you know this because?"

"It's on Google. Everything is on Google."

Lewis folded his arms across his chest. "And who in the hell are you? Open your shirt and show me there's no wire."

The man laughed. "I'm the last person who would be wearing a wire. I'm Joe Singletary."

Lewis had heard that name before, and he knew this man didn't have anything to do with law enforcement. "What did she do to you?"

"Cost me millions of dollars. Now she's on some trip with the FBI to avoid me. I've had people try to get her, but she's like a cat with nine lives."

"That's true. So, the FBI is keeping her safe, huh?"

Joe nodded. "But I have a plan, and I need your help. And it's going to be very lucrative. Once she's dead, you'll be able to get away and start over. Don't you think you deserve that?"

Lewis nodded. "How are we going to make this happen?"

"We're going to North Carolina to flush her out. She cares about her family, and that's where we're going to hit her."

Lewis smiled, realizing that this man was the real

deal. "Let's head over to Pelham Bay and hash this thing out. Are you driving?"

Joe shook his head. "We should probably take a cab so that we aren't captured on too many cameras."

"Good idea." Lewis hadn't been this excited since he set the bomb at Zoe's office a week ago. If this guy was the real deal, then they would be dancing on Zoe's grave. He figured that he would settle into an island life after the job was done. A couple of girls in bikinis pouring him drinks and feeding him exotic fruits would make up for everything he lost in New York.

Carver had gotten over his jet lag after two days. Zoe, however, seemed to hit the ground running. While she was out on patrol with her sheriff friend, Carver linked up with the Shadow Team through a videoconference on their secure server.

"Wendy was Singletary's inside contact at the Bureau," Sarah said. "And it looks as if she was the only person working with him. Since her death, it doesn't look as if he's been having any communication with anyone else."

"That's good to know," Carver said.

Sarah nodded. "Now, we have to wait for the official announcement from the Bureau about her death and ties to Singletary. But knowing them, they are going to gloss over it."

Ray picked up a cup of coffee. "Of course they will. Wendy dying trying to stop Singletary will make a better story for the Feds than a rogue agent."

"Why haven't you guys outed Wendy yet?" Carver asked.

"Because," Ken began, "that's going to bring heat on you as well."

Carver nodded. "I didn't think about that."

"She was pretty cunning," Sarah said. "I'm thinking she worked with Singletary because she was upset about the way her sister's case was handled."

"Of all the people to saddle up with, she chose that monster?" Ray shook his head. "If he knew her sister, he probably would've put her on the stroll."

"Probably?" Carver said. "Joe doesn't respect women. If he could make a buck off his mother, he would."

"Here's the question, though: How much longer are you going to be able to keep Zoe on this wild-goose chase?" Sarah asked. "She's going to catch on sooner or later."

"To everything," Ray said.

Carver gritted his teeth and fought the urge to flip his friend off. He knew that comment had a lot to do with how he felt about Zoe. But now that she knew, and he knew she felt the same way, he wasn't as worried about how she would react to the fact that he'd been lying to her.

After all, he'd done it for her safety.

"Carver, you all right?" Ken asked.

"Yeah. Any idea where Singletary is now, though?"

"He left Virginia and we haven't been able to get eyes on him. That bastard is smart. He bought a plane ticket to Memphis, but never got on the flight." Sarah sighed. "I should've put a bullet in his head when I had a chance a year ago."

"So you could be out of a job?" Ken asked. "We're going to get him and we're doing it the right way."

"We need to hurry up and do it, because until he's locked up or dead, Zoe isn't safe," Carver said.

Zoe yawned as she and Dale James, her sheriff's deputy friend, rode around the famed Vegas strip.

"Zoe, you know this Jessica Dolan case is about three years old, and the only thing we're going to find—if we find anything—is bones."

"Listen, her parents just need to know where their daughter's remains are and how they can find closure with her death. Could you imagine losing a loved one to a crazed serial killer?"

"No. But I remember losing the love of my life to New York."

Zoe rolled her eyes. "You got over it. You have a beautiful wife and family."

"True. But I'd still marry you."

"Too late for that," Zoe quipped. "I didn't think bigamy was legal."

"Courtney loves *Sister Wives*. She'd be cool with it. You know you were my first love. And first heartbreak."

"Can we leave the past in the past? You said you were going to help me find this girl's body."

"Yeah. I just wanted to drop that on you real quick. Since you're not on the force in New York anymore, have you thought about leaving the city and joining another department?"

"After working for myself, I can't go back to following someone else's rules."

Dale nodded. "I can see that. Now, this neighborhood right here is one of the places where people settle after moving to Vegas. It's cheap and transient. We've also found bodies here before."

Zoe nodded.

Dale parked the car and glanced at Zoe. "You got a gun?"

"Yes, and it's legal."

"Good, because this isn't the safest hood in Vegas."

"Thanks, Dale. See you in an hour."

Zoe walked around the neighborhood for about fifteen minutes, looking for ground that looked disturbed, and she tried talking to a few people milling about, but she was ignored. Then she wondered, how do you ask people where's the best place to bury a body?

Sighing, she felt as if she wasn't going to be able to get the Dolans closure, and she'd all but given up hope that Jessica was still alive. When her phone rang, she almost jumped out of her skin.

"This is Zoe."

"Hey, it's me," Carver said. "Any luck?"

"Nope. I feel like I'm going in circles."

"Why don't we call it a day and try tomorrow. I can come and pick you up."

"Not yet. I told Dale to pick me up in an hour and it's only been about forty-five minutes."

"How far are you from the Hilton?"

"I don't know. I just know it's getting hot out here and I'm frustrated." Zoe sighed into the phone.

"I'm coming to get you. Just text me the address."

"You rented a car?"

"Yep."

"Why?"

"Because you shouldn't have to depend on this deputy to get around."

"Your eyes are turning green as you speak. Dale and I are friends, and being around him gives me more access to police reports and missing persons cases than rolling around a town I don't know in a rental car." She laughed. "Though he did ask me to marry him this morning."

"He did what?"

"Yep, you have some nerve to be jealous."

"Let me go on record and say, I don't want my woman riding around with some man who wants to marry her."

"He was joking because he's already married."

"Whatever. Text me the address and I'll see you in a few."

Zoe laughed, then hung up to text him her location. She started walking back toward the apartments, hoping to find someone who she hadn't talked to earlier. When she didn't, Zoe decided that Carver had a point. Maybe tomorrow they could cover more ground together and find this girl.

Carver watched Zoe walk down the sidewalk and knew when she got in the car she was going to pepper him with questions he didn't have answers to.

He blew the horn to get her attention. He'd rented a Corvette because it had been the only car available at the time.

"Wow. Having a midlife crisis or what?" Zoe laughed as she got into the car.

"This was all they had."

Zoe nodded. "Right. Please tell me you've found some food."

Carver handed her a brown paper bag. "Turkey sandwich and fries for now."

"God bless you, Carver Banks. If you have a bottle of water for me, I might love you forever."

"You're going to do that anyway. I got you a sports drink. I figured you'd broken a sweat in this desert heat."

He glanced at Zoe as she devoured her sandwich. She was sexy even when she ate like a homeless woman.

"What?" she asked as she swallowed.

"Nothing. Glad I made the right decision with the sandwich."

She gave him a thumbs-up, then took a huge bite. "So," she said after swallowing, "where should we actually be looking for this girl's body? Did you talk to your friend at the field office?"

"He's off today. Haven't had a chance yet."

She was about to pull out her tablet when Carver grabbed her wrist. "Eat," he ordered.

Zoe took the last two bites of her sandwich. "Fine. And I'm only doing it because these fries smell amazing, not because you told me to."

"I'll accept that, but I know the truth." He winked at her, then revved the engine.

Chapter 27

Joe and Lewis had been plotting for two days to get Zoe's family. They'd decided to snatch her sister-in-law for two reasons. Joe knew Zoe would be scared that he would put Chante out on the stroll.

Chante Harrington was fine, but too old to get the money his younger girls commanded.

And Zach Harrington would pay anything to get his wife back. He was stupid enough to love and trust a woman. That's why it had been so easy for Natalie to get inside his office and give him the list of high rollers. *If she had been loyal, she'd still be alive*, he thought as he and Lewis ate breakfast in silence.

"So, when are we going to North Carolina?" Lewis asked.

"That's going to be a little tricky. I can't just hop on a plane. Driving is going to take about twelve hours."

"Why don't we just drive out there in the morning? I know she's a lawyer, so we can easily get into her office."

Joe nodded. "But we have to be smart about it. I'm

sure there are cameras and shit at her building. We need a couple of days to watch what she does. And I have a girl in North Carolina who can go inside and check out what's going on."

"What about her husband? Zoe's brother will probably be around."

"Not during the workday. And I can keep him busy, but we have to be precise. We can't afford mistakes."

"Right. No more than ten minutes, and I have to spike her drink."

Joe handed Lewis a vial of a clear liquid. "That's right, and don't put too much in it, so that you aren't dragging a dead weight."

Lewis nodded. "Two drops, right? I think we're ready. All we need to do is get down to the Carolinas and put this plan in motion." Joe and Lewis clinked their coffee mugs together.

"That bitch is finally going to get hers," Joe said.

Carver and Zoe had been in Vegas for four days and she wasn't any closer to finding Jessica. And she felt as if Carver didn't have a huge problem with it. She glanced at him as they sat down to eat at the Spice Market Buffet.

"We need to talk," Zoe said.

"That's never a good sign."

"What if we don't find Jessica? Maybe this case was cold for a reason," she said with a sigh.

Before he could respond, his phone rang and it was Sarah. Rising to his feet, he turned to Zoe and said, "I have to take this." He walked outside. "What's up, Sarah?"

"Well, we did track Singletary to New York. Looks like he's getting desperate. What's Zoe's connection to Lewis Martinez?"

"That's her former partner, and there's bad blood between them."

"Not good. Singletary was seen on camera with him, but we've lost their trail."

"How?"

"That man is a ghost. He appears and disappears when he wants to. It's like he's taunting us."

"He is. Son of a bitch."

"We're closer to getting a tail on him. We're going to switch tactics because what we've been doing isn't working."

"At least he doesn't have anyone else on the inside that we know of. Tell Ray to keep an eye on Lewis. He may be an ex-cop, but he's going to slip up—use a credit card, get caught somewhere he shouldn't be."

"His cell phone has been shut off, and we're going to have local stores that sell those disposable cell phones monitored, all up and down the East Coast."

"Good idea. I have to go, Zoe is on her way to the car with the sheriff's deputy."

Carver got out of the car and shook hands with Deputy Dale. He gave the man a sidelong glance, wondering what in the hell Zoe ever saw the skinny, *Goof Troop*-looking dude.

Well, if he was being honest, Dale wasn't that skinny, but he could toss him a few yards if he had to.

"How are you doing, sir?"

"Agent Banks." He glanced at Zoe, who seemed to be hiding a laugh.

"Excuse me, Agent Banks. I was telling Zoe that I was able to uncover some reports that might help you in the Dolan case. We did unearth a body about two years ago that we couldn't identify. I have those reports."

"Thanks. When can we see the reports?"

"We can head over to headquarters now and take a look at them."

"What happened to the body?" Carver asked with his arms folded across his chest. Zoe shook her head and looked away from both men.

"A body that doesn't get identified usually ends up in a potter's field. I'm sure you wouldn't know anything about that since the FBI usually leaves the hard work to local agencies."

Carver narrowed his eyes at Dale but didn't say anything. He was so sick of these local cops and their complaints.

Zoe turned to Dale. "Thank you for all of your help. Both of us appreciate it."

"Zoe, you know I'll *still* do anything for you." He winked at her and Carver wanted to punch him in his schoolboy face. But Carver was playing it cool, so he thought.

Opening the car door for Zoe as Dale walked away, Carver offered her a small smile.

"You're not slick," Zoe said. "And I know you're having a little pissing contest with Dale."

"What are you talking about?"

"Play dumb if you want to, but I know you." Zoe laughed. "It's cute."

"Whatever."

"We need to focus on what we might find in these reports, and not a long-lost relationship from college."

"So, if I find my Woo-Woo, you're going to be cool with it?"

"This is what you want to talk about right now?"

"Just tell me you'd be ready to have dinner with her and hop in her car, then I'll apologize to Howdy Doody."

"You're so childish."

"So you say." Carver revved the engine as he took off behind Dale.

Arriving at the Clark County Sheriff's Office, Dale led Zoe and Carver into a conference room, which was stacked with three boxes of reports. "Have fun, guys."

Zoe sighed and took a seat at the table. "I guess we have a lot of reading to do."

Carver smiled and opened the boxes. Even though he figured they were going to be reading a bunch of reports that didn't mean anything, this was the safest he'd felt Zoe was since they'd gotten to Vegas.

Four hours later, they decided that it was time to go. "I can't believe we still haven't found a clue," Zoe said as she yawned.

"Me either," Carver said. "I didn't think there was going to be so much paperwork that shows nothing."

"Do you want to get a drink?" Zoe asked.

"Sure, but not in some crowded bar."

"We can order room service. My room or yours?"

Carver smiled slyly. "Well, you know my door is always open, but since you offered, your room."

She shook her head. "Just so you know, we're just having a couple of drinks and talking about this case."

"Whatever you say." He winked at her.

Chapter 22

Singletary sat across the street from Zach and Chante's house. They had to be the most boring people in the world. That man was always kissing or hugging on that woman.

Idiot. If another man came through with more money, she'd be gone. He dropped his night vision binoculars and waited for Lewis to return to the car. Lewis was dressed as a jogger and was scouting out the Harrington household. They didn't have security cameras, but they had those motion-detection lights and a standard home security system.

The garage seemed to be the easiest way to enter the house or leave a ransom note. Lewis thought he and Singletary should at least get some money from the Harringtons before they killed Zoe and her sister-in-law.

Singletary didn't agree, because he knew that would do nothing but bring the FBI out in force, and he wasn't trying get caught because he didn't need the money. Singletary thought about killing Lewis after he got rid of Zoe.

This man was getting on his nerves, and Singletary was starting to wonder if he'd made a mistake in bringing Lewis with him. Though having the extra body was a good thing, and in the last two days, Singletary had a lock on Chante Harrington's schedule and her routine. She was predictable. She was beautiful, as well. Joe knew he was going to sample that before he slit her throat. Or maybe he would just shoot her and toss her body in one of the rivers around Mecklenburg County.

Just like her sister-in-law, this bitch made enemies, and anyone could be a suspect.

"Are we ready to make this thing happen?" Lewis asked as he hopped in the car.

"Tomorrow morning, my girl is going in to look at how her office works. Then we'll put the plan in motion," Singletary said.

"And the ransom?"

"For the last fucking time, we're not asking for ransom. That was never a part of the plan, and it adds a layer that we don't need. Neither Chante nor Zoe is returning to this man, no matter how much money he throws our way." Singletary wanted to speed down the street, but the last thing he needed was to call attention to them.

"You're thinking too small, man."

"And you're thinking like a common hood. Just shut the fuck up and let me handle this."

Lewis glared at him but didn't say a word.

* * *

Back in Las Vegas, Zoe and Carver sat in the middle of her queen-size bed. They had a cornucopia of food—lobster tails, crab legs, jasmine rice, shrimp, and chicken salad—and an empty bottle of wine. Zoe had suggested eating after they'd downed the wine like water.

"What kind of wine was that?"

"Rosé. I figured since it has its own hashtag that we might as well give it a try."

"Good call," she said, then gave him a kiss on the cheek. Carver took her chin between his forefinger and thumb.

"Now, you can do better than that." He captured her lips in a hot and wet kiss. Zoe pressed her hands against his chest.

"You know the rule for tonight, right?"

"And you know rules are meant to be broken." He pulled her into his arms and kissed her again. This time, Zoe was powerless to resist the burgeoning passion growing between her thighs.

He pulled back from her and smiled. "But, if you want to follow the rules, I understand."

"Just move the food."

Carver moved the tray of uneaten seafood to the table across the room and returned to the bed. He was thankful that Zoe was wearing a pair of boy shorts and a tank top. She'd given him the easiest access to everything he wanted. Pressing her against the pillows, he ran his fingers across her lips.

"So soft."

She licked the pad of his index finger. "If we're breaking the rules, you better make it worth it."

Carver knew when he was being challenged, and he was ready. Pressing her back on the pillows, he ran his fingers across her wetness. Zoe moaned in delight as he slipped his finger inside her shorts.

In and out. In and out.

"Carver!"

He pulled her shorts down, spread her legs and planted his face between her thighs. He licked and sucked Zoe as if she were a lollipop.

"Yes, yes, yes," Zoe cried as she writhed underneath his sensual kiss. Carver reached up and palmed her breasts until her nipples were rock hard and pressing against her shirt.

Locking eyes with his woman, Carver's heart swelled with love. But in the back of his mind, he hated lying to her, hated pretending that they would find a body he was sure wasn't in the Vegas desert.

"Baby?"

"Zoe, you're so beautiful," Carver said. "I love you."

"I love you, too." She leaned forward and stroked the top of his head. "Now, make love to me."

Carver kicked out of his denim shorts and dove deep inside his woman. Thrusting harder and deeper as she silently willed him to do so, he didn't think about the fact that he hadn't protected them.

Zoe drew him in deeper, tightening herself around him as they rocked back and forth. Carver wanted to pull out before he reached his climax, but the heat of Zoe's body rendered him senseless. He exploded. Zoe's explosion was seconds behind his. As they clutched each other's sweaty bodies, Carver realized two things:

He never wanted to let Zoe go, and if he had to continue this lie, he would until she was safe.

"There is a lot of cold seafood over there that we should eat," Zoe said after a beat. "And now that I've had an unexpected workout, I'm starving."

"You knew you were going to get that workout when you opened the door in those so-called shorts." Carver winked it her.

"I actually expected you to follow the rules. I guess I should've known better."

"When it comes to you, there are no rules. Zoe, you're going to get it real soon—I'll do anything for you."

She followed a bead of sweat down his chest. "Does that mean you're going to bring me some crab legs?"

"I will get you crab legs," he said as he rose from the bed.

Zoe watched Carver as he crossed the room. His body was artistic, like a better version of Adonis. As much as staying in bed seemed like a great idea, Zoe wanted to solve this case, because her heart was starting to ache for the Dolans and she wanted to know what happened to Jessica. She hoped that if something happened to her, she wouldn't end up in some shallow hole that people walked over.

"Carver," she said. "Do you think we're going to find Jessica at all?"

He set the platter of crab legs on the side of the bed. "I don't know. We can work on that in the morning. My mind is fried after looking through all of those reports."

"Why does it seem like you're not very plugged in to

finding Jessica Dolan? You were the one who walked in my office dropping the president's name and you act as if this is some romantic romp. That's not true. I've—we've—been following the leads as they come. What else can we do?"

Zoe expelled a frustrated sigh. "Isn't this why you came to get me? We're supposed to be doing more."

Carver took a crab leg from the tray and cracked it open. He pulled the meat from the shell and brushed it across Zoe's lips. "Eat."

She bit into the crabmeat and smiled after she swallowed. "You're not feeling some kind of way about all of these dead ends?"

"Zoe, I'm not trying to make you pass out from exhaustion."

"This is my job, and I know when I'm tired. I don't need you to police what I do and how I do it." Zoe hopped out of the bed and slammed her hand against Carver's shoulder. "Just because we're sleeping together, it doesn't change the way I work this case."

"I didn't say you should change anything, but there is no need for you to—"

"Just stop. I need to take a shower." Zoe slammed into the bathroom. Turning the shower on, she waited until she heard the hotel room door close before she got in.

Inside his room, Carver called the Shadow Team. As their faces came up on the screen of his tablet, Carver hoped they would tell him that Singletary had been captured.

"Where do we stand?"

Sarah shook her head. "Same place. No sign of Lewis or Singletary."

"I have a trace on Lewis's credit and debit cards. Did get a signal from his cell phone, but it was in Brooklyn," Ray said.

"Did you follow it?"

"Yes. Led straight to a homeless shelter. Joe is training him up right."

"Banks," Kenneth said. "Have you checked in on Zoe's twin brother? Singletary isn't above going after folks' family."

"Being that Zach Harrington is still hating my guts because of the investigation into his ex-wife, I can't just call him up and say hello."

"That's true," Sarah said. "And I don't want to get another office involved. I checked in on the official investigation into Singletary, and they don't have anything either. What I do know is, Wendy was the only person working with him from the FBI, but he could have a nationwide web of crooked cops."

"I still don't understand why she worked with him." Carver ran his hand across his face.

"Either money or blackmail, but we'll never know because dead women don't answer questions," Kenneth said.

"So, let's move on. Since I'm in Virginia, I can get to Charlotte before anyone else. I can get eyes on the

Harringtons just in case Singletary has plans to make a move on them," Ray said.

"And you guys are sure no one knows Zoe and I are in Las Vegas?"

"You're cloaked by shadows," Sarah said with a smile. "You're officially in Texas. You might want to check in with your new field contact, Michael Silvers. I programmed your FBI-issued phone to ping off a tower in Dallas."

"Damn, I'm glad you're on our side," Ray said with a laugh. "Banks, how is Zoe?"

"She's starting to smell a rat. She's starting to get attached to the idea of the Dolan family finding peace, and she thinks I'm an uncaring asshole."

"That sounds about right," Ray said with a laugh.

"Go to hell, Ray. I have to do something to keep her busy until Singletary is dead or in jail."

"I know that's right," Ray said. Carver rolled his eyes at him. Before he could say another word, there was a knock at the door. He ended the call, then crossed over to the door. He looked out of the peephole and wasn't surprised to see Zoe standing there.

Carver opened the door and stood against the doorjamb. "You calmed down yet?"

"Carver, I'm sorry if you think I'm overreacting, but this isn't how I work. And you seem like you've just lost interest in this case."

"Zoe, I'm doing all that I can to find her, but I don't get why you think that I'm not trying to help."

"Are you going to let me in?"

"Should I? I mean, you just kicked me out of your

room, with an attitude." Carver chuckled. "If you come in, do you promise to keep your hands to yourself?"

"If you don't let me in, I'm going to punch you in your face now."

"So violent, yet so beautiful." Carver stood aside and allowed Zoe to enter. She stood next to the his bed and looked around the room. Carver closed the space between them and lifted her chin. "Have you figured out that I love you and I worry about you? I know you're trying to pretend that this is just another case. It isn't."

She tilted her head to the side and stared into his eyes. "I know that. And I know you're concerned. But you need to realize this: When this case is over, I'm going to have others, and you won't be tagging along with me."

"So that means I'm going to have to put a GPS tracker on you?"

She sucked her bottom lip in. "That's not funny, and if I find out that you did, I'd fight you."

"And you'd lose, babe." Carver kissed her on her forehead.

"You're funny. I'll make a deal with you; help me eat the rest of our room service and I'll get back to work in the morning."

"Deal. Because a brother was still hungry."

Zoe smiled. "I got dibs on the crab legs." They headed out the door and Carver was happy that he had another few hours to keep Zoe away from the truth.

Chapter 23

Charlotte, North Carolina

Zach woke up and kissed his wife on the cheek. "Wake up, beautiful."

"No," she moaned as she turned her back to him. "I'm tired and your baby is draining my energy."

"Oh, he's my baby now?"

"Yes, she is."

"But you're the one with the full schedule today." Zach pulled the blanket off Chante and tossed it aside. "So, get up and get in the shower. I'll even join you."

"That sounds like a good reason to get out of bed," she replied with a smile. Chante rose from the bed and Zach followed, wrapping his arms around her waist.

"Soon, I'm not going to be able to do this," he whispered against her ear. "And I can't wait."

"You're ready for me to be as big as a house?"

"I'm ready for our son to grow and make you even more beautiful." Zach spun her around. "Chante, I love you more than life, and now that we're having a baby, I can't tell you how much you mean to me."

She smiled. "You can try. And I think I'd better tell my parents that they're going to be grandparents soon."

"A trip to Charleston?"

"Aww, no. But we can invite them here. I'm sure my mother can stand that harsh city air for one weekend and not crack her skin."

Zach laughed. "I like your mom. Even if she still calls me a Yankee every now and then."

Across the street, Lewis watched the Harrington household and saw lights come on in the upstairs bedroom. It was about six o'clock and he knew that Chante and Zach left the house while it was still a little dark outside. That would make it easy for him to grab Chante if it didn't work out at her office.

Lewis didn't understand why Joe didn't plan to ask for a ransom. He could get the money he said Zoe had cost him, kill both women, and then disappear. If Lewis was going to be all the way down here in North Carolina, he wanted more than just the satisfaction of knowing that Zoe would be hurt and disappointed that her sister-in-law was dead. He wanted to watch that bitch suffer *and* get paid.

And just like that movie *Seven*, he wanted Zoe's head in a box and delivered to her brother. He hated what she had done to him and a few other officers who were in their division. She could've ignored what they'd done. Did they use excessive force in some cases?

Yes, but each one of those animals deserved it. Drug

dealers and thieves, they hadn't been Rhodes scholars out helping the community. And if some of the drug money went missing, then so what? They had families to feed, and a beat cop's salary wasn't going to feed three kids and a wife.

But because of fucking Zoe, he didn't even have his family anymore. And it was time for her to pay as well. Bitch.

Lewis's burner cell phone chimed, indicating a text message. Since he was tired of taking orders from Singletary, he ignored the text and continued to watch the Harringtons. Lewis was going to devise his own plan to get everything he wanted.

About thirty minutes later, Zach and Chante were walking out of the house. Lewis saw how close the couple was and remembered when he and his wife shared kisses in the morning before he went on duty.

His blood boiled thinking about how Zoe ruined everything for him. She had to pay, and her brother was the avenue to make that happen.

"Why are we down here?" Zoe asked as she pulled the lever on the slot machine.

"Because even Wonder Woman needs a break." Carver dropped another quarter in the machine. Then the lights and buzzers went off.

"We hit the jackpot!" Zoe laughed as Carver spun her around and lifted her into his arms. She wrapped her arms around his neck and kissed him gently on the lips. "So what are we going to do with these riches?"

Carver put her down and collected the payout vouchers.

"Looks like we should go to an island and be naked all day," he said.

Zoe slapped her hand on her hip. "And just forget about the family we're supposed to be getting closure for?"

Carver sighed and glanced at Zoe. "You're right, but can you blame me for wanting to get away with you for a little while, to get away from all of this?"

She thumped him on the shoulder. "That's pretty much the most insensitive thing ever!"

"Whatever, Zoe. You know this has been a wild ride, and I need a break."

"You know I don't stop and I don't give up until the job is done."

"One of the many things I love about you."

"How about we go double or nothing?" she said as she took the voucher from his hand. "I feel lucky tonight."

"No. Look at the time. We need to get to bed and start over in the morning."

"Gambling or looking through more reports?"

"Both. Right now, I want to take you to bed—and I mean just to sleep," Carver said. He knew he couldn't continue to lie to Zoe tonight. He hoped the Shadow Team would get some information on Singletary soon so that he could stop this charade.

"You're no fun." She tweaked the end of his nose. "Let's go. I see how people come to Vegas and lose it all. These casinos make you suspend reality."

Carver nodded, then wrapped his arm around Zoe's waist. "That's why there are no windows."

"Well, my body knows what's up."

"And what is your body saying?"

"To go to bed and take you with me."

"Is that so?"

She nodded. "I want you to hold me tonight, while we sleep."

"Technically, it's morning, but I'll hold you just the same."

Zoe stifled a yawn as the doors to the elevator opened. She reached down for her phone, then remembered that she'd left her phone in her room. She had an overwhelming urge to call Zach.

"What's wrong?" Carver asked when he noticed her frown.

"I was going to call Zach. I . . . Never mind."

"What?"

"It's a twin thing, you wouldn't understand. I'm just glad he married a woman who does."

"Well, explain it to me, so that your man can be just as understanding."

"I will in the morning." She stood on her tiptoes and kissed him on his cheek. "Carver, this is really nice and you're something special."

"Define *this*."

"Us. You and I finally being in a space where we can make this work."

"We could've made this work a long time ago, if you weren't so hardheaded. Zoe, that night—"

"Carver—"

"Hear me out. That night when we met and made love, I've never forgotten it. I dream about it, and if things had been different, I would've told you everything.

But I was undercover and working on a case that had a lot to do with national security."

"I get it." The door to the elevator opened and they stepped off. Carver took the key card from from her hand and unlocked the door. Zoe stepped inside and Carver closed the door, then stroked her cheek.

"I wanted to make you mine that night. Wanted to spend the next morning finding out everything about you and how to keep you in my life."

"Yet, the next time I saw you, there was this big FBI badge between us," she said as she slipped her shoes off.

"That happened. Let's build a bigger bridge to get over it."

She hopped on the bed and smiled at him. "Done. I'll never bring it up again."

Carver pulled off his shirt and joined Zoe in the bed. He wrapped his arms around her waist and rested his head in her lap.

"And how am I supposed to get any sleep like this?"

He shrugged. "I'm comfortable."

She pushed him off her and squeezed his cheek. "Good night."

Lewis drove four car lengths behind Chante. He wanted to make sure she didn't see him as he tracked her. Just as she made a right turn, his phone chimed again. "Damn it," he groaned as he picked up the phone. "Yeah?"

"If you keep ignoring me, I'm going to think you're working against me and my plan," Joe said.

"I'm following Chante and you're breaking my concentration."

"That's not a good excuse as to why you haven't answered the phone."

Lewis sighed. "What do you need, Joe?"

"Details. Have you noticed a pattern in the routine? What have you found out about them?"

"They start off early. She'd be easy to grab from the house."

"That's not the plan."

"Your plan is stupid."

"Lewis, I'm going to chalk that up to you being tired and not that you're a fucking idiot."

"The Harringtons are loaded, and you could get your money, still exact revenge and make Zoe suffer."

"And get the FBI involved. Don't be stupid. We have a plan and we're sticking to it."

"If you threaten this man's wife, he will pay and won't call in the authorities. I saw them together this morning. He loves her."

Joe sighed. "Are you kidding me? No man loves unconditionally like that, and the minute you start asking for money, you will see the truth. I don't care what you think you saw this morning, we're not changing the plan."

"Fine," Lewis snapped. But he didn't care what Joe said, he was going to get everything he could out of this trip to North Carolina. Zachary Harrington would pay, and probably lay down his life, to get his wife back. When he snatched Chante, there would be a ransom note.

But Lewis knew he had to be smart about the note. It couldn't be handwritten. It needed to be on paper that wasn't traceable, like a notepad from the hotel. Glancing out of the window, he saw an office store. Smiling as he turned his attention back to Chante's taillights, Lewis knew he was going to make the money he lost because of Zoe, and he'd be the one to stick the knife in her heart when he killed her sister-in-law.

Slipping out of Zoe's arms, Carver quietly stole out of the room and headed to his own. It was noon in DC and he needed to talk to the Shadow Team to find out what was going on with the search for Singletary.

He booted his tablet and called Sarah. Her face appeared on the screen. "And I thought you'd forgotten about me," she quipped.

"I'm in a different time zone, remember."

"Yeah, the Zoo zone."

"Sarah, what do we know about Singletary's whereabouts?"

"Don't know where that ghost is, but one of the cameras in Charlotte picked up Lewis Martinez."

"What? In Charlotte?"

"Yep. I'll keep you posted on what we find out. I have a meeting in five minutes."

As soon as he ended the video call, there was a knock at his door. Carver smiled, because he knew it was his woman.

"After all that talk last night, you still left me alone

in the bed," she quipped as she offered him a cup of coffee.

"I'm sorry, I had to check in with my team back in DC to see if they needed me or any of my files, and I didn't want to wake you."

Zoe walked in the room and perched on the edge of the dresser. "Likely story, G-man. Do they need you? Because I can stay out here and keep looking for Jessica without supervision."

"And leave you here with Deputy Dale? Nah."

She sucked her teeth. "That man is married. You're something else. I know why you're staying."

He set his coffee down next to her and leaned in. "And why is that?"

"So that you can put this work in at night." Zoe wrapped her leg around his waist. "And I don't mind a bit."

"You know, I can work the morning shift, too," he said as he pulled her closer and brushed his lips against hers.

"Is that so?" Zoe licked his bottom lip.

"I'd rather show and prove." He captured her mouth in a hot kiss, sucking her full lip while their tongues danced. Carver slipped his hand between Zoe's thighs, thankful for her lace nighty and lack of panties. He felt her desire dripping immediately and he was turned on like a roaring shower.

Moaning as he fingered her wet slit, Zoe shivered at his touch. When she closed her eyes, Carver shook his head. "Look at me," he commanded gently. "Tell me how you feel."

"Damned g-good."

He pulled his finger from her wetness and brought it

to his lips. He licked her juices from his fingertip. "And you taste good, too." Before she could reply, he had two fingers inside her, stroking, teasing, touching her most sensitive spot.

She threw her head back and cried out his name. "Carver, please, not the two fingers again."

He continued stroking. "I remember the last time you got the two-finger treatment. You enjoyed yourself."

"Need you. All of you inside me."

"Not. Yet. I haven't even had breakfast yet." Carver planted his face between Zoe's thighs and feasted on her. Her moans and screams filled the air like music at the symphony. Just as he took her to the brink of an orgasm, Carver pulled back.

"Why—what are you . . ."

"I got this," he said with a wink, then lifted her from the dresser. "I'm about to give you what you need."

Zoe sighed as he laid her on the bed and stripped out of his pajama pants. He slid a condom on his dick and dove into her wetness, thrusting in and out as she wrapped her legs around him. It was as if she was begging him to go deeper. And he did. "Zoe, Zoe," Carver groaned as she ground against him.

"Yes, baby. Yes!"

He wanted to hold his climax back just so that he could admire the look of satisfaction on Zoe's face as she came over and over again. But one last thrust and he exploded. Holding her in his arms, Carver was once again filled with guilt and afraid of what the truth would do to them.

Zoe wasn't the kind of woman who trusted easily, he

knew that. He knew that had been the source of her anger when he'd been investigating her family. Winning this woman almost took an act of Congress, and the moment she learned that he'd lied to her again, he knew she was going to bolt.

He opened his mouth, but Zoe kissed his confession away.

"Whoa," he said when their lips parted. "I don't know what I did to deserve that, but I'll do it again."

"And I thought I was rewarding myself," she said.

"Keep on doing it." He squeezed her bottom. "What do you say we go try the breakfast buffet?"

"Umm, that would be nice, but I don't think I can move right now."

"There's always room service."

Zoe nodded and yawned. "As soon as I wake up from my nap."

Carver kissed her forehead and wrapped his arms around her waist. "Good idea." As they drifted off to sleep, Carver dreamed of waking up to Zoe every morning, just like this one.

Chapter 24

It was afternoon when Zoe and Carver pulled themselves out of bed. As much as she didn't want to get out of bed, she knew she'd wasted valuable time that could've been used to find Jessica Dolan's remains.

Glancing at Carver's sleeping frame, she wondered why he'd stopped being focused on finding this girl's remains and closing this case. She wanted to ask him about that, but before anything else, she needed to call Zach. Looking at the clock, she figured that he and Chante were wrapping up their workday and probably heading back home. She grabbed her phone and headed for the bathroom. She turned the shower on, then dialed her brother's number. She hoped that everything was going to be all right with him and that she was just being paranoid.

Voicemail. Now, she was worried.

"Hey, Zoe! You plan on leaving me any hot water to shower with?" Carver called from behind the door.

She walked into the bedroom. "Carver, something's

wrong," she said. "I can't explain it, but there's something going on with my brother and I need to talk to him."

Carver shut off the shower. "What do you mean?"

"He always answers my calls, but he didn't. Then I had the dream."

Rubbing his hand across his face, Carver knew that he had to come clean with Zoe. Especially since he knew Singletary and Martinez were in Charlotte. "Zoe, your life is in danger. I asked you to take this case because Joe Singletary put a hit out on you. The information you gave the FBI about Natalie put a sizeable dent in his organization and cost him a lot of money."

Zoe's mouth dropped open and her knees went weak momentarily. Regaining her composure, she hauled off and slapped Carver with all her might. "You son of a bitch! I had the right to know this. And you had the gall to keep this away from me while taking me on this damned wild-goose chase? Is there a missing girl out there, or is that a lie, too?"

Rubbing his jaw, Carver shook his head. "We're not going to find Jessica Dolan's body here. This case hasn't been reopened. But, Zoe, if I walked into your office and told you the truth, you would've gone off half-cocked and tried to find Singletary yourself."

"And?"

He palmed his face. "And you might be dead! He sent someone after you in Santa Fe, the bombing at your office was probably his handiwork as well."

"I can take care of myself, and if I knew there was a threat, then I could've prepared myself. You robbed me of that, and from what I can tell, you haven't done shit to protect me."

"You're breathing, aren't you?"

"I'm out of here," Zoe snapped. She started for the door and Carver grabbed her arm.

"You can't go, because we don't know where Singletary is, and I'm not going to let you put yourself in danger. For all I know, Singletary still has other moles in the FBI who are watching your moves. What do you think is going to happen if you hop on a commercial flight right now?"

"I don't give a shit, but I know if I spend another minute in this room with you, I'm not going to be responsible for what I do to you." She slammed out the room and returned to her own.

Zoe paced back and forth, wondering what she should do next. Carver was right about getting on a commercial flight. She had two firearms that she couldn't get through security, and obviously they had been under someone's watchful eye.

How could Carver do this to her? If someone was trying to kill her, she needed to know that. What if Singletary was behind the bombing? She knew how to stop him and she was going to do just that. Pulling out her phone, she opened her cloud drive and pulled up the active file she'd kept on Singletary. The last time she'd checked on the pimp, he'd been in Virginia.

"Close to the interstate," she muttered as she read over her notes. She'd planned to share her files with Delvin Smallwood after Natalie had been sentenced, but Zoe had gotten so busy with her own cases and checking into Chante's background, that she'd forgotten about it. And Zoe hadn't been convinced that stopping Singletary was a priority of the FBI. He was only harming young girls of color, and Zoe knew how things like that went in law enforcement circles. There had been no media coverage of the sex trafficking ring after Natalie's conviction. And the only reason Natalie had made headlines was because of being Zach's wife, her client list, and the judge who'd worked her case and tried to get her off.

Had not sharing her information with the FBI helped to put her life in danger? *No! Carver put my life in danger with this fake case. I'm going back to New York and I'm going to find this bastard myself.*

Carver knew Zoe was about to make a hotheaded decision that was going to put her life in danger. How was he going to stop her? She could be mad, but he was going to make her understand why he'd done things in this manner. Stalking over to her room, he banged on the door.

"Zoe, please open up."

"Go. Away."

"Either open the door or I'll get a key from the front desk. Remember, I paid for the rooms. We have to talk about this."

She snatched the door open. "Listen to me and listen good. I don't have to talk to your lying ass."

"You do, because I'm not about to allow you to put yourself at risk because you're mad at me."

"I'm not mad at you. I'm disappointed, and I'm hurt, but mad? No, I'm not mad. You have two choices right now: get me back to New York on that private jet or pay for my flight to New York. But I'm not spending another day in Las Vegas with you."

"Fine, we can go back to New York."

Zoe slammed her hand on the dresser. "There is no *we*! Once the plane lands, you need to go ahead and file a plan to take your black ass back to Washington."

"That's not going to happen. I know you're going to try and hunt him down on your own."

"You're damned right. I'm not going to live my life in fear because you withheld information I needed."

"I've done all of this to protect you, and it's not going to stop now. If you want to track him down, then I'm going to help."

"Well, the FBI has done such a great job of finding this man, so yes, I'm going to welcome your help," Zoe snapped.

"You don't have a choice in the matter."

"Bullshit!" She pushed him away from her. "Carver, was any of this real?"

"Any of what?"

She narrowed her eyes at him. "Forget it."

"Zoe, I—"

"Shut up. You're still everything I've always thought you were. A lying bastard. You used me, and how I felt about you, to manipulate me into this cross-country trip. But you really don't give a damn about me. If you did, you would've been honest. Now, get out of my room and get the jet ready."

He closed the space between them and grabbed her shoulders. "I do love you, Zoe, and that's why I did all of this. I don't want anyone to hurt you."

"Then why do you keep doing it? Get. Out."

"I'm not leaving until you hear me out. I have a team working on finding Singletary, and we're close. You have to let us do our job."

"For the last time, I don't have to . . ."

Carver took her chin in his hand and forced her to look in his eyes. "Damn it, Zoe, listen to yourself right now. You want to walk around here and pretend you don't need anyone, that you're fucking Cleopatra Jones. There are people out there who want you dead, and I'm not going to let anyone hurt the woman I love. I lied to protect you. I took you out of the reach of killers, and I'm not sorry for it. You can stand here and question what I did, but I'd do the same thing again."

She blinked twice, and Carver's heart broke as tears welled up in her eyes. "I hate you."

"No, you don't. I understand how you feel right now. But if we're going to capture Singletary, you got to let me and the Shadow Team help you."

She dropped her head. "Fine. But once this is over, I never want to see your face again."

"We're flying to DC. I'm going to file the flight plan and we should be ready to go within the hour."

Rolling her eyes, Zoe walked over to the bathroom and slammed the door. Carver shook his head. He knew things were going to end like this. But he wasn't sorry at all. Heading back to his room, he called Sarah.

"What's up, Banks?"

"Zoe knows the truth."

"Wow, how did she take it?"

"How do you think? We're going to fly to DC. She's going to work with us to find Singletary."

"Carver, that might not be such a good idea. She's his target and she's a civilian."

"And if I don't keep her in the loop as to what's going on, she's going to be a loose cannon in New York. I'm not going to find her dead . . ."

"Is this about how you feel about Zoe, or are you trying to make up for what happened to Monica?"

"Seriously, you want to go there?" Carver gritted his teeth.

"Yeah, I do. Because I was there that night. I watched my sister die as well. You loved her and wanted to protect her—even though she had the same damn training as you. Just because you love a woman, it doesn't mean you have to be her knight in shining armor. If you and Zoe are coming here to help take this monster down, then you better make sure you two have this personal shit worked out. I don't want to see you turn into that person again."

"Sarah, it's not like that. Zoe doesn't—"

"Zoe is a former cop, and from what I've heard, pretty good with a gun. She might need help staying away from a hit man, but she can take care of herself. You know what, you never questioned my skill on the battlefield. Do you think that once you fall in love with a woman and stick your dick in her that she loses the ability to kick ass?"

"I'll call you when we land."

"Truth hurts, doesn't it. See you soon."

Carver looked down at his phone and shook his head. He mulled over what Sarah said. He hated that she was right, and had him pegged.

He knew Zoe could take care of herself, just as

Monica could. But growing up, he'd watched his mother work herself to death while his father did nothing. She'd been the breadwinner, the housekeeper, and the head of the household. His father tried to play the disciplinarian, but at the end of the day he'd only been a leech who'd sucked the life out of his mother.

Carver knew that wasn't how love was supposed to be, so when he fell for a woman, he was overbearing. He wanted to protect his woman at all costs.

But why do I keep losing them? he thought as he started packing.

Chapter 25

"Gabby," Chante said into her intercom, "I'm not feeling very well. Can you clear my calendar for the rest of the day? Make sure Diane is available to meet with Katy Turner, please."

"Yes, ma'am," Gabby said. "Do you need another ginger ale?"

"No. I think Baby Harrington is trying to tell me something and I should listen."

Gabby laughed. "That's a good idea. Zach will appreciate that."

"Has he still been calling you, asking for updates?"

"Well," she said, "at least it's not on the hour anymore."

Chante sighed. "He's such a dork. He better be glad we love him around here."

"You get out of here and get some rest."

Chante placed her hand on her belly as the baby kicked like David Beckham. "You're busy in there today. I hope you're in there alone, but Daddy seems to think that he might have dropped two of you in there."

She yawned as she rose to her feet and grabbed her purse. Chante hated to leave, being that she had a full day, but she and Zach had already decided that the baby would dictate how hard she worked until she left for maternity leave.

Chante pulled her iPhone from her purse and Face-Timed Zach.

"Hey, beautiful."

"Babe, I'm about to go home. Your child doesn't want me to work today."

"Want me to meet you at the house and massage your feet?" He wiggled his eyebrows. "My meeting ended early."

"You don't have to, but I won't be mad if you do. Can you bring me two slices of barbecue chicken pizza from Fuel, and some fries?"

"Let me guess, the baby wants that?"

"Yes. As a matter of fact, the baby wants to share. Why not get a whole pie?"

"Sounds like a plan. Text me when you get home."

She nodded and blew him a kiss. After ending the video call, she stuffed her phone in her purse and headed for her car.

Lewis watched Chante leave the office. She was leaving too early. There was no way he could grab her in the middle of the day. After trolling the parking lot, he'd spotted all of the cameras and decided that he needed to figure out how to disable the cameras without his face being seen. That's why he'd been in the parking garage that afternoon. He was going to grab her after the cameras were down. Now, he had to call Singletary and tell him the plan wasn't going to work.

Lewis followed Chante and wasn't surprised to see that she was going home. He remembered days like this. He'd turn off his radio, go home in the middle of the day and make love to his wife. They had been so close, so in love, and he thought they would weather any storm.

When he and Chellie got married, their racial differences didn't matter. They were both products of Spanish Harlem. Went to high school together and dated since they'd been freshmen.

But once Zoe's investigation came to light and he was linked to being a racist cop, Chellie left him. She wouldn't even let him explain that he'd only hurt criminals; he'd been on the streets making sure he could return home to her.

But she'd taken Zoe's side and called him racist. Then she left. And when she left him, everything changed. He knew he'd never love again. Seeing Zach and Chante reminded him of what he used to have.

He was going to take pleasure in ruining their love. Despite Joe's objections, Lewis had the ransom note and he was going to leave it at the site where he grabbed Chante. He thought about taking her now, but as he was about to park the car, Lewis saw Zach pull into the driveway.

"I knew it," he muttered. "Afternoon delight." Lewis drove off and dialed Singletary's number.

"Do you have her?"

"No, she left the office early, and when I followed her home, her husband came behind her."

"Damn it, the sooner we get her the sooner we draw Zoe out from wherever she's hiding. I'm tired of waiting."

"This was your plan, remember?"

"You need to execute it, or maybe I should execute you."

"Motherfucker, I'm out here putting myself at risk, following a lawyer! So, don't think your threats mean anything."

"I don't make threats, I make promises. You have twenty-four hours to make this happen or you're going to take your last breath."

Lewis threw his phone on the floorboards of the car after Joe hung up on him. He was getting tired of that man acting like he was a king. This wasn't what Lewis had signed on for, and there was still no sign of Zoe. The money that Joe had lured him to North Carolina with was damned near gone, and that black bastard hadn't given him another payment.

That's why the ransom was going to be important to him. Lewis circled back around the block and parked across the street from the Harringtons' house. He wanted to peep in the window and see what the couple was doing. In his mind's eye, he knew they were making love, just like he and Chellie used to do in the middle of the day. Having his wife for lunch had been one of the most delightful things of his day. It made his patrols a lot easier.

Sighing, Lewis knew the best thing for him to do was to return to the roach-infested hotel where he'd been staying and tweak the plan to kidnap Chante.

* * *

Meanwhile, Zoe and Carver boarded the jet in silence. She turned her back to him as she took her seat. He wanted to reach out to her, remembering their flight to Las Vegas and how they'd made love to each other.

However, the cold look in her eyes silenced him. When Zoe buckled her seat belt and turned toward the window, Carver knew that she wasn't going to talk to him at all. He actually said a silent prayer for turbulence.

An hour of smooth flying passed before Zoe turned and looked at Carver. "What is this Shadow Team?"

"It's three of the Marines I served with in the war. We went into intelligence agencies after leaving the Corps and we help each other out when things get tough. We're like family."

Zoe sucked her teeth. "Did the president really reach out to the FBI to find Jessica Dolan, or was she randomly chosen so you could keep this farce going?"

"The case is real, but it isn't a priority."

Zoe turned back to the window. Carver wanted to hold her, kiss her anger away and go back to the carefree days they'd shared before everything imploded. But he knew better.

"So," he began, "you want a drink or something?"

"Silence. That's all I need."

"Zoe, you have to understand this was the only way I thought I could help you."

She whirled around and glared at him. "Through all of your service, you somehow have become this wannabe superhero. Captain Save the World. But guess what, I've never needed to be saved."

"Did you know you were being targeted?"

"No! Because you didn't tell me! How could I know? Why does Singletary want me dead anyway?" Zoe folded her arms across her chest. "How do you know this is a credible threat?"

"You and Delvin Smallwood were about to bring him down. You had information that you were going to give Smallwood, right?"

"Was he in on this, too?"

Carver nodded. "But he's dead now."

Zoe gasped. "What happened?"

"We've discovered that an agent was working with Singletary. She was feeding him the information about our whereabouts, and I think that she's the reason why that hit man came after you in Santa Fe."

She nodded. "So, we ended up on this private jet because you didn't want our names to show up on watch lists or flight plans. Makes sense."

Carver nodded, then waited to see if she was going to continue talking to him. Silence filled the cabin for a beat.

"Carver, why did you take it upon yourself to be the one to find me and protect me?"

"That's the easiest question you've ever asked me. It's because I love you."

She rolled her eyes. "Whatever. You've proven that you'll do anything for a case. I don't believe you."

"You can question a lot of things about me, but don't ever question how I feel about you, Zoe."

"You can save all of that," she said, "because I'm not

buying it, Carver. I'm guessing capturing Singletary is going to be a nice feather in your cap. Probably get you a regional director job, put you on the fast track for a promotion or something like that. Again, just like two years ago, I was a means to an end for you."

"That's not true."

"Do you even know what the truth is? What it feels like?"

Carver crossed over to her and touched her cheek. "Yes. I. Do." He captured her mouth in a soft kiss, begging her for forgiveness, pleading for her to believe in his love. She pressed her hands against his chest, and when Carver thought she was going to push him away, Zoe gripped his shirt, pulling him closer. He said a silent thank-you to God. Maybe he and Zoe still had a chance to make this thing work.

Why am I kissing him? Zoe ripped her mouth from Carver's and stared into his eyes. Could she forgive him? Did he really love her? Could she ever trust him?

"Zoe."

"Carver, you really hurt me. I don't want to always wonder if you're being honest with me."

"I'll never lie to you again, even if it is to save your life."

"That's no excuse. You don't think we could've caught Singletary together? I find people for a living. And I'm not going to stop until I find this son of a bitch. If he wants me, he can come and get me."

Carver shook his head. "This is why I didn't come to your office and tell you what was going on. Zoe, he's dangerous, and if you think I'm going to allow you to paint a target on—"

"Babe," she said. "You don't have a choice. We've tried it your way, now it's my turn."

"At least work with me and the Shadow Team."

"It's my life, Carver. You've had me waste weeks of it, and I'm taking it back right now. If you and your shadow crew want to work with me, I'm cool with it."

"Hardheaded."

"Whatever."

He stroked her cheek. "Zoe, if something happens to you, I wouldn't . . ."

"Working together, we can make sure that doesn't happen."

Carver sat beside her, and Zoe leaned her head on his shoulder. While she could understand what he had done, she still didn't like it—but she wasn't going to write him off for loving her that much.

"Is there anything else you're keeping from me about killers that I should know about?"

"No. But what do you know about Singletary?"

She pulled her phone out of her purse and opened the file she'd been keeping on him. "I was going to share this with Smallwood, but things got hectic in my life, and when the news died down after Natalie's arrest, I figured the FBI had its pound of flesh."

Carver read over Zoe's detailed file and rubbed his forehead. "And you never wanted to work for the Bureau? I mean, this has more detail into his organization than our task force ever got."

"It helps that I wasn't working for Smallwood. How

much evidence do you think the double agent got rid of to help Singletary stay out of the reach of authorities?"

"Looking at this, a lot. I wish you'd come to me with this."

She raised her right eyebrow at him. "You do realize that I was still pissed at you for arresting me when I started this, and I went above your head for a reason."

"Cold. Just cold."

"You know what else is cold? Handcuffs, a suspended PI license, and being trotted out in front of cameras as a person of interest in a sex-trafficking ring." Zoe smiled sardonically. "I was pissed. And you're the last person I wanted to talk to or share anything with."

"Well, we're going to have to work on your sharing skills."

"I'm sorry, pot, what did you say?"

"Hush, woman." Carver kissed her on the cheek. "When we get to DC, we're going to rest at my place for a little bit before heading to meet with the team."

"And resting is all we're going to do."

"What about eating?"

"Eating food is allowed. Carver, we have to get serious about finding Singletary, and I don't need you distracting me."

"Here's my promise: Until we find Singletary, that's going to be our focus. But once he's no longer a threat, I'm taking back every minute I missed making love to you."

Zoe's lip trembled. "Is that so?"

He nodded. "Sure is."

"How much time do we have before we land?"

"About another three and a half hours or so."

Zoe stroked his knee. "This is the part where we make up, right?"

"Yes, it is." Carver brought his mouth down on Zoe's. This time the kiss was hot, wet, and filled with passion. She sucked his tongue as he lifted her leg to gain access to her wetness. And Zoe was dripping wet, filled with need and want.

"Carver," she moaned as he fingered her slit. Her desire dripped like warm honey. "That feels so good."

"I can make you feel better," he said as he slid her panties off. Then he eased between her legs, lapping her sweet juices. Zoe pressed her hips into his lips and Carver deepened his kiss. His tongue danced across her throbbing bud. Just as her thighs started to shiver and she was about explode, Carver pulled away. Zoe gasped, wondering why he'd stopped at that moment.

In a flash, Carver had discarded his shorts and lifted Zoe from her seat. He drove into her, whispering in her ear how much he loved and needed to be inside her.

"Carver. Carver!" They matched each other thrust for thrust—as if they were trying to disappear inside each other. Zoe gripped his neck as she bounced up and down on his erection until she did explode. Her hot juices dripped down his thighs. Carver's climax came right after. They fell back on the seat and Zoe placed her hand on his chest.

"We're definitely going to need a few hours of sleep before we dive into finding Singletary," she said.

"Umm-huh."

Before too long, they'd both gotten a head start on the rest they needed as the couple drifted off to sleep.

Chapter 26

Zoe woke up with a start when the jet hit a pocket of turbulence. "Oh, God!"

"What's wrong?" Carver asked, his voice groggy.

"I thought we were about to crash. Jesus, I'm not getting on another plane anytime soon."

"It's going to be fine. We're not going to crash and I got you." Carver kissed her forehead.

"I need to call Zach and let him know what's going on."

Carver shook his head. "Zoe, the fewer people who know about this, the better. I know you and your twin are close, but he doesn't need to know what we're doing."

She nodded, realizing that Zach had been through enough because of Natalie and Singletary. "I'll keep him out of this."

Carver nodded. "Besides, you're the one Singletary is trying to get."

"Then I need to stop hiding. If he wants me, he can come and try to get me. If you and this shadow group are big and bad, then you guys can protect me."

"I'm not willing to take that risk, Zoe."

She narrowed her eyes at him. "It's my life, and we're doing it. Let him know where I am. If he's in Virginia, then I need to make myself seen in Washington. He probably has more than one mole in the FBI."

Carver sighed, though he figured Zoe was wrong about that. He'd hoped that she would settle down a little, but he should've known better. Zoe's fuse was lit and she was poised to explode. "Let me make a call." He glanced at his watch. "We should be landing in about thirty-five minutes."

She nodded and walked over to the bar to pour herself a drink. Landings were another thing she hated about flying. Planes crashed on the runway all the time—at least in her mind.

"Are you all right over there?" he asked after watching her down her second bourbon.

"I'll be fine. I think we should skip resting and head straight to your crew. I have a plan, and you're just going to have to go along with it."

"That's still up for debate," Carver said as he walked over to her and drew Zoe into his arms.

Charlotte, North Carolina

Chante was in heaven as she lounged on the sofa. Zach massaged her swollen feet and she moaned in delight. Dinner had been delicious, but she was sure her doctor would frown on her putting French fries on top of that greasy pizza. But it seemed to calm the baby down.

"I don't know what I did to deserve you, but I'm so thankful," she said.

"Please, I'm the lucky one. I think there are two babies in there, if your dinner is any indication." Zach kissed her big toe.

"Oh, hush. This is just one little girl who was hungry."

"If you say so. Are you feeling better?"

Chante nodded. "I think you're right about me doing too much. I'm going to hand off some of my cases to my associates and get used to the changes in my body."

"Not you."

"I'm finally listening, but forgive me for not knowing how being pregnant would change my life."

"But in a good way, right?"

"Of course." She placed her hand on her belly. "I love our baby already, and I can't wait to welcome her into the world."

"I can't wait to meet him, either. Chante, I love you so much." Zach scooped his wife up in his arms. "Now, let's go to bed."

"I'm not sleepy."

"Who said anything about going to sleep?"

Lewis sat in the ratty motel room waiting for Joe. He made sure to tuck the ransom note away. Both men were frustrated that the plan for the kidnapping had stalled. Joe burst into the room with a scowl on his face.

"This is taking too long."

"I know that, but I'm going to take the cameras out and—"

"No," Joe said. "Grab her from the house. You've been over there long enough to know how they operate. When you get her, bring her to this address." He handed him a piece of paper. "It's an abandoned warehouse. I've set up a meeting with Zachary at seven a.m. to talk about one of his properties. He should leave home before she does. That will give you time to bring her to the warehouse. We don't have any room for errors. Make sure you don't get caught."

"Got it." Lewis smiled, thinking that the ransom note was going to drive Zach crazy. His wife was probably the most important thing in his life.

"Zoe's PI agency has an answering service, and once we have her sister-in-law, I'm going to leave her a message."

"What happens when she shows up?"

"The bitch dies." Joe headed for the door. "It's time to get our revenge."

Landing in Washington, Carver didn't want to go through with Zoe's plan to mark herself as Singletary's target, but his woman was determined. He could tell by the way she marched off the jet and stood on the tarmac with her arms folded across her chest. Whether he liked it or not, she was going to do everything he was trying to keep her from doing.

He never wanted her to be a target for this man. How was he going to make sure she didn't end up like Monica?

"Come on," Zoe said as she locked eyes with Carver

as he stood at the top of the stairs leading from the plane.

"Here we go," he said as bounded down the steps. "I called a car service and it should be here shortly, but if you want to walk about twenty blocks, we can do that, too."

"Just hush," she said as she squeezed his arm. "I'm not walking. But I did post that I just landed in DC on Facebook. If Joe is really stalking me, he's watching my social media."

"Can you slow down?"

"I've been in a holding pattern for weeks," she said. "Fine, I'll meet with your people before I do anything else."

"Thanks." Carver wrapped his arm around her waist. "Looks like that's our car, or a hit man."

She hip checked him. "Will you stop it?"

"Not until he shows me some identification." Carver walked up to the car and spoke with the driver for about five minutes before he waved Zoe over.

"He's not a killer, right?"

"That's right. I'll get our bags. You can get in the car, get off your feet."

She offered him a mock salute. "Sir, yes, sir!"

Carver grabbed the bags and joined Zoe in the car. She turned and looked at him. "Where are we heading?"

"If I tell you, are you going to tweet it?" Carver quipped.

"No." Zoe rolled her eyes. "I'm just ready to get this thing off the ground and put this man behind bars or in a grave. He's going to learn that I'm not one to mess with."

"He should be afraid."

"Yes, he should."

They rode in silence for the next twenty minutes; then the car pulled up at a white building that reminded her of a doctor's office.

"Let's go," Carver said as he opened the door.

"What is this place?"

"Just an office building." Carver pulled the bags out of the car and smiled.

"Don't say a word about social media."

"I wasn't." They walked to the building, and he punched in a code, then opened the door. When they walked into the building, Zoe looked around at the computers and equipment lining the walls.

"Control central?"

"Something like that."

"Banks," Sarah called out.

"Sarah," he said as he crossed over to the statuesque woman with her hair pulled back in a ponytail. "Where's the gun?"

She lifted her pant leg and showed him her holstered .22. "I'm always strapped." She glanced at Zoe. "Miss Harrington?"

"Just call me Zoe."

Sarah walked over to her and shook her hand. "You're beautiful."

Carver cleared his throat. "Can we get down to business? And where are the others?"

"Ray went to get some food and Kenneth is following up on a lead on Singletary in Richmond."

"How many people are involved in this?" Zoe asked.

"There are only four of us," Sarah said. "One thing that we've learned is that you have to be careful who you trust these days. We've all been though the fire together and have each other's backs."

Carver nodded. "War creates family."

"Or destroys it," Sarah said.

"That's all well and good," Zoe began as she looked from Carver to Sarah. "But this man wants me dead, and I don't plan on letting him get what he wants. So, how are we going to find this bastard?"

Sarah smiled, then nudged Carver. "I like her, Banks." She led them to a set of monitors in the back of the room. She sat down in front of the monitors. "We've been tracking Singletary's financials and we see that he withdrew about ten thousand dollars from an offshore account. We ran his face through the facial recognition system and got a hit in New York."

"That son of a bitch," Zoe muttered. "He really wanted to get me on my home turf?"

"Zoe, this man is dangerous. He killed two FBI agents and he may be behind the death of your former sister-in-law."

Carver shook his head. "She was going to be the linchpin in the case against him."

Sarah nodded. "I'm guessing Wendy told him that, and that's why she was killed in prison."

Zoe started pacing and Carver wanted to draw her into his arms. Maybe now she was starting to understand how brutal Singletary was. Sarah glanced at him, then rose from the monitor.

"I'm going to get some water. You guys need anything?"

"No, thank you," Zoe said.

Sarah left the room and Carver pulled Zoe into his arms. "Are you starting to see why I—"

She placed a finger to his lips. "I know what you're going to say, and I don't want to hear it. I can't believe he killed Natalie."

"And didn't even get his hands dirty. Zoe, we have to be careful."

"Forget being careful, we have to capture him."

Carver sighed and dropped his arms from Zoe's waist. "Hardheaded and reckless. That's going to be on your tombstone."

She narrowed her eyes at him. "Carver," she said, "I'm tired of people telling me what to do and how I'm supposed to do it. That's why I work for myself. That's why I don't work with my brother. Don't let your need to control things be the reason I walk away from you."

Carver folded his arms across his chest. "Let me be clear about this situation. Joe Singletary is a killer who doesn't give a damn who he hurts. He thinks that you cost him millions of dollars because you took Natalie down and unraveled his organization. Whatever I have to do to keep you safe, to keep you alive, I'm going to do it. You can love it or hate it, but I'd rather you walk away from me than see you buried."

* * *

Zoe's mouth fell open and nothing came out. She'd never been shut down so fiercely in her life. Carver lifted her chin and stared into her eyes. "You're going to do what we say to keep you safe and get Singletary."

"All right," she said.

"No more going rogue and broadcasting your location to the world," he said, then held his hand out. "Give me your phone."

"If you break it . . ." She held the phone out to him.

"Not going to break it, just turning off your location services." Carver entered the setting and turned it off, and deleted her Facebook app. "You should turn the phone off. So if you need to call your brother, do it."

"I'll call him in the morning," she said, stifling a yawn.

"Tired?"

She nodded. "But we have to find him. Sleep can wait."

"Tired Zoe isn't going to be a lot of help. There is a room in the back where you can take a quick nap and join us later."

As much as she didn't want to, Zoe headed to the room where Carver told her she could rest. She took a seat on the soft sofa and smiled. At least he was including her in the search for Singletary. But she was still a bit miffed that he'd wasted so much time on a wild-goose chase when they could've been looking for Singletary. She leaned back on the sofa and grabbed her phone. Before turning it off, she sent Zach a text message.

I'm in DC. Going to be out of touch for a while. Love you.

Zoe turned the phone off and closed her eyes. Drifting off to sleep, she dreamed of putting a bullet in Singletary's head.

Carver leaned back in his chair as he tracked Joe's electronic footprint. The trail went cold in New York.

"Where do you think he went?" Sarah asked as she slurped her chow mein noodles.

"That's what frustrates me to no end. We get a glimpse of him and then he disappears." Carver slapped his hand across the desk.

"You're really upset, huh," Ray said with a smirk.

"Shut up."

"She's really pretty," Kenneth said. "I'd put my nuts on the line for her, too."

Carver glared at them. "Can we just get over how she looks?"

"Nah," Ray said. "Let's talk about why we're really here."

"Because Singletary is a fucking killer."

"Yeah, right," Kenneth said. "That might be part of why the FBI is looking for him, but this little reunion is all about sweet pea back there."

"That's a damned . . . Look, Zoe isn't the only one at risk because of Singletary and she has—"

"Calm down, cowboy." Sarah grabbed two egg rolls and tossed one at Ray. "We all want to get Joe."

"Some more than others."

"Ray, shut the f—"

"Guys, calm down. Now we need a plan to get Singletary. We can talk about the lovely Zoe later."

Everyone laughed, except Carver. "While you-all are cracking jokes, keep in mind that we have to figure out why Singletary was in New York. Was he the one behind the bombing of Zoe's office?"

"Got video on that," Raymond said. "And it looks like someone dressed as an alarm tech set the devices. But he was smart enough not to show his face."

Carver released a frustrated breath. "How do you know it wasn't Singletary?"

"Was smaller than Joe and shorter."

"Maybe it was the mob, like the old man said," Carver said as he rose to his feet.

"Or," Kenneth said, "maybe your girl has more enemies than you think. I looked at some of her older cases. She's pissed a lot of people off and the NYPD is at the top of that list. She's investigated some of the same officers that she worked with. Her old partner lost his job because Zoe uncovered some abuse."

"You think more than one person wants to kill Zoe?" Carver asked as he paced back and forth.

Sarah snapped her fingers. "You said Zoe got her ex-partner fired, right?"

Kenneth nodded. "I've checked to see if there is any activity on his credit or debit cards and we got nothing."

"But we do know he and Singletary were together in New York," Ray said. "If they teamed up, Zoe is in trouble."

Chapter 27

Zoe woke up in a cold sweat. She'd been spooked by her dream about Zach. She saw him in trouble, in a sea of fire, reaching out for her. His mouth was open but no words came out. Sweat dropped down her back like rain. Did that dream mean something, or had she allowed the fact that Singletary wanted to kill her make her paranoid?

"Calm down," she muttered as she sat up. But a feeling of impending doom kept her rooted on the sofa. Zoe could hear muffled voices coming from the other room. She figured the whole team must be back.

Glancing at her watch, she saw it was after midnight. "Didn't mean to sleep this long." Rising to her feet, she stretched her arms above her head. Then she headed toward the main room.

When she entered, all of the conversation stopped. Looking around at the new faces, she had to say that Carver surrounded himself with good-looking people. One of the men in front of one of the computers reminded her of the Rock, with his smooth caramel complexion and expressive brown eyes. Underneath his shirt, she could see the outline of his rippling muscles.

The other man, who looked to be of Middle Eastern descent, with his jet-black hair and full beard, looked as if he could be a superhero. His coal-black eyes were mesmerizing. Zoe wondered how Sarah kept her wits, surrounded by these men.

"Hello."

Carver rose from his chair and crossed over to Zoe. "You all right?" he asked.

It didn't go unnoticed by anyone that Carver wrapped his arm around Zoe's waist in a possessive manner.

"Yeah, I'm fine. Didn't mean to sleep that long."

"You obviously needed the rest. Let me introduce you to the other guys on the team."

They crossed over to the computers and Carver pointed to the Rock look-alike and introduced him as Raymond.

"And this joker right here is Kenneth. A man of many faces."

Kenneth stood up and kissed Zoe's cheek. "That's how the French do it. Nice to meet you."

Carver glared at Kenneth and hip checked him as he walked Zoe over to Sarah's monitor.

"Singletary's trail goes cold in New York. We have evidence that he linked up with your former partner, Lewis Martinez. But we don't know where they went. All they really have in common is that they both want you dead."

Zoe shook her head at how matter-of-factly Sarah spoke. But if this woman was a Marine, she looked at death all the time. There was no need for her to get emotional about Zoe's life.

"Is there anyone else in New York with a grudge?" Sarah asked.

"That could be half the city." Zoe shrugged her shoulders.

Kenneth grunted. "More specifically, have you heard from any of the other cops you investigated?"

"Lewis is the only person I've heard from directly," she replied. "Would be just like that damn prick to team up with Joe to get me."

"Guys, we got to shut down. Our hack has been discovered," Sarah said.

Kenneth hit a kill switch on the system and all of the screens went dark. Zoe felt as if she were in the middle of a spy movie. Part of her wondered, if these four people could get as much information on Singletary as they had in a few weeks, what stopped the FBI from bringing him down?

"So, what are you guys? If you have access to all of this information, why is Singletary still free?"

"Do we look as if we're doing this within the confines of FBI protocols?" Ray asked.

"What Mr. Sensitivity is trying to say," Kenneth said, "is that what we do is deep, deep undercover and we don't—"

"We're called Shadows for a reason," Sarah said, and rolled her eyes. "We help each other with hard cases and sometimes we bring down rogue agents. We're trying to figure out who else is helping Singletary, and the only people we trust are in this room."

Carver nodded. "Sometimes we break the rules."

"Oh," Zoe said as she folded her arms across her chest.

"And some of us use this space for personal reasons," Ray said, then rose to his feet. "Are you worth it, Zoe?"

Carver crossed over to Ray and pushed him in his massive chest. "You're fucking out of line!"

"We're all taking a risk here. I'm not out of line at all."

Sarah moved liked lightning to split the men apart. "We decided to do this because this is what we do. You two need to take this beef and grill it, or I will shut it all down!"

Zoe took a deep breath. "You know what, I'm not trying to cause problems and I didn't ask any of you to take a risk for me. I didn't know this was going on." She shot an accusatory glance at Carver. "If you don't want to help me, I can take care of myself. I'm not a damsel in distress."

"Zoe, excuse Raymond. He was obviously dropped on the head as a child." Sarah punched him in the forearm.

Ray rolled his eyes. "Twenty-four-hour protocol, right?"

Sarah nodded. "We're going to go silent for twenty-four hours and pretend we haven't seen each other in months."

"Then I'm going to New York to see if they left any clues as to where they are now."

Zoe furrowed her brows, confused that Raymond would continue to work the case when he seemed to be so against it. Carver walked over to her and placed his hand on her shoulder.

"Don't worry about him," he whispered in her ear. "He's the devil's advocate of the group."

"And here I thought he was just the asshole."

"Let's get out of here and go to sleep."

"Sure, though I am wide-awake. Maybe we should go over the information that I have on Singletary and see if there's a pattern or something."

"No, you need to relax. Zoe, are you sure that you're all right?"

She looked deep into his eyes and was about to tell him about the dream she'd had when Kenneth walked over to them. "Hey, guys, we got to go."

Carver nodded. "Come on, we can talk on the way out."

Kenneth looked from Zoe to Carver. "I hope you understand why Ray was asking those questions."

"I really don't care," Zoe said.

"Let it go, K," Carver said. "We'll deal with this in the morning."

"Breakfast at your place?" Kenneth asked.

Carver nodded as he and Zoe walked out the door. She turned to him once they were on the sidewalk. "You cook breakfast?"

"No, we're just going to have a discussion about what we need to do to take Singletary down. There is a Dunkin' Donuts about three blocks away."

"Ooh, apple fritters. Is it open twenty-four hours?"

Carver laughed. "I don't know. Let's find out."

Charlotte, North Carolina

Lewis parked his car across the street from the Harringtons' house. He knew there wasn't much time to make sure everything went well. It was two a.m., and in four hours, the Harringtons would be starting their day. Joe said that he was going to make sure Zach left the house first because of their bogus meeting. Picking up his night-vision binoculars, Lewis looked at the house. He didn't see anything, but he imagined the couple inside making love.

He remembered early mornings and late nights with his wife. She'd brush her taut ass against him and his dick would stand at attention. She'd always sleep in a sheer nightgown, giving him access to her wetness at all times. He'd slip his hand underneath the gown and stroke her until she purred. His little sex kitten had always been ready to please him.

Lewis imagined that Chante was the same way when it came to Zach. That's why he looked so happy all the time and so in love. That's why Lewis was going to leave the ransom note. He'd done everything necessary to make sure he couldn't be traced.

Lewis had a separate cell phone and he left that number on the bottom of the note. He made sure when he wrote it that he used gloves and an envelope that was self-sealing so that he wouldn't leave DNA.

One of the last cases he'd been involved with at the NYPD had been a kidnapping, and the suspect got caught because he'd licked the envelope. Lewis knew that couldn't happen. Leaning his seat back, he watched the dark house and thought of all he'd lost because of Zoe Harrington. He'd known the bitch was trouble the first time they'd done a stop and frisk together.

"Put your hands up!" Lewis yelled at the hooded

black man running away from him and Zoe. He drew his gun and she glared at him.

"What are you going to do, shoot him in the back?" She ran up behind the man and pushed him into a pile of trash on the corner. "Why are you running?"

"Because you motherfuckers are chasing me. I didn't do shit! And that bitch with you is crazy! Always around here robbing people!"

Zoe pulled the man to his feet. "What are you talking about?"

Lewis walked up behind Zoe. "He has weed. I bet he tossed it."

"I don't have shit and I didn't have shit!"

"Calm down," Zoe said. "Against the wall. Let me just make sure you're clean, then you can go."

"But he fits the description of—"

"If he's clean, he's free to go!" Zoe snapped, then patted the man down. Finding nothing illegal on him, she nodded for him to take off. He ran away from them and Lewis jumped in Zoe's face.

"You're supposed to have my back out here, not some—"

"Some what? Some nigger? Some innocent guy?"

Lewis shook his head. "You better figure out whose side you're on or you're not going to make it."

"I'm not working with a dirty cop, and if that guy is telling the truth about what you're doing out here, then I'm going to the Internal Affairs Bureau."

"Oh, so you're a rat?"

"Call it what you want, but you can't use that badge to terrorize people." She strode off to the patrol car and Lewis knew that she was going to be trouble.

"Bitch," he muttered. "It's time to make you suffer like you did me."

Inside the house, Zach woke up and picked up his cell phone. Glancing down at the screen, he reread Zoe's message and still didn't understand it. What was she doing in DC, and why did she have to turn her phone off?

"Babe?" Chante said, her voice husky with sleep. "Are you all right?"

"Not really. I'm still trying to figure out what's going on with my sister." He set his phone on the nightstand. "I didn't mean to wake you."

"With all of your tossing and turning and your daughter's kicking, I wasn't sleeping anyway."

Zach inched closer to his wife and drew her into his arms. "Sorry about that, babe. I know you need your rest."

"Yes, because today is going to be my last day going into the office, and I'm not going to do a lot of working from home."

"I love the way that sounds. I guess that means I'm going to have to pamper you and start working from home as well."

Chante stroked his cheek. "Do you miss New York?"

"Sometimes, but not enough to leave you here while I'm there."

Chante sighed and rubbed her belly, which had expanded overnight—in her mind. "If you ever wanted to move back there, I'd be willing to compromise with you."

"What made you change your mind?"

Chante shrugged. "You don't seem as if you're really happy here."

"Darling, I'm happy wherever you are. I'm worried about Zoe. Something just hasn't been right with her lately, and my sister has been known to take risks."

"I get that vibe from her. But she's a detective, Zach."

"Zoe used to be a cop and she quit because she had a dirty partner. After she quit, she took on those cops. Dad and I wanted Zoe to come into the family business and have a nice safe desk job. Maybe we should've let her play with those military boys during Fleet Week so that she could've gotten all of this out of her system."

"Wait, what does Fleet Week have to do with anything?"

"Zoe wanted to go to Manhattan for Fleet Week when all the Marines and sailors come to the city."

"And you stopped her."

Zach laughed. "Locked her in the basement."

"Harsh!"

"And that probably turned Zoe into the hardcore feminist that she is now."

"You say that as if being a feminist is a bad thing," Chante said. "Your sister is probably saving the world and we'll never know about it. I think Zoe is really some sort of superhero."

"Whatever. Don't ever say that in front of her. She might believe it and start wearing a cape." Zach kissed Chante's cheek. "Should we go back to sleep or use this energy that we have for something else?"

"Sweetheart, I will have to make it up to you later because I'm so tired."

"Party pooper," he whispered as they both drifted off to sleep again.

Zoe couldn't sleep. She found herself walking around Carver's living room as the sun came up. He'd been sleeping ever since Kenneth left. But Zoe couldn't turn her mind off. She'd put her location out there and Singletary hadn't taken the bait. Did he know she was working closer to the FBI now and was on to him? What was he waiting for?

She headed for the kitchen and grabbed a bottle of water from the fridge. Gulping the cold liquid, she decided that she was tired of hiding. She was going to go back to New York and return to her normal life. If Singletary was waiting for her there, then she'd be ready.

"Did you sleep at all?" Carver's question startled her and she dropped the water bottle.

"No," she said as she kneeled down and picked up the bottle. Carver grabbed some paper towels to mop up the water.

"Zoe, whatever you're thinking, you shouldn't do it."

"You can read my mind now?"

"Yes, I can. Are you planning to go back to New York?"

Zoe leaned against the sink as Carver dumped the wet towels in the trash. "I appreciate what you and your team tried to do, but I can't keep depending on you guys. Especially when some of you don't even seem to think I'm worth the trouble."

"It doesn't matter what they think, Zoe. And Raymond obviously thinks you're worth it, since he is in New York trying to trace Singletary. But the most important thing is, I know you're worth it, and I'll be damned if I'm going to watch you risk your life because you think you have something to prove."

"I never said that I had something to prove. But I don't hide, and that is what this feels like. If he wants to get me, then I'm ready for him to come for me."

"And if he does come for you and you die?"

"Why do you think I can't take care of myself?"

"This man is dangerous, and even if you can take care of yourself, you don't know his plan. You don't know if he's going to have some little kid come up to you with a bomb in a box. Zoe, please. Let me help keep you safe. I can't lose you."

"And I can't keep hiding under your slacks! Had you told me the truth about what was going on when you came to my office that day, we could've come up with a plan and taken care of this."

Carver folded his arms across his chest. "When I showed up on your doorstep, you looked as if you wanted to kick me out of your space. Now, be honest with yourself—had I told you that someone wanted you dead and I was there to protect you, would you have listened?"

"Well, may—"

"I said be honest."

"No, but at least I would've known what was going on."

"And you could be dead right now. Zoe, you know

what I'm not going to do—apologize for what I've done—and if I had to do it again, I would. Get over it."

She shook her head. "That's why I'm going back to New York, because your attitude is pissing me off. You act like I should drop down on my knees and thank you for lying to me. Fuck you, Carver. Fuck you." Zoe stormed out of the kitchen and grabbed her bags. When she headed for the bathroom, Carver stopped her.

"Can we talk and not argue or place blame?" he asked.

"I don't have anything left to say to you."

"But I have plenty I need to say to you, Zoe." He led her to the sofa and she shot him a nasty look before sitting down.

Carver sighed and took her hand in his. Zoe slipped it out of his embrace. "Say what you have to say so that I can go."

"I know you think I have some savior complex, but that isn't what this is about. You know I love you and it would kill me if I lost you."

"You're dangerously close to that happening right now," Zoe murmured.

Carver gritted his teeth. "Just listen to what I have to say, please. I lost a woman I loved, and it nearly destroyed me. Monica and I served in the Marines together. We were both in intelligence with the rest of the Shadows. One night, we got into an argument about some of the risks she'd been taking in the war zone. She didn't appreciate what I said and went outside. Unfortunately, she walked right into a Taliban ambush and was killed instantly."

Zoe's mouth formed the shape of an O, but she didn't say anything. Carver stroked her arm. "I can't go through that again, and that's why I did this."

She rose to her feet and started pacing. "So, you are using me to replace the love you lost?"

Carver rolled his eyes. "No. Zoe, you aren't Monica. No one will ever be Monica, but I'm not going to watch you go out there and put your life in danger because you feel like you have something to prove."

"Like you said, I'm not Monica. I'm not walking out into a war zone and I'm not staying here while that man is hunting me like I'm some deer in the headlights."

"I'm not going to let you be his prey, and I need you to understand that!"

Zoe crossed over to him and punched him in his chest. "It's not your decision! Why don't you *understand* that?"

"Fine, you want to die. Then let's go to New York— blind, not knowing what's going on. But you aren't going alone. I don't give a damn how hard you want to fight me."

Chapter 28

Charlotte, North Carolina

A beam of sunlight woke Lewis up. He cursed himself for going to sleep when he knew he needed to be alert. Glancing over at the Harringtons' house, he smiled when he saw both cars were still in the garage. He looked at his watch and realized that he hadn't overslept, but he had missed his chance to see the couple wake up and do their early morning dance. Part of him almost didn't want to kidnap the wife, but Zoe had brought this hell on her brother when she ruined Lewis's marriage and his life.

Lewis wished he had a cup of coffee to rinse the sleep out of his system. But he knew he had to do this. He opened the door and crossed the street. He walked behind the garage and lay down on the ground. The ransom note was underneath his arm and he had his face covered with a bandana and a pair of sunglasses.

What he'd forgotten, though, had been his latex gloves. When Lewis realized that, he started to head to the car to grab them, but he heard the door open in the garage.

"I can't believe you're actually leaving before me," he heard the wife say.

"Early meeting to get rid of that warehouse property. It's a good thing."

Silence. Lewis figured they were kissing.

"Pizza for dinner?"

"Again?"

"Yes. Again. And fries, too."

"You pick it up, since I'm not sure how long this meeting is going to be."

"All right."

More silence. Probably more kissing.

"Love you," he heard the wife say.

"Love you, too. Now, you go get dressed."

Lewis held his breath as he heard a car crank up. He watched Zoe's brother back out of the garage, and as the car disappeared down the block, Lewis slithered like a snake on the ground and entered the garage. He dropped the note on the steps and turned the knob on the door leading into the house. Like most people living in the burbs, the garage door leading into the house was unlocked. Lewis smiled and walked over to the coffeepot. He dripped a few drops of GHB in the pot. He figured that she would come downstairs and fix herself a cup before heading to work.

Lewis listened for the shower to start. When he heard the water, he decided to take a look around the house. He stopped in the den as he looked at their wedding picture.

Standing on a beach, they looked like the happiest couple in the world. And Zach's wife was just beautiful.

The shower stopped and Lewis crossed back into the kitchen to sneak out of the house. He posted up in the garage and waited for the moment when he'd grab that woman. Because he didn't want Joe to interrupt him, he sent a quick text.

I'm in place.

Now, he just had to wait in silence.

Back in DC, Carver and Zoe walked to the boarding area at Union Station. She glanced at him, still trying to deal with what he'd told her about Monica. On one hand, she did feel for him. She had never lost to death a man she'd loved. But, on the other hand, she still felt some kind of way about his justification for keeping her in the dark about Singletary's plot because he'd watched Monica die.

"Am I going to get the silent treatment all the way to New York?"

Zoe rolled her eyes. "What's left to say?"

"That you understand. That you forgive me."

"I'm not there yet, and you're going to have to give me time."

"Will three and a half hours be enough time?" Carver smiled at her. "Zoe, we're going to have to figure out a plan together at least."

"Not right now, and I'm not sitting beside you." They

boarded the train and she headed to a seat in the back. Carver sat three rows in front of her.

About an hour into the train ride, Zoe walked over to Carver. "Mind if I sit?"

He shook his head and moved over to the empty seat next to him. Zoe took his seat. "How long were you and Monica together?"

"Five years. We met in basic and fell for each other."

"I thought that wasn't proper in the military?"

"Only if I'd been her commanding officer. We kept our relationship a secret for as long as we could, but my crew knew the truth. Raymond thought it was a bad idea for us to be together."

"I'm not surprised." Zoe rolled her eyes.

"And when I asked her to marry me, I told her she should leave the Marines, but she wasn't having it. We weren't ready to be married, but I thought getting her out of the Corps and out of danger would mean that we could build our lives together. Of course, Monica wasn't feeling that and she tossed my ring back in my face and told me to go fuck myself."

"Wow."

"Though we broke up, we were still in love, and I thought we'd have a chance after the war." Carver sighed. "But when she died, things changed."

"Changed how?"

"I shut myself off to love, took a lot of risks, because for a few years I wanted to die. Give everything to my country. The other Shadows had to get me back on track."

"Are you over her?" Zoe's voice was barely above a whisper.

"She's always going to have a place in my heart because she was my first love." He touched her chin and forced her to face him. "But you're not sleeping with a ghost."

She nodded. "I hear what you're saying, but what's changed about you and how you deal with women now?"

"Zoe, just know this. I love you and I want to protect you with everything in me. Maybe I went about this the wrong way, and I'm sorry, but I don't regret it, and if I had to do it over, I wouldn't change a thing. You may disagree with me, but at least you're still here to do that."

"All right," she said. "Maybe I have been acting like a jerk. But I just don't want you to think that I need a savior. I can take care of myself, and if you want to have my back, then that's fine. Just let me in on it. Don't keep secrets from me."

I'll never do it again. Do you want me to cue up Babyface?" Carver smiled and cleared his throat. Zoe covered his mouth with her hand.

"Don't even do that," she said. He licked her palm and she jerked away from him. "That was so nasty."

"Oh, please, when my tongue does that to you in other spaces, you don't mind at all." He wiggled his eyebrows and slipped his hand between her thighs.

Zoe couldn't even argue with him about that. "You need to stop." Leaning her head against his shoulder, Zoe felt as if she and Carver had a chance to move beyond this.

"If you say so."

"Oh, I know so," she said.

"I could demonstrate, but people might hear you screaming."

"There's always tonight," she said as she ran her hand across his cheek.

"I like the way you think, woman."

Zoe pulled her cell phone out of her purse and told Carver that she was going to check her voicemail at the office. "Since you're going to be watching my six, I guess I could get back to work."

"Yeah, because I'm sure the FBI is going to stop paying me to pay you now. And the cheating husbands of New York have had a break long enough."

Zoe rolled her eyes. "I investigate wives, too. Although, those cases are a little harder to crack because women are better at hiding things."

"Good to know."

Zoe pressed the code on her phone to access her voicemail and listened to the first fifteen messages. Insurance adjusters, clients asking when she'd return, a lawyer reminding her that she needed to testify at a divorce case next month, and then she heard a voice that sent chills down her spine.

"Zoe Harrington, you're a slippery bitch. Cost me millions of dollars, but I know you value family more than anything else. That's why I snatched your pretty little sister-in-law. If you ever want to see her alive, you're going to do exactly what I say. See you in North Carolina, bitch."

The phone slipped from her hand. "Zoe? What's wrong?"

"Singletary has Chante! We have to get off this train and get to Charlotte." Zoe rose to her feet and took off running for the doors. Carver followed her in vain as she grabbed the ticket attendant and begged him to get the conductor to stop the train.

"Ma'am, we can't do that."

"Zoe, calm down," Carver said. She whirled around and glared at him.

Pointing her index finger in his face, she roared, "No, you put my whole family in danger with this wild-goose chase of yours. If you'd just told me the truth about what was going on, we could've avoided this! You better get me off this train."

Carver flashed his FBI badge at the ticket agent. "We need to stop this train."

"What's going on?" the frazzled agent asked.

"We have a situation and we need to get off the train and get to North Carolina."

"Yes, sir," the agent said, and took off down the corridor. Zoe started to follow her, but Carver grabbed her arm.

"Zoe, stop."

She snatched away from him and pointed her index finger in his face again. "Carver, playing this game with you has put my family at risk, and now that murderous bastard has Chante."

"I had no idea that—"

"Because you didn't trust me with the truth. If anything happens to Chante, her blood is on your hands."

Charlotte, North Carolina

Chante banged her hand against the lid of the trunk, hoping someone would hear her. "Hello! Let me out!"

Silence.

She banged again until her hands were raw and her palms started to bleed. Chante didn't understand what was going on. She'd walked out of the house and felt a hand over her mouth, then everything went black. By the time she came to, Chante realized that she was in the trunk of her own car. She couldn't understand who would be after her. When she'd reached for the emergency trunk release, it didn't work, as if something was on the lid stopping it from opening.

Chante took a deep breath and said a silent prayer that she wouldn't die in the trunk of a car. Then she felt her baby move. There was no way in hell that she was going to let her child suffer.

"Let me out, please. Please, I'm pregnant. Please let me go."

Lewis would've felt sorry for Chante had she not been a Harrington. He wouldn't have kept a pregnant woman in the trunk of a car, but Zoe needed to know that her sister-in-law was in danger. He was about to take one of the boulders off the back of the trunk and give her some air, but Singletary walked over.

"My man! Good job."

Lewis nodded. "Thanks."

"She still crying and banging on the trunk?" Joe laughed, then walked over to the car and slammed his hand against the trunk lid. "Don't worry, you won't be in here much longer. I'm going to take real good care of you."

"Please! Why are you doing this to me?"

"You married into the wrong family," he said.

She started banging again. "Please, I can't breathe and I'm pregnant! Let me out."

Lewis leaned in to Singletary. "We can tie her up and let her breathe."

"Doesn't matter what we do, the bitch is going to die anyway." Joe slapped the lid again. "I left Zoe a message, but she hasn't called yet. You better hope your sister-in-law steps up."

"Don't keep me in here," Chante said. "I can't breathe and my baby—"

"Shut up. Shut up!"

Zach was pissed. His day had gone from bad to worse in the span of six hours. First, his morning appointment had been a no-show. He'd waited for the man for two hours. And when it became clear that he wasn't coming, Zach left and headed to Dunkin' Donuts to grab some apple fritters. As he drove to the doughnut shop, some idiot rear-ended him.

Waiting for the police and getting a rental car took up most of the morning and half the afternoon. And Zach still didn't get his sweet treat. He called Chante to see if she'd left the office and gone home yet.

Voicemail.

"Babe, I hope you're on your way home and your day was better than mine. I'm going to stop by the grocery store and get some of those cupcakes you love." He ended the call and headed to the store.

Things were starting to look up for Zach as the lines in the grocery store were short and the buttercream cupcakes he and Chante enjoyed were readily available. He started to get a bottle of wine, but then he remembered he'd be the only one drinking it. Zach grabbed two bottles of craft beer instead, because after the day he'd had, he needed a drink.

While standing in line to check out, Zach's phone rang. He answered the phone, hoping it was Chante.

"Hey, babe."

"Zach," Zoe said. "Where are you?"

"Zoe? What's wrong, you sound weird."

"Is Chante with you? Have you talked to her?"

"Zoe, what in the hell is going on? Chante is at the office. I just called her and left her a voicemail message. She's starting maternity leave today."

"Zach, listen to me. Chante has been kidnapped."

"What are you talking about? Who would want to . . . How do you know?"

She sighed into the phone and told her twin that she was about two hours away from Charlotte and he needed to get home.

"Zoe, tell me what the hell is going on. Who has my wife? Does this have something to do with that psycho Robert Montgomery?"

"No, this isn't about her ex, Robert. It's much worse. Zach, just wait for Carver and me. Okay?"

"Zoe, tell me what the hell is going on!"

"I'll tell you everything when we get to your house."

Zach set the cupcakes and beer down on the edge of

the register's conveyer belt and ran out of the store. Speeding to his house, Zach was confused about what to do. Did he call the police and report his wife missing? What if Zoe was wrong? *Please let Zoe be wrong. I can't lose Chante and our baby.*

When Zach arrived home, he saw that the garage door was open and Chante's car was missing. Something was wrong. They always closed the garage door because the lock on the door leading inside was broken. He wanted to punch himself in the face for not getting it fixed.

But their neighborhood was safe; at least he thought it was. Pulling into the driveway, he noticed an envelope on the step. Zach didn't even turn the car off as he jumped out.

Maybe Chante had left him a note or something. Ripping the envelope open, Zach read the note as fear ran up and down his spine. Chante had been kidnapped, and they wanted three hundred thousand dollars.

"Fuck! Fuck! Fuck!" Zach pulled out his phone and called his sister back.

"Zach, are you at home?"

"Yes. And there's a ransom note."

"What does it say?"

"That Chante's going to die if I don't get them three hundred thousand dollars in twenty-four hours. There's a number at the bottom. I'm calling—"

"No. Don't do anything until we get there."

"Zoe, my wife and child could be dead. I don't have time to waste."

"You and Chante aren't the target. I am. A man named

Joseph Singletary is behind this and he wants to kill me, not Chante."

"Who is this man, and am I supposed to feel better that someone wants to kill you?"

Zoe sighed. "Zach, trust me—no one is dying—except Joe."

Zach heard a voice telling Zoe to slow down.

"Should I call the police?"

"Not yet," she said.

Zach released a frustrated breath. "How much longer before you get here?"

"Just wait for me."

Zoe hung up with her brother and turned to Carver. "What are we going to do?"

"The Shadows are coming and we have a team of FBI agents who recover hostages coming as well. We're going to save Chante, but, Zoe, you've got to calm down and you're going to have to let us do our job."

She was about to say something when her cell phone rang, showing a blocked number.

"Hello?"

Loud screaming pierced her ear. "Chante, are you okay?"

"Not for long," Singletary barked. "It's a shame that you're going to take another wife from your brother."

"Why don't you let her go? Chante has nothing to do with this."

"I know. And had you kept your nose on your face and not in my business, this wouldn't be happening."

"What do you want from me?"

"Do you know how much money you cost me?"

"No, I don't, and I really don't give a fuck. Let my sister-in-law go!"

"You have a mouth on you, bitch. You're not in charge here, I am!"

"Fine, you're in charge."

"Wait for my instructions, and you better do exactly as I say."

"Yes, sir," she snapped. The line went dead and Zoe banged her hand against the steering wheel. "I'm going to kill him."

"Zoe, this is what he wants. We have to come up with a plan and make sure we nail him before—"

"You didn't hear her screaming. She's pregnant, she's scared, and there's no telling what he's doing to her."

"We're going to save her, Zoe."

"If we don't, Carver, I will never forgive you." Zoe looked forward, trying to keep her fear and anger from boiling over. Carver reached out to her, but she put both hands on the steering wheel.

"Can we talk about this?"

"What's left to say? It was one thing when I was the only person at risk, but now Chante is in the clutches of this thug who doesn't even give a damn about human life."

"That's why I have the Shadows in place. Kenneth is already at your brother's house analyzing the ransom note."

Zoe was about to get into how all of this could've been avoided had he been honest about what was going on, but she didn't want to have the same argument again. She had to be laser focused on finding Chante before Singletary killed her. Deep down, she knew that no matter what she did, Singletary was planning to kill Chante. And she couldn't let that happen.

The rest of the ride to Charlotte was in total silence. When they pulled up to Zach and Chante's, Zoe jumped out of the car and walked in the open front door. "Zach!" she called out.

"In the kitchen."

Zoe walked into the kitchen and ignored the other people around her twin. She wrapped her arms around him. "I'm sorry. I'm so sorry."

"It's not your fault," he said as he took a step back from her.

"Zoe," Kenneth said as he crossed over to her. "We dusted the place for fingerprints and we got a hit on your former partner, Lewis Martinez."

"That son of a bitch! So, he kidnapped Chante for Singletary."

"We don't—"

"He called me on the way here and said he had her." She looked at Zach and chose her next words carefully. "I heard her."

"What did she say?" Kenneth asked.

"Is she hurt?" Zach asked.

Zoe took a deep breath. She couldn't tell her brother the torment and terror she heard in Chante's screams. Carver walked in and nodded toward Kenneth. "Let's talk in the back."

"What number did he call you from?" one of the FBI agents asked.

"It was a blocked number." Zoe handed over her phone. "He's supposed to be calling back with instructions."

"Was Chante all right?" Zach asked again.

"I think so," Zoe said. She hated lying to her brother, but what choice did she have?

He glared at her. "Don't lie to me." Then he turned to the FBI agent. "What did you find out about the number on this note?"

"It's a throwaway cell phone, Mr. Harrington."

Zach muttered curse words that would make a sailor blush. Zoe grabbed her brother's arm. "Let me get you a drink or something."

Zach snatched away from his sister. "I don't want a drink, I want my wife back. How did this happen?"

"Natalie."

"What?"

Zoe told him how Natalie was working with Singletary during her time as the Harlem Madam. After Natalie had gotten Zoe arrested, Zoe started investigating the trafficking ring and uncovered Natalie's connection to Singletary. She'd given most of her findings to the FBI. When Natalie found out that she was going down for all of Singletary's sins, she started talking. Then the heat was on him and his nationwide organization. Natalie had been sentenced and was going to cooperate with the FBI, but once Singletary got a mole inside the unit of the FBI investigating him, he started eliminating people.

"So, Natalie's dead?"

Zoe nodded. "As well as two FBI agents. I'm next on his list."

"This makes no sense to me. If the FBI knew this was going on, why weren't you warned?"

Kenneth and Carver walked into the kitchen and Zoe

nodded toward Carver. "I'll let him tell it." She crossed over to the refrigerator and grabbed a bottle of water. As much as she wanted to pretend that she wasn't going to have a problem working with Carver, she was pissed. She wanted to punch him in his face for putting her brother through all of this.

"What is she talking about?" Zach asked as he looked from Zoe to Carver.

Carver cleared his throat. "We had intel that Singletary was targeting Zoe, so we took her out of New York and tried to apprehend him while Zoe was out of his reach."

Zach crossed over to Carver. "I'm about sick of you and your meddling in my fucking life. Now you're the reason my wife is in the clutches of some psychopath!" Without warning, Zach hauled off and punched Carver in the face. Carver stumbled backward and Kenneth took a step toward Zach. Zoe blocked the big man from touching her twin.

"You know he deserved it."

Sarah and Ray walked into the kitchen and surveyed the tense scene. Zach was shaking his hand and Carver was stroking his sore jaw.

"Can everyone take a breath and calm down? Fighting in here isn't going to save Chante," Sarah said.

Zoe was about to respond when her cell phone rang. Blocked number. It was him. She waved for everyone to be quiet as she answered the phone.

"Hello?"

"You must not care about Chante."

"What are you talking about?"

"You have a bunch of FBI agents at your brother's

house. Bad idea. You said this is between you and me, but you got all of these people in our business. *Tsk, tsk.*"

Zoe felt nuclear anger building inside her. "I'm tired of your bullshit. What do you want?"

Sarah shook her head frantically at Zoe and mouthed, "Don't engage with him. Listen what he has to say."

Zoe sighed and rolled her eyes. "Joe, what do you want me to do? You're in charge."

"Whoever is coaching you is smart. You need to come see me alone. So, tell them that you're taking out the trash and wheel the green bin to the curb. Once you do that, I'll know that you're ready to play ball."

"Then what?"

"Wait and see."

"How is Chante? I want to speak to her to know that she's all right."

"She's alive." Joe laughed. "For now."

"Prove it."

"I don't have to prove a damned thing to you. But, since I'm a gentleman, I'll let you speak to her."

A beat passed and Zoe heard Chante's voice. "Zoe. Zoe, please do what they say. Tell Zach I love him."

"Chante, where are you?"

The line went dead and Zoe shoved her phone in her pocket. Without a word, she walked outside and pushed the trash can to the curb like Joe told her to do. Looking around the area, she searched for signs that Joe was watching the house. There were a lot of places where he could be hiding. The house across the street was for sale, there was an empty house catty-corner from Zach's place. She figured that was the spot. It looked as if you would have a clear view of the house from that place. She wondered if Joe was cruel enough to have Chante that close to her home. *He's a psycho, it's possible. He's probably making her watch everything that's going on right now.*

"Zoe?" Zach said, putting his hand on her shoulder. "What are you doing out here?"

"Thinking. Singletary is a ticking time bomb. He's a psycho and I'm scared."

"But all of those people in the house say that we can get Chante back. You think we can't?"

"I didn't say that. I just said—"

"Zoe, don't lie to me. What are the chances of me seeing my wife alive?"

She placed her hands on his shoulders. "She's going to come home and wrap her arms around you. Just wait." Zoe kissed her brother on the cheek and headed back into the house.

Chapter 29

Carver stroked his cheek as he watched Zoe and Zach talking on the curb.

"He doesn't like you much, huh?" Kenneth asked.

"Shut up."

"He clocked you pretty hard." Kenneth laughed. "I know he's upset, but that seemed really personal."

"I'm not going to sit here and joke with you right now. I have to figure out what the twin summit is out there."

Raymond walked up and said, "That ransom note was from Lewis. The fool sweated on the envelope."

"Really." Carver folded his arms across his chest. "So, Zoe has two people out there looking to kill her and we don't know what direction they're going to be coming from."

"We will if we can control the situation. Zach has to call the number on the letter, and we need to trace the call."

Carver blew a frustrated breath. "Raymond, go out there and talk to them."

"You really think that's wise?" Sarah asked. "I'll go."

Carver nodded, then turned to Ray and Ken. "What's the plan?"

"Once we draw Lewis out, he's going to lead us back to where he and Singletary are keeping Chante. But everybody has to be on the same page. They're watching us," Raymond said. "We need to clear the agents out of here."

Kenneth nodded and headed for the living room, where the other agents were staged. Carver was about to walk out to where Zach and Zoe were standing when Raymond grabbed his shoulder.

"Are you sure you can handle this?"

"Can we not start this again?"

Ray folded his arms across his chest. "Let's see, you have a woman standing out there mad as hell because you tried to play Captain Save—"

"This is not the same situation, and I wish you would stop comparing Zoe and Monica."

"I'm not comparing them; it's you. Don't try to do something that's going to lead you down a road where that woman is going to hate you."

"At least she will be alive. Zoe has a point. Had I trusted her with the truth, we might not be here."

Ray shook his head. "So, at the end of the day, if you save her sister-in-law, she tells you to go to hell. You're putting everything on the line and—"

"I'm doing my job, and as long as we rescue Chante and keep Zoe alive, that's all that matters. Now, let's get to work."

Raymond nodded and walked over to the kitchen table to set up his laptop. Carver didn't want to think about what his friend had said, but the truth was, he knew at the end of all of this he could lose Zoe. Could he really live with that?

"Why would I call this man?" Zach snapped at Sarah. Zoe touched her brother's arm.

"Let's go inside," Zoe said. "Sarah knows what she's doing."

Zach glared at the women. "Whatever it takes to get my wife back. But your fellow agents told me not to pay any money or call this man."

"That's what the FBI is supposed to tell you. But Singletary and his accomplice aren't playing by the rules. They don't want your money, they want your sister."

Zoe swallowed. "And we're going to give them what they want."

"No!" Zach shook his head. "I'm not losing you to save Chante."

"Mr. Harrington," Sarah said. "As long as the Shadows are here, you're not losing anyone. Now, I need you to shake hands with the agents who are leaving your house, then we're going to get down to finding Chante."

Zoe's phone rang as Zach and Sarah headed inside. "Hello?"

"I see you cleared everyone out. Good job," Singletary said, clearly unaware the Shadows were still in place. "I don't want to kill your sister-in-law, but you're going to make that happen if you don't do what I say."

"I'm listening."

"There's a lake up near a Hilton hotel off of Harris

Boulevard. Be there in an hour and you better come alone."

"Are you bringing Chante?"

"Who's in charge? You just be there."

Before Zoe could say another word, the line went dead. Zach turned around and locked eyes with his sister.

"What was that about?" he asked.

She shook her head and followed him and Sarah inside. Raymond waved them over to the kitchen table.

"If we're going to extract Chante, we have to make the writer of this note think he's going to get the money he's asking for," Raymond said.

Zoe rolled her eyes. "And that's probably the most dangerous thing you can do."

Raymond looked up at her. "How many hostages have you saved?"

"Three," Zoe snapped.

Carver walked into the kitchen with bottles of water for everyone. He handed one to Sarah, but when he walked over to Zoe, she turned her back to him.

"Fine," Raymond said. "You're not a rookie, but these people don't want to hurt Chante. Zoe, they want to kill you."

"I'm not trading my sister for my wife," Zach exclaimed.

"That's understandable, but if you want to save your wife, then you're going to listen to me." Raymond shot a frosty glance in Zoe's direction. "We know who has your wife and we know that this is about something else. Believe me, I don't want to see your wife hurt."

"She's pregnant," Zoe said. "That's why we have to

bring her home, no matter what." She looked up and locked eyes with Carver. "If I have to give Singletary and Lewis a pound of flesh to save my sister-in-law and my unborn niece or nephew, then I will."

"It's not going to happen like that. We're going to bring her home safe and sound," Carver said.

"Excuse me if I don't trust that you're going to be the one to save my wife," Zach snapped. "But I know one thing is for certain, you're not using my sister as bait."

"Don't I get a say in this?" Zoe asked.

"No," Zach and Carver said in concert. She rolled her eyes and walked outside on the back patio. Leaning on the railing, she looked out over the quiet neighborhood and prayed that Chante wasn't being hurt by her captors. Just as she was about to return inside, her cell phone rang. Blocked number. It was Singletary.

"Hello?"

"Tell your brother that I'm serious about giving him his wife back, as long as you play along."

Zoe gritted her teeth but didn't respond right away. "How do I play along?"

"Well, I want my revenge, and that ends with you in a grave."

Son of a bitch, she thought.

"You have one hour to show up at the lake. Alone." The line went dead and Zoe wanted to toss her phone across the yard.

"What's going on, Zoe?" Carver asked. His voice startled her, because she hadn't even noticed that he'd come outside.

"Where did you come from? I thought you-all were in there brainstorming."

"Zoe, that was Singletary, wasn't it? He keeps calling you, and I know you're going to do something reckless."

"Like you did?"

"We're going to work up a plan, but you have to let us, and be honest about those calls."

She folded her arms across her chest. "What's the plan?"

"That ransom note didn't come from Singletary," Carver said. "And if we're going to bring your sister-in-law home alive, then we have to follow this lead."

"What if that note is just to throw us off track? Why would he leave a note and continue to call me?"

"Your former partner's DNA was found on the envelope from a drop of sweat."

Zoe balled her hands into fists. "That bastard. If anything happens to Chante because of Lewis, I hope you can keep me out of prison."

"Zoe, you can't go after these men alone."

She pointed her finger in his face. "I shouldn't have to, but I'm not going to let my brother down."

"I understand that. How do you think he's going to feel if you don't make it home with his wife? What did Singletary say?"

Zoe looked away from him and stroked her forehead. "He's taunting me. Telling me that he wants me dead and whatnot."

"Has he given you a clue as to where he is?"

She shook her head. "I need to take a drive. Where are the keys to the car?"

"Zoe, where are you going?"

"I just need to think and I need some quiet. Sitting around here feeling useless is driving me crazy."

She saw the suspicion in his eyes as he turned and walked away. Zoe didn't care. Her phone chimed, indicating that she had a text message. Blocked number.

Tick-tock.

Zoe walked into the house and stealthily grabbed the key to Zach's rental car while the Shadows and Zach huddled around Raymond's computer. Backing out of the house and into the garage, Zoe got into the car and peeled out of the driveway. She didn't have time to waste.

Zach looked up at Carver as Kenneth set up the phone call to the number on the ransom note.

"Where's Zoe?"

"She was on the patio."

Raymond shook his head. "She's not out there."

Carver headed for the garage and swore when he saw that Zach's car was missing. "Zoe's gone."

Zach leapt from his seat and ran out to the garage. "How did you let her walk out of here without being noticed?"

Carver pulled his cell phone out of his pocket and dialed Zoe's number. His call went unanswered. "Shit," he muttered. Carver shoved his phone into his pocket and returned inside.

"Zach, is there GPS on your car?"

"It's a rental. I don't know."

Raymond snapped his fingers. "It has GPS. Where did you rent it from?"

Zach told him the name of the rental car company

and Raymond quickly hacked into the company's database.

"Looks like she's heading down Harris Boulevard," he said.

Carver grabbed his keys and told Ray to text him the directions. "I'm going with you," Zach said.

"No." Carver threw his hand out. "You need to stay here and make that phone call. I'm not going to let anything happen to Zoe." He dashed out of the house before Zach could reply. Speeding down the street, Carver prayed that he would reach her and could stop her from doing whatever she was about to do.

Lewis stroked Chante's forehead as she slept. She'd been crying and screaming so much that Lewis spiked her water to calm her down. He hated to see a pretty woman cry. She kept saying she was pregnant, but Lewis found that hard to believe. Her body was svelte and toned. When his wife was pregnant, she'd gained ten pounds a month. He'd still loved her and thought she looked beautiful with the extra weight. Lewis placed a hand on Chante's stomach. He felt her flinch.

"It's okay," he whispered. "Not going to hurt you, yet."

Chante's eyes fluttered open. "Where am I?" Her voice was thick and groggy.

"You're here, where you need to be."

"Why are you doing this to me?"

Lewis pushed her hair back and smiled sardonically at her. "This isn't even about you, babe. You just married into the wrong family."

"Please let me go. I'm pregnant and my baby didn't hurt you. I don't even know you."

"You'll get to know me very well if your husband doesn't pay."

Chante sighed and tried to sit up, but she couldn't move. "Can I sit up?"

"Are you going to be a good girl and be quiet?"

She nodded and Lewis helped her sit up. Chante wished she had the strength to fight this man and run out of the warehouse. She glanced around to see if she could get an idea as to where she was.

"Did Robert Montgomery have you do this to me?"

"Who?"

"What happened, you two shared a cell and he told you to ruin my life?"

"I've never been to prison, sweetheart."

"Then why me?" Chante coughed and felt as if she was about to vomit.

"Because your sister-in-law ruined my life."

"Zoe?"

Lewis nodded and handed Chante an untainted bottle of water. She opened it and took a swig.

"She made me lose my wife, my child, my career, and my pension. Did she really think she was going to get away scot-free?" Lewis laughed. "Not going down like that."

"Please let me go. I'm sure Zoe didn't mean to—"

"Fuck that." Lewis slammed his hand on the wooden slab underneath Chante. She winced and inched away from him.

Lewis rose to his feet and paced back and forth like

a madman. "She ruined me. Stole what was important to me."

"What does that have to do with me?"

"You're all she has. Sorry that you have to pay the price, beautiful."

Tears welled up in Chante's eyes. She could read between the lines. Even if Zoe brought him the ransom money, she was going to die.

Chapter 30

Zoe realized that she hadn't heard from Joe. Pounding the steering wheel as she parked in the hotel parking lot, she bowed her head and said a prayer.

"God, please let me save Chante. Zach can't take this heartache." She got out of the car and walked toward the lake. The area was crowded with couples holding hands, families walking dogs and eating ice cream cones. She couldn't understand why Singletary chose this spot. Especially if his plan was to kill her and get away scot-free.

"Zoe Harrington. Glad to see you can follow instructions." Turning around, she looked into the face of evil. Seeing Joe Singletary in person didn't leave a great impression.

Bearded and portly, he looked like any geek off the street trying to be trendy. Zoe narrowed her eyes at him. "Where's Chante?" She slowly moved her hand to the waistband of her jeans, where she'd hidden her .22 caliber pistol.

"You think I'm just going to hand her over to you

because you asked?" He laughed, then inched closer to Zoe until he stood in her face. "You're going to have to suffer first. I suffered because of you and as they say, turnabout is fair play."

"What do you want from me? You want me to apologize for helping little girls avoid you?"

He gripped Zoe's cheeks. "You talk too damned much, and that mouth has cost me millions."

She kneed him in his nuts and then pushed him on the ground. With lightning-fast reflexes, Zoe pulled her gun out and pointed it at Singletary.

"And I'm not sorry, you bastard. Where is my sister-in-law?"

"Kill me and you'll never find her. You have a lot of enemies, and I have your biggest holding her hostage." He spit at her and Zoe kicked him in his privates.

"Where is she?"

"People are watching you. The cops will be here soon and you're going to jail. You're the one with the gun."

"I'm about to use it." She cocked the revolver. "Where is Chante?"

"Shoot me and you will never know where she is. Can you live with that? Knowing that you're the reason both of your brother's wives died?"

Zoe's hand trembled as his words weighed on her. "I should kill you right now and let the FBI find Chante."

"Should? Bitch, if you're going to do it, then pull the trigger." Zoe's finger hovered around the trigger and Joe kicked her ankle, knocking her down. Zoe gripped the gun as she fell and fired off a shot. The crowd near them started screaming and running. In the chaos, Joe was able to gain the upper hand on Zoe and kick the gun away from her.

"Ooh, you should've used it when you had the chance. Now, you have these people running for their lives." He stomped on her wrist and Zoe howled in pain. Joe leaned down and grabbed her hair, then slammed her head into the ground. "You're a worthless bitch!"

Everything went black.

Swirling blue lights and police sirens greeted Carver as he pulled up to the lake. Raymond had sent him the coordinates of where the car was parked. Fear trickled down his spine like ice water. Had something happened to Zoe? Was he too late to save her? Hopping out of the car, he pulled out his FBI badge and showed it to the uniformed officers pulling out the yellow crime scene tape.

"What happened here?"

"Reports of a shooting. Why would the FBI care?"

"We've been tracking a suspect who was in this area, and if he's involved, then we have serious problems."

The other officer pressed his radio and called for his supervisor. "We got the Feds out here asking about the shooting. Said a suspect they were tracking might be involved. Ten-four." The man turned to Carver. "My sergeant is on her way."

"I need to get to the crime scene, I don't have time to wait." Carver took a step forward and the officer tried to stop him.

"FBI or not, we can't let you on our crime scene until our supervisor says so."

"Listen, this is linked to a kidnapping, and time is of the essence. I need to get past."

"Why haven't we been called in to help?"

"So, you want to have a fucking pissing contest now?" Carver pushed his way through and bounded to the spot near the lake where the crime scene markers were. A woman in uniform approached him. "You can't be here."

Carver pulled out his FBI badge. "This shooting is related to a kidnapping we're investigating, and I need to know what happened out here."

"This is the first I'm hearing about a kidnapping. We're investigating a shooting."

"And who's your suspect?" Carver narrowed his eyes and fought back the urge to tell this woman where she could go and how she could get there.

"We're investigating that."

Carver pulled out his cell phone and showed her a picture of Joseph Singletary. "This is who you need to look for. Joseph Singletary. He's probably trafficking women out of your city right now and you know nothing about it."

"Then why haven't we heard about this man from the FBI?"

"I'm not going to sit here and explain things to you when we have two women who are in danger!"

She folded her arms across her chest and glared at Carver. "What do you need?"

"Do you have a description of the suspect from the shooting?"

"From what the witnesses said, the shooter was a woman. She seemed to know the man who wrested the gun away from her."

"What did they look like?" Carver tried to keep his voice even. The officer pulled out her cell phone.

"A witness sent me this picture."

Carver winced when he saw Zoe on the ground and Singletary on top of her.

"So," the officer began, "looks like this was a domestic—"

"That is Joseph Singletary and that woman is in danger. You need to put out an APB right now."

"Are you sure about this?"

"*Yes!*" Carver nearly shouted. "Where did they go? Are there cameras out here?"

The woman nodded and pointed Carver in the direction of her lieutenant. "He's getting the video from the surveillance cameras. Lieutenant Williams! This is   "

"FBI Agent Carver Banks," Carver said as he flashed his badge again. "We need an all-points bulletin on Joe Singletary and Zoe Harrington. She's the woman he assaulted."

"Done," Williams said. "Why is the FBI involved in this?"

"We've been tracking this suspect for a while and he's kidnapped Chante Harrington."

"What do we need to do?"

Carver gritted his teeth. "Stay out of my way." He pulled out his phone and called Sarah. "Joe has Zoe."

* * *

Zoe opened her eyes and found her arms and legs bound together. She'd been stripped down to her underwear and left in a dark room. She tried to find something that could identify where she was as she glanced around. All she saw was emptiness. She regretted underestimating how brutal Singletary was. She should've shot his ass. But he did have the upper hand because he knew where Chante was. Killing him would've meant that Chante was lost and possibly dead. The door opened and Zoe locked eyes with Lewis Martinez, her former partner.

"Look at you." He smiled and Zoe's blood ran cold.

"Bastard," she muttered.

Lewis spat in her face. "I can't wait to watch you die."

"Where is Chante? You and Singletary have what you want, now let her go."

"Your sister-in-law is a sweet piece of ass. I hope she has a nice, healthy baby." Zoe wiggled in her constraints. Had she been free, she would've punched him in the face with all her might. "If you laid a hand on her . . ."

"What are you going to do?" Lewis snorted. "You think you can do something? I should kill you right now. But it will be better to make you suffer first." Lewis kicked Zoe in her stomach. She closed her eyes as the pain vibrated through her body.

"You're not even worth this. Joe should've just tossed you in the lake."

"Why don't you man up and do it yourself?"

Lewis spat on her again. "Don't worry, I'm going to make you suffer; just like you ruined my life."

"You ruined your own worthless life!"

Lewis grabbed a chunk of Zoe's hair and slammed her head against the floor. "I'm going to show you worthless."

"Leave her alone," Joe said from the darkened doorway. "I didn't bring her here to be your punching bag. Whatever happens to her happens because of me."

"Where is Chante and why haven't you let her go? You wanted me and you got me. She has nothing to do with this!"

Joe shrugged as he walked over to Zoe and kneeled over her. "You keep thinking that you can make demands, sweetheart. Maybe I'm going to send you and your sister-in-law back to your brother in pieces." He pulled out a knife and ran the blade down Zoe's cheek. Blood trickled from the small cut, and Zoe closed her eyes. As he moved the blade lower, her body tensed.

"I'm going to untie you for now. You're going to be a good girl and stay put, right? The next cut is going to be deeper."

Zoe lay still as he unbound her, but her mind was working overtime. She had to find a way out of this hellhole. If Singletary untied her, he did it for a reason. She was going to be sure that he regretted it.

Carver tried to keep his poker face as he walked into Zach's house. How was he going to tell this man that his sister was now missing? Not only missing, but in the clutches of two men who wanted to kill her. He walked into the kitchen and Sarah motioned for him to join her at the table and be quiet.

"And my wife is unharmed," Carver heard Zach say. "Fine, I will bring the money alone. It will be in a box as you requested." Zach sighed but continued talking. "I want to speak to my wife."

Kenneth nodded at Zach and held up two fingers. Sarah grabbed a notepad and wrote: *We know where Chante is now. Got a signal from the phone. Sending an extraction team with Zach. Where is Zoe?*

He wrote back: *Missing. Singletary has her. Shooting at the lake and the police issued an APB.*

"Fuck," she mouthed.

Raymond walked out of the kitchen as he whispered into his cell phone.

Carver wondered if Zoe and Chante were in the same place. He sprinted toward Ray and grabbed his shoulder. "Joe grabbed Zoe."

"What? I told you to keep an eye on that girl. Where is she?"

"Don't know. The car is at the lake. Her cell phone is off and I have no idea what Singletary is driving."

"Locals out there looking?"

Carver nodded.

"This is a cluster. You know that, right?"

"I know, but I'm not going to lose her."

"Lose who?" Zach asked from behind them. "Is there something y'all not telling me?"

Carver started to shake his head and keep the truth from Zach, but Ray spoke up.

"Your hotheaded sister is missing."

"What?"

"The police are looking for her, and I think she may be with Chante."

Zach palmed his face and started pacing. "How did you let this happen?" He grabbed Carver by the throat. "You keep putting the women in my life in danger. I swear to God, if you—"

Ray pushed Zach off Carver. "Listen! We're all on the same team."

"That's my family out there! My wife and my sister. This isn't about some goddamn team." Zach gave Ray a shove and stormed outside.

"Hotheadedness runs in the family, huh?" Ray said.

"Don't do that. His wife and his sister are out there with that maniac."

"The team is ready to go. How are we going forward with this?"

"I'm going with you. If Zoe is there, we have to save her and Chante."

Zoe found a sharp stick and placed it underneath the pallet where she'd been tied up. She couldn't wait for Joe or Lewis to come inside and try to touch her again. She had to play the role of being afraid. Walking to the door, she heard a phone ring. Then Lewis started talking.

"No cops, or I will kill your wife. I want the money in a box and the bills had better not be marked."

So this is about money? she thought as she placed her hand on the doorknob. It was locked. When she heard Lewis end the call, she walked over to the pallet where she'd hidden the stick.

Gripping the stick, she hoped he would come inside. When he didn't, she took the stick and walked over to the door to listen for any activity on the other side. She heard Chante's muffled voice and said a silent prayer of thanks, because Chante was still alive. But was she safe? Zoe shook the handle, hoping the lock on the door would wiggle loose. *If that slimy bastard hurts Chante!*

Just as she was about to beat the knob until it fell off, the door opened.

"Thought you agreed to be a good girl and stay put." Joe took a step toward Zoe and she cracked him over the head with the stick. Then she jabbed the sharp end in his eye. He fell to his knees, howling in pain. Zoe took another swing at his head and the blow knocked him backward.

She kicked him in the groin, then stomped on his belly. "You sick bastard!" Zoe took the stick and crashed it across his forehead. She didn't stop until she felt his blood splash on her face. Looking at his motionless body, she gave him a shot to his rib cage to see if he would move. He didn't, and she searched his pockets for his cell phone. Finding it, she was about to call Carver when she heard a gun cock behind her head.

"I told him he should've put you out of your misery," Lewis hissed. "Get up, slowly."

Zoe lifted her hands above her head as she rose to her feet slowly. "Lewis, you don't have to do this. Just take the money and run."

"The money is not enough, bitch. I'm taking the money and your life. Look at me. When I shoot you, I want to see how scared you are."

Zoe sighed and slowly turned around. "Just do it. If you're going to shoot me, then do it." She lifted her chin and locked eyes with him.

Lewis fingered the trigger, and then a loud explosion boomed behind them. Zoe ducked and threw herself at Lewis's knees. He fell to the ground and the gun went off.

"Shots fired, shots fired!" Zoe heard a voice exclaim. Three men in black SWAT uniforms rushed into the room and pointed long rifles at them. Zoe backed up and threw her hands up. One of the officers rushed to her side and wrapped his flack jacket around her shoulders. "Ma'am, are you all right?"

"My sister-in-law, Chante Harrington, is she okay?"

"Yes, we found her in the next room, but you're the one covered in blood." He helped Zoe to her feet and led her out of the room while the other officers restrained Lewis and tended to Joe. She shot him an evil glare and forced herself not to spit in his face.

Chapter 31

Carver ran toward the SWAT officer walking with Zoe. "Zoe! Zoe!" He drew her into his arms and she collapsed.

"Get an ambulance!" Carver yelled, noticing all of the blood covering Zoe.

"There's one waiting outside, Agent Banks," the officer said.

Carver rushed outside and handed Zoe over to the paramedics. "Has she lost a lot of blood?" he asked as the medic began examining Zoe.

"Sir, please step back."

"I have to know if she's all right." Carver's voice wavered. Zach crossed over to them.

"Zoe!"

"Gentlemen, I need to examine her, and neither of you are allowing me to do that."

Carver turned to Zach. "How is Chante?"

"Fine, no thanks to you. All of this shit could've been avoided if you would've been honest with Zoe. You better pray to every God you can think of that Zoe wakes up and Chante doesn't lose our baby." Zach stalked away from him and returned to his wife's side. The paramedics were loading Zoe on the ambulance and Carver hopped on with them. Much of the blood that had scared him had been wiped away, but he saw the wound on her face.

"How is she?"

"Stable. The blood wasn't hers. Looks like your lady beat the hell out of somebody today."

Carver stroked her hand, wanting her to wake up so that he could see those sparkling eyes. He wanted to tell her that he was sorry and should've told her the truth from the beginning.

Zoe felt a soft touch on her shoulder. Opening her eyes, she smiled at her father. "Daddy."

"Baby girl, you know a hard head makes a soft bottom. You gave everyone a scare."

"Well, I didn't mean to, but I had to help save Chante and the baby."

"By getting yourself killed?" He smiled and his face lit up like a bright star. "You're going to have to listen sometimes. Especially to Carver. He loves you."

"Daddy. Don't go."

"You're going to be fine, and I don't have to stay and look after you. You can take care of yourself, and you got someone who is going to always have your back, if you let him."

"Daddy."

Zoe took a deep breath and her eyes fluttered open. The first face she saw was Carver's.

"Zoe," he whispered. He stroked her cheek and a tear ran down his cheek.

"C—"

"Shh," he said as he brought his finger to her lips. "Don't talk. Rest."

She closed her eyes, just as Carver leaned in and said, "I love you, Zoe."

The next time Zoe opened her eyes, she was in a hospital bed. Her head pounded like a snare drum.

"Ms. Harrington," a doctor said. "Do you know where you are?"

"Charlotte."

"What day is it?"

Zoe narrowed her eyes. "Umm, I'm not sure. How long did that bastard keep me in that warehouse? A day? A few hours?"

"How's your head."

"Throbbing. I'm hurting."

"Well," he said as he checked her vitals, "that's to be expected. I'm giving you an antibiotic to make sure the wound on your face doesn't get infected."

Zoe lifted her hand to her cheek and cringed, thinking about Joe's knife. She wanted to know if he was dead, wanted to know if the bastard was burning in hell where he belonged. Glancing past the doctor, she saw Carver sleeping in the corner. "How long has he been here?" she asked the doctor.

"Your husband has been here since you were admitted."

"That's not my husband," Zoe said. Her declaration seemed to wake Carver.

"Okay," the doctor said. "Should I have him removed?"

The door opened before Zoe could reply, and Zach walked in. "Zoe? Are you all right?" He pressed past the doctor and grabbed his sister's hand.

"How is Chante?"

"She's fine. Worried about you and trying to get the doctors to let her out of her room to come see you."

"And the baby?"

"He's fine."

"He?"

Zach smiled, then looked up at the doctor. "I'm sorry, am I interrupting another examination?"

Zoe snickered, imagining that Chante's doctor had kicked him out of her room.

"We just finished up," the doctor said. "Zoe, I'll be back in about an hour."

When the doctor left, Zach turned to Carver. "What in the hell are you doing here?"

"I'm here to make sure Zoe's all right," Carver replied.

"Look what looking after her got her." Zach narrowed his eyes at him. "Why don't you get out?"

"Zach," Zoe said. "Please, I don't need this right now."

"Yeah, Zach, she needs her rest," Carver said. Zoe locked eyes with him.

"But you can leave," she said. "Your case is over and you handled your duties. Feel free to go back to Washington now."

Zach folded his arms across his chest and nodded.

"Zoe, we need to talk about this," Carver said as he rose from the chair. "You know this was more than a case to me."

"My sister-in-law is lying in a hospital bed because of you. I think you should get out before I throw your ass out. You've done enough *for* my family."

Carver gave Zoe a fleeting look, but she turned her head away from him—hiding her tears. How could she believe anything that he told her, when this whole thing was based on a lie?

How could she believe that Carver loved her, when she knew that he'd only been trying to keep her from being murdered? Carver had succeeded in his quest, so now he could move on to his next case. Zoe turned around as she watched him walk out the door. Had she just been another case to him?

She released a deep breath and turned back to her brother. "I want to be alone."

"Zoe, you did the right thing telling him to leave. He—"

"Zachary! I want to be alone." She closed her eyes tightly and waited until she heard the door close. Then Zoe let her tears flow freely.

Carver wasn't surprised to see his Shadow Team waiting for him in the hospital's family room.

"How is she?" Raymond asked.

"She's going to be fine. Possibly a concussion."

Sarah took note of Carver's tight face. "She kicked you out, huh?"

Carver nodded. "Guys, thank you for coming together to help me with this case."

"That's what we do," Kenneth said. "You'd do it for us as well."

He nodded, then sighed. "And we got Singletary."

"He's on life support. Your girl put a beatdown on him."

"Too bad she didn't kill him," Carver muttered as he paced back and forth. "We'd better get out of here."

"We?" Ray asked.

Carver didn't say another word as he walked out the door. The Shadows followed him, no one sure what to say.

"Guess we better get back to DC and write up some reports," Kenneth said, breaking the silence among them. "The Charlotte agents are going to take Lewis into federal custody and handle things from here."

"Back to our corners," Sarah said with a sigh. "It was fun while it lasted."

Raymond stopped walking and looked at Carver. "Was it worth it?"

"Don't start this shit," Carver snapped. "She's alive."

Raymond shook his head. "Alive, but she kicked you out—right? You keep risking everything for these women and in the end, you wind up back at square one. You're not Captain—"

Carver wanted to punch his friend in the face, but he couldn't help but hear a bit of truth in his words. He also knew Raymond was still harboring a grudge toward women because the love of his life disappeared without a reason or even a Dear John note.

But he couldn't think about Raymond and his feelings right now. He needed to get Zoe back into his life, and if that meant giving her time to be alone for a little while, he'd do it.

Zoe opened her eyes when she heard the door open. Two men in black suits walked in and stood at the foot of her bed. She pushed a button to lift the head of the bed so that she could look into their faces. "Who are you people?" she asked.

"Ms. Harrington, I'm Agent Simon Baker from the Charlotte field office. Are you up to answering some questions about what happened?"

She looked at the other man, who hadn't said a word. "I need to see some identification and I want my lawyer present. However, being that she's in a hospital bed down that hall, that's not going to happen. So, get the hell out of here."

"Why the hostility?" Simon asked.

"You're going to have to excuse me, I almost died today because the FBI decided to lie to me. I have nothing else to say."

The other man cleared his throat. "Ma'am, what Agents Banks and Smallwood did was to save your life."

"Get out of my room."

"Just FYI," Simon said as he and his partner headed for the door, "Joseph Singletary died about twenty minutes ago."

"May his soul burn in hell." Zoe pressed the button for the nurse as the FBI agents left. She had to find out when she was going to be released from the hospital because she needed to be alone.

* * *

Carver pulled up to Charlotte Douglas International Airport with every intention of flying back to Washington, DC, and giving Zoe a little time to get her head together. But when he started to return the rental car he'd been driving, Carver changed his mind. He didn't plan to end up bitter and disgusted like Raymond. And he wasn't going to allow the woman he loved to just move on without him.

Zoe might never understand what he did and how he went about things. But she was going to know that he loved her, and he wasn't giving up on her again.

Making a U-turn at the return counter, he headed back to the hospital.

Chapter 32

Zach climbed into Chante's hospital bed and drew his wife into his arms. "Zach," she said with a smile on her lips. "You're not going to smother me like this when we get home, are you?"

"Woman, I might not let you out of my sight for the rest of your life."

"Oh, Lord."

"Oh, Lord, nothing. Do you know how scared I was when I got that ransom note? Then you and my sister went missing. Zoe's going to be lucky if I don't lock her in the basement."

"Like she would go for that. Are you sure she's all right? I really want to see her."

"You need to rest and let the doctor monitor the baby. If anything . . ." Zach's voice trailed off and he held his wife a little tighter. "Zoe's going to be fine. All she has to do is stay away from that stupid ass Carver Banks and her life will be so much better."

"Stay out of your sister's love life," Chante said, then yawned.

"No. It's not like she's ever stayed out of mine. You know she ran a background check on you."

"After the last woman you married, I can't say that I blame her." Chante dropped her hand to her belly.

"Are you all right?"

"Yes. It's just a habit. When I feel the baby, it makes me realize what I have to live for. She kept me fighting while I was in there with those men."

Zach kissed her cheek. "If I could get my hands on those—"

"Zach, it's over. The last thing we need is more violence. Let's just work on putting our lives back together."

"I know. But, baby, I was so scared and . . ."

"Let's not talk about it right now," she said. Chante reached up and stroked his cheek. Zach kissed her palm. A few minutes later, Chante fell asleep for the first time in eighteen hours, and she felt safe.

Zoe decided that she was going to get out of the bed alone. Maybe if she showed the nurses and her doctor that she was more mobile, they would let her go home in the morning. Granted, she'd been in the hospital less than twenty-four hours and the doctor was monitoring her concussion, but she was restless and she wanted to see her sister-in-law to make sure she was all right.

As soon as she got out of the bed, the room felt as if it were spinning. Right before she hit the floor, she felt strong arms lift her. She focused her eyes on her savior, expecting to see her brother.

"Carver?"

"Why are you out of bed by yourself?"

"What are you doing here? I could've sworn you went back to Washington."

"Started to, but aren't you glad I didn't?"

"At this point, if you can get me to the bathroom, I'd be very thankful." Zoe expelled a deep breath and tried to pretend that she wasn't happy to have his arms around her.

Carver helped her into the bathroom and waited outside while she handled her business. Zoe sat there for a moment, wondering if she should continue being angry with him or if she should let him know about the agents who had come to see her.

Maybe I should trust what Daddy said, she thought as she opened the door. Seeing Carver standing there ready to help her melted her anger and brought tears to her eyes.

"You all right?" he asked as he took her into his arms.

"No, I'm not. Carver, I know you were trying to help me and you wanted to keep me safe from the danger I put myself in. We could've worked together on this and kept my family out of it."

"I know I messed up, and I'm sorry, but I know you wouldn't have listened to me if I'd come to your office and said you were in danger."

She nodded as he helped her into her bed. "That's probably true. But when we were in Santa Fe, you couldn't tell me? That man in the hotel who tried to shoot me, that was because of Singletary, wasn't it?"

Carver nodded and told her about Wendy and her double cross. He revealed that he hadn't wanted to believe that Wendy was working with Singletary, but when things started adding up, showing that she was, he decided that he had to keep Zoe safe and made her his priority.

Then Smallwood's death made him realize that he was right about Wendy and Singletary working together. "No matter what I would've done, we could've ended up right here, just like this."

Zoe stroked his cheek. "I'm sorry I told you to get out of here when I really wanted you to stay."

"I'm here, baby, and I'm not going anywhere."

Zoe sighed. "Two FBI agents came into my room earlier and they said I owe you my life."

"Well, I knew what I was getting into and why I was doing it. You don't owe me anything. Zoe, I meant it when I said I love you."

"I know, and I love you, too. This whole thing has been a nightmare and I just didn't know what to do."

"Here's what we're going to do. We're going to get through all of this together. Lewis is probably going to spend the rest of his life in prison."

"Probably? If he doesn't, then the system is fraudulent because no other asshole deserves life in prison more than he does. He could've killed Chante and her baby."

"But he didn't. And he's facing federal charges."

Carver took a deep breath and clasped Zoe's hand. "Did he hurt you?"

"What are you really asking me?"

"Did he . . ." Carver's voice trailed off.

"Hell no! But do you know if he harmed Chante?"

"No, from what I've been told, but she did say he creeped her out talking about his ex."

"Where is he now?" Zoe asked as she shifted in her bed.

"Locked up in the Mecklenburg County Jail."

Zoe rolled her eyes and sighed. "And Singletary is dead."

Carver glanced at the bandage on the side of Zoe's face. "He did that to your face?"

She nodded. "Sadistic bastard. I really wanted to kill him, and I've never been that angry before. It was like something inside me snapped." Tears poured down her cheeks and Carver held her tighter.

"You were justified in everything you did," he said. "Both of them wanted to kill you and you had to survive."

Zoe sighed and leaned against his chest. "Thank you for coming back."

"I'm not going anywhere until I know you're all right. If I have to stay with you forever, I'm down with that, too."

Zoe drifted off to sleep with a smile on her face. Forever with Carver didn't seem like a bad deal at all.

* * *

Zach eased out of Chante's bed as his wife slept soundly. He needed to check on his sister. Zach said a silent prayer as he walked down the hall and thanked God for saving the women in his life. Losing either of them would've killed him.

Zach stopped at the door of Zoe's room and gritted his teeth when he saw Carver holding her. "This son of a bitch," he muttered. Opening the door, Zach willed himself not to start muttering curse words at Carver. "Well, this is unexpected and cozy."

Zoe woke up abruptly and shook her head. "Zach, don't come in here and start a fight."

"You guys need a minute?" Carver asked. Zoe touched his elbow.

"Don't go," she said, then turned to her brother. "How is Chante?"

"Resting," Zach said. "How are you?"

Zoe nodded and smiled. "I'm good. Ready to go home."

"You have no idea what it means to be observed for twenty-four hours, do you?" Zach asked. "My head is still hurting, so I know yours is, too."

Zach and Zoe rubbed their foreheads at the same time. Carver chuckled. "Never saw the twin thing up close and personal," he said.

"If you hurt my sister, you're going to get more than you bargained for, understand?"

Carver shook his head. "I'm not in the business of hurting the woman I love."

"I'm holding you to that," Zach said. "If you don't take care of my sister, you will regret it."

"Still threatening a federal agent, huh?" Zoe quipped.

"Still not a threat. It's a promise." Zach smiled as he left the room and figured that he could possibly give Carver a chance. He could tell from the way that man looked at Zoe that he really did love her.

Chapter 33

Three months later

Lewis walked into the federal court building in Charlotte. He couldn't believe he was going to face trial because of Zoe Harrington—again.

This time, though, he was going to make her wish she'd never met him. He thought Singletary would've been able to get her, but that loser was all talk. No wonder he trafficked young girls; he couldn't handle adults. How in the hell did he let Zoe get the best of him?

"Martinez, let's go," said the deputy.

"My lawyer said I was supposed to get a change of clothes." Lewis folded his arms across his chest.

"You can change in the courtroom. Let's move," he said as he crossed over to Lewis and grabbed his arm.

"Don't touch me!" Lewis snatched his arm away. "I know my rights. I used to be a cop."

"You're a long way from that now, aren't you?" The deputy prodded Lewis to move. He shuffled along and wanted nothing more than to chop that deputy in the throat. But he'd wait until the time was right. Lewis wasn't going to prison, and he was going to get his revenge on Zoe Harrington.

Zoe sat in the prosecutor's office, waiting. She'd been in Charlotte for three months, healing and prepping for Lewis's trial. Zach and Carver had been annoying and helpful.

Zach wouldn't allow Zoe to sleep more than three hours a night without waking her up to make sure she wasn't suffering from any concussion effects. Then Carver would come over to make sure she was eating, and if he wasn't satisfied with her meal choices, he'd go out and buy her what he thought she should eat. Usually something with bacon on it, and Zoe hated bacon.

"You know what," Chante said one day after Zoe passed her grilled-cheese-and-bacon sandwich to her. "I think you are the luckiest woman in the world."

"And why would you say something that crazy? Between your husband and Carver, I'm the most annoyed woman in the world."

"You need to stop acting like you don't light up when Carver walks in this house." Chante poured a little more coffee in Zoe's already full mug.

"I know you can't have coffee, but, Chante, I would like to sleep this week."

"Come on, you know I live vicariously through your mug. And don't try and change the subject, Zoe. You're just as stubborn as your brother."

"You really hurt my feelings, Chante," Zoe quipped. "Carver is great, but—"

"No buts. That man loves you. I mean, he takes Zuch's abuse to be by your side."

"My brother is trying to end up in a federal prison the way he threatens that man." Zoe laughed and checked her watch. "And it's about time they come in here to harass me."

"Ooh, your niece just kicked because she wants Carver to be her uncle."

"You're doing the most, sis. Carver isn't the uncle type."

As if they'd heard Zoe, Carver and Zach walked into the house and, surprisingly, they were laughing and talking as if they liked each other. Chante nudged her sister-in-law and rose to her feet.

"Thanks for the sandwich, Zoe. I'm going to get some juice."

Carver turned to Zoe. "You're not eating?" He sat down beside her and Zach followed Chante into the kitchen. "Are you feeling all right?"

Zoe stretched her hands above her head. "Yes, I'm fine. A little nervous about this trial, though. The defense is going to be brutal."

"Zoe, you don't have a thing to worry about." Carver kissed her on the cheek. "But you still need to eat."

"What I need is to get out of this house. Clearly, I don't have a concussion anymore, and you and Zach are driving me crazy. I need to work out, go for a run and burn off pent-up energy."

"Then let's get out of here while your brother isn't watching. I know how you can burn off that energy, babe."

"I bet you do." She leaned in and kissed him, slow and deep.

"Aww, damn it," Zach said. *"This is not what I want to see when I walk in my living room."*

"Then turn around and walk away," Zoe said. Carver rose to his feet and offered his hand to Zoe.

"Come on. We're going to take this party somewhere else." Carver winked at Zoe and they dashed out of the house.

"Ms. Harrington, sorry to keep you waiting."

Zoe's head snapped up and locked eyes with the federal prosecutor. "It's all right. So, are we going to go over my testimony now?"

"Well," the prosecutor began as she crossed over to her desk and took a seat. "Lewis is thinking about a plea deal."

"What?"

"I got a call from his attorney a few hours ago. We're working on the details."

"You're joking, right?" Zoe shook her head. "If he's not spending the rest of his life in prison, then why are we here?"

"I like to let victims know what's going on with their cases. Zoe, Lewis could help us dismantle Singletary's organization."

"Singletary is dead. You kill the head, the snake dies."

"What about those girls in other parts of the country who don't know the head has been killed? There are other pimps out there that are a part of this organization."

"And you think Lewis has insight into this?" Zoe laughed. "The only thing those two had in common was me."

"Zoe, we're trying to save girls who have been abused

and raped. It would've been a lot easier if Singletary could speak."

"Are you blaming me for this deal with the devil?" Zoe rose to her feet, knocking her chair backward. "I had to save my life because you guys didn't do your fucking job!"

"Calm down."

"Whatever," Zoe said as she headed for the door. When she exited the office and saw Carver standing in the hall waiting for her, she calmed down instantly. Flinging herself into his arms, she felt comforted as soon as he wrapped his strong arms around her.

"What's wrong?"

"Lewis is copping a plea and that *woman* acts as if it's my fault."

Carver frowned. "What the hell? How is this your fault?"

"Maybe I should've let Singletary cut me up."

"Hell no, you shouldn't have, and if they are too weak to put . . . Let's go, Zoe."

"No. I want to sit in the courtroom and watch this son of a bitch say he's guilty."

"Sure that's what you want to do?"

She nodded. "How did things go in DC?"

Carver didn't want to tell Zoe about his meeting with the FBI. The Shadow Team had been called into headquarters.

As the four of them walked into the J. Edgar Hoover Building, Sarah sighed.

"This should be fun."

"It's not like we haven't been here before," Raymond said.

Kenneth nodded. "Yeah, remember the Thomas affair."

Carver chuckled. "Think we're going to get more than a slap on the wrist this time." And Carver knew that he was going to have to fall on his sword. He needed to take responsibility for bringing the team together to protect Zoe.

Raymond noted his silence and turned to him. "Carver, don't go in here and do something stupid."

"What are you talking about?"

Sarah and Kenneth exchanged knowing looks. "If you think we're going to let you go down alone, you're wrong," Sarah said.

"I'm thinking about retirement," Carver replied.

Raymond rolled his eyes. "Guess you have an engagement ring in your pocket to take to Zoe, huh?"

"Simmer down," Sarah said as they stepped on the elevator. "If you're giving up your job for Zoe, then you better make sure she's worth it."

"She's worth it," Carver said with a smile. The elevator doors opened and they headed for the office of the Special Agent in Charge. His secretary led them to a conference room where their boss sat at the head of a long table.

"Here we go," Raymond said as they took their seats around the table.

"Look at the four of you. Squad goals, right?" Timothy Clarke said as he folded his arms across his chest. "And they say our intelligence agencies don't work together."

"We're not millennials," Raymond said.

"If you-all keep hacking our servers, you won't be

government agents either." He slammed his hand on the table.

"That's my bad," Sarah said.

Clarke raised his eyebrow at her. "You expect me to believe you did all of this by yourself?"

Sarah shrugged her shoulders. "You're going to believe what you want to believe. I just want to know why we're all gathered here today."

He narrowed his eyes at the group. "We're here today because you four decided to go rogue and ruin a case that we'd been working for two years. Our main suspect in two murders and a sex trafficking ring is dead instead of being taken into custody and giving us the information we need to save his victims."

"So, Zoe Harrington was supposed to die so that you could question Singletary?" Carver snapped.

"Did I say that? But you took away our right to question him and his right to a fair trial."

"He tried to kill that woman. She defended herself."

"Agent Banks, you are too personally involved with this case to even be speaking to me right now."

Carver leaned back in his chair. "Then why in the hell am I here? Why are we all here?"

"Good question," Kenneth said. "Because in two weeks, we got more on Singletary than you got in two years. You should be thanking us."

Clarke laughed and shook his head. "You people have some fucking nerve. You're lucky to still have a job. Things are about to change around here and you-all are going to fall in line. Smallwood may have been okay with insubordination and the like, but I don't play that shit."

"Are we done here or not?" Carver asked, his voice nearly a growl.

"Not until I say so."

Sarah tapped Carver's shoulder. "Chill out."

"Here's the deal," Clarke said. "This little crew is disbanded. I know that you-all have been working together on cases. That's it. The end. Stay in your corner. If I hear about any covert operations involving any one of you, all of you are fired."

"How about you stop taking out how you feel about me on my friends?" Carver said. "You want me gone, grow some balls and fire me."

Raymond groaned and shook his head. Kenneth palmed his face and turned away from Clarke.

"Well, Banks, if you want to tender your resignation— go right ahead."

"How about I just retire?" Carver rose to his feet, opened his jacket, and dropped an envelope on the table. "I'm out."

"What is this?" Clarke said as he stood. "Banks . . ."

"I've put in my papers for retirement. So, like I said, I'm out." Carver pointed to his friends. "They had nothing to do with this botched investigation. You want to talk about rogue agents. What about the people who are and have been on Singletary's payroll for years? Wendy wasn't the only one, and you're going to have to find them. On your own." Slamming out of the office, Carver knew he was going to stand by Zoe, no matter what.

"Carver," Zoe said, snapping her fingers in front of his face. "What's going on?"

"Was just thinking about that meeting. I retired today."

"What?"

He nodded. "After all that's happened, I can't continue

to work for the Bureau. I know there are other people who were working for Singletary, and I'm not going to take the risk that I might have one of them on my team and—"

"You didn't do this for me, did you?"

Carver stroked her cheek. "So what if I did."

"You're crazy," she said.

"I'm crazy in love with you, Zoe." His eyes fell on the faint scar on her cheek. "I wasn't there when you needed me, and that's never going to happen again."

"I love you, Carver."

He leaned in and captured her lips in a hot kiss. Zoe melted against his massive chest as his hands roamed her back. Pulling away from him, Zoe smiled.

"Kiss me like that again and we're not going to make it into the courtroom."

Carver smirked at his woman. "You say that as if it's a bad thing."

"Come on, horn dog," she quipped as she took his hand.

Chapter 34

Lewis walked into the courtroom, knowing that he was going to have one shot to escape. His guard had stopped to talk to another deputy after he led Lewis to the defense table. Lewis noticed the guard had been distracted when they walked into the courtroom. But he hadn't uncuffed him yet.

Sighing, he urged himself to be patient. Once his hands were free, he just needed to be fast enough to get the gun, fire off a shot, and get out of the courtroom. Lewis figured if he grabbed a civilian on his way out, he would have a chance to make it out of the building alive. He wasn't going to prison, especially not over Zoe Harrington.

"That bitch," he muttered.

"You say something?" the guard asked.

"No, sir. These cuffs are just a little tight." He held up his hands and wiggled them.

"Give me a second," the guard said, and walked over to another deputy. Lewis gritted his teeth, wanting to bang his fist against the table. But he knew he needed to remain calm. A few seconds later, the deputy walked over to him and unlocked the handcuffs.

"Thanks." Lewis smiled at the deputy and noticed where the man kept his gun—on his right hip. When his attorney approached the table, the deputy moved to his left. Once again, Lewis was all smiles because the gun was in reach.

"All right, Lewis," his lawyer began. "We're just going to enter your plea and see if we can get you released on bail. Now, that's probably not going to happen."

Lewis nodded. Bail didn't mean anything to him because he was going to get out of this courthouse for free.

"Is everything all right?"

"Yeah, I'm fine." Lewis started coughing and leaned forward as if he was having stomach pains.

"Guard," the lawyer exclaimed. When the guard walked over to the table, Lewis bent over deeper so that he was closer to the gun. As the deputy tried to help, Lewis grabbed the gun and shot the deputy in the stomach. Horrified screams filled the courtroom. Lewis pointed the gun at his lawyer. "Move!"

She held her hands up and shifted out of his way. Lewis faced the two guards who were moving in his direction. "I will kill everything in here," Lewis exclaimed. He fired another shot, in the air this time. The guards stopped moving and Lewis backed out of the courtroom.

Once he made it to the hallway, Lewis saw Zoe and Carver heading in his direction. Lewis turned around and pointed the gun at Zoe. "This day just keeps getting better. Bitch, get over here!"

"Put the gun down, Lewis. You're not going to make it out of here alive," Zoe said as she held her hands up.

"Neither are you!" Lewis pulled the trigger and in a flash, Carver threw himself in front of Zoe, taking a bullet in the shoulder and falling to the ground. Lewis started to run. Zoe launched herself into him, knocking Lewis to the ground. She wrestled the gun out of his hand, then punched him in the face until two deputies pulled her off him. Zoe kicked at Lewis as two other deputies handcuffed him.

"You son of a bitch. I hope I get the chance to flip the switch when they electrocute your ass!" Zoe pulled away from the deputies and rushed to Carver's side. The sight of his blood on the white tile floor made her knees weak.

"Ma'am," a deputy said, "step aside, we have to get to him."

"Please," Zoe murmured as she touched Carver's cheek. "Don't leave me."

Chapter 35

Carver's mind was in the war zone. He'd taken fire, but how was his squad? He tried to sit up, but a hand across his chest forced him to stay on his back.

"Mr. Banks, we're heading to Carolinas Medical Center. You've been shot and lost quite a bit of blood."

He felt a soft hand squeeze his and he opened his eyes. Seeing Zoe by his side, Carver's mind snapped to the present. The worry lines on her face and her red-rimmed eyes broke his heart. He tried to open his mouth, but something stopped him from talking. Carver tried to reach up and pull the tube from his mouth, but another hand stopped him.

"Sir, we're going to have to strap you down if you keep trying to pull your tubes out."

He blinked, then focused on Zoe as she stroked his forehead. "Calm down. Please, let them help you."

Carver nodded, then closed his eyes, and instead of darkness, he saw a white light.

* * *

"Crashing! He's crashing!" the lead EMT exclaimed.

"No, no!" Zoe screamed. "Please, God, don't let him die." Another EMT pushed Zoe aside and started life-saving procedures on Carver. It hit Zoe like Thor's mythological hammer that she was watching Carver die. The EMTs broke out the electronic paddle to start his heart again. Her mind raced, replaying all of the mean things she'd said to him, every moment when she'd downplayed her feelings just to save face. Wasted moments that she could never get back, and now he was . . .

"We have a heartbeat."

Zoe closed her eyes and silently thanked God and her dad. "Is he going to make it?" she asked one of the EMTs.

"It's going to be up to him and what the doctors do at the hospital, ma'am. But your husband seems like a fighter."

Zoe took a deep breath. "He is a fighter and I'm going to be right by his side."

Once the ambulance arrived at the hospital, Zoe pulled out her cell phone and called Zach.

"What's up, Zoe?" he asked when he answered the phone.

"Zach, Carver's been shot. We're at the hospital right now and I'm scared. He might not make it."

"What happened?"

She told him about the scene at the courthouse with Lewis and how Carver threw himself in front of her and took the bullet that was meant for her.

"I'll be there in fifteen minutes," Zach said.

Zoe hadn't realized that she was sobbing until a

nurse walked outside and tapped her on the shoulder. "Ma'am, do you need some help?"

Zoe shook her head and walked inside. She headed to the admitting desk. "Where's Carver Banks been taken?"

The woman typed in his name. "He's in surgery. Are you family?"

Zoe nodded.

"You can wait over here, and when the doctors have any information, I'll let them know where to find you."

Zoe shivered as she walked over to the waiting room. She sat down for about five seconds; then she started pacing back and forth. She didn't know how much time had passed when she felt herself being drawn into a pair of strong arms.

"Zach," she murmured as she hugged her brother.

He took her face into his hands. "Are you all right?"

She shook her head. "He's in surgery and . . ."

"Come on, let's sit down. I know how you get in situations like this. Have you eaten anything?"

"I don't give a damn about food right now," she exclaimed. Zach nodded and walked her over to a row of chairs.

"Understand that, sis, but you're also in a state of shock. If you don't take care of yourself, how are you going to be there for Banks?"

Zoe took a deep breath and sat down. Zach held his sister's hand. "You know, it's okay to be scared."

She leaned her head on his shoulder. "We keep putting the people we love in danger."

"Actually, that's all on you," Zach quipped. Zoe shot him a cold look. "Okay, too soon. Listen, sis. I know you've been in dangerous situations that you've never talked about. I know you've kept your heart intact because you didn't want to be sitting here feeling like this. Zoe, you're not Wonder Woman, and that's okay. You love Carver and God knows he loves you. But y'all have dangerous jobs."

"Did you just say *y'all*?"

"I'm trying to be deep and insightful. All you got from this was the fact that I said y'all?"

Zoe smiled for the first time in hours. "Zach, I do love him and I wasted so much time trying to pretend that I didn't. What if I don't have another chance?" Tears dripped from her eyes and Zach pulled her closer to his chest.

"You're going to have another chance."

"You don't know that."

"Yes, I do. I know everything."

Zoe playfully punched him in the chest. "Jerk."

Carver opened his eyes and looked around the room for one face. Zoe. Had she left? Was he dead?

"Mr. Banks?"

He looked up and took note of the young face staring back at him. Was his doctor Doogie Howser?

"Yeah?" he croaked.

"Good to see you awake. I'm not even going to ask you how you feel because I'm sure you're in pain. The surgery went well and we were able to remove the bullet. We also had to give you a few blood transfusions. But we're expecting a full recovery."

Carver nodded. "Zoe."

"The young lady in the waiting room, I assume. Because she's very adamant about seeing you, I'm going to send her in shortly."

"I love her. Need to let her know that I'm going to be fine."

The doctor smiled. "I'll get her now." As the doctor walked out of the room, a wave of pain washed over him and he closed his eyes. He didn't hear the door open, but he smelled her perfume.

"Zoe," he said.

She stroked his forehead. "Carver, don't you ever do anything that stupid again." He opened his eyes and watched her wipe her eyes.

"How long have you been crying? Baby, I've been shot before, and I'd rather take that bullet and this pain so that I can look into your eyes."

"I'm sorry."

"Sorry?"

"For wasting time, for allowing my heart and soul to finally open up when I saw you bleeding on the floor. Carver, we—"

"Have a future together, and when this pain goes away, I'm going to show you how great our life together is going to be. But there is one thing," he said, then coughed. Zoe poured him a cup of water.

"What's that?"

"I need a job. You know a PI who might want to hire me?"

She shook her head. "Nope."

"Come on, Zoe, you know I can't live in New York without work."

Her mouth dropped open. "You're moving to New York?"

Carver closed one eye. "Only if you get me a pain-killer right now." Zoe pressed the call button and held his hand until the nurse arrived.

When Carver took his pills and drifted off to sleep, Zoe slipped out of the room. She went to the waiting area to find her brother, but he wasn't there. Then she headed for the cafeteria.

"Hey," she said when she saw Zach loading a plate with food. "You can go home and get some real food. Carver's out of the woods."

"That's great."

Zoe nodded. "I'm going to stay here with him."

"As you should," Zach said as he took his food to the register.

"Yeah, but you don't have to."

"I'm not. Chante wants this mystery hospital meal."

"Why?"

"Because she's seven months pregnant and eats weird shit."

Zoe laughed and looked at the food Zach had stacked on the plate. "Good luck to her and my niece."

"We're having a boy."

"How do you know?"

"Because God wouldn't do that to me. I can't handle having a daughter who would be a lot like her aunt."

"You say that as if it is a bad thing."

Zach pulled his wallet out and paid for the food, then shot Zoe a frosty look. "Whatever." He leaned in and kissed her on the cheek. "You know I love you, but you were a hotheaded little girl who grew up to be a nuclear warhead. Can't lock my child in the basement until she's thirty."

"You didn't do that to me."

"Only because Dad thought it was a bad idea."

Zoe picked up a ketchup packet and tossed it at her brother. "You make me sick."

"Yeah, yeah. Love you, too. Call me if you need anything," Zach said, heading for the exit. Zoe glanced at her watch and headed back to Carver's room. She needed to be by his side today and forever.

Epilogue

Zoe wasn't sure if she was more nervous than her brother as she listened to Chante's screams. Carver chuckled as Zoe paced back and forth.

"What's funny?" she asked, stopping midstride.

"You acting like the expectant father. Sit down, babe."

Zoe sighed and took a seat beside her man. "This is torture."

"Imagine being the one giving birth."

She closed her eyes. "I think adoption will be our option."

"Oh, really?"

"Yes. But I'm putting the cart before the horse. We have to work out our other partnership." She patted his knee. "I'm not changing the name of my firm."

"Nope. We need a new name," he said. "And we should move out of the Bronx."

"But I love the Bronx. What if I go with the name change and we stay in the Boogie Down?"

"So you know how to compromise?"

Zoe narrowed her eyes at him. "You're evil."

"Now, now, that's not what you said last night."

"Keep messing with me and it will be a long time before you have a night like last night." Carver leaned into Zoe and kissed her slow and deep. Zoe moaned as she pressed her hand against his chest.

"That's just wrong," she replied.

Chante screamed one last time, then the sound of a baby crying filled the air. Zach stuck his head out the door with a huge smile on his face.

"It's a boy."

"Aww," Zoe said. "Please tell me my nephew looks like me."

Zach grinned like a Cheshire cat. "Maybe."

"Zach!" Chante exclaimed. "We're not done."

Zoe's eyes widened with excitement. She turned to Carver. "Okay. Zach had twins, we're good."

Carver shook his head. "I'm not sure it works like that, but I'll take it."

She wrapped her arms around his waist. "Carver, I love you. Thanks for settling in with me and my crazy family."

"You know, I was serious about the name change for our agency," he said as he pulled Zoe into his arms. "Banks Investigations."

Zoe narrowed her eyes at him. "How are you trying to take over my business like that?"

"Not taking over anything, beautiful. We're going to have the same name." Carver reached into his pants pocket and pulled out a black velvet box. "Marry me, Zoe."

"What?" She stopped in her tracks, looking up at him with her mouth agape.

"I don't think I can be any clearer. I can't see myself living my life without you in it."

"Carver."

"You're the only woman I've ever taken a bullet for, and I'd take a hundred more."

"Carver."

"Say yes."

"I will if you shut up!" Zoe smiled and stroked his cheek. "I love you, and the rest of my life, I want to be Mrs. Carver Banks."

Carver pulled her into his arms and kissed her with a hot passion that made her knees weak. Pulling back from him, Zoe looked into his eyes—her heart filled with love and devotion—and knew that for the rest of her life, she was going to spend it with the man she loved.

Carver slipped the ring on her finger, then kissed her hand. "So, Banks Investigations. That way when we have the twins, we can rename it Banks and Sons Investigations."

Zoe shook her head. "We are so having twin girls," she quipped.

"Let's get started practicing then," Carver said with a wink.

ALSO AVAILABLE

I Heard a Rumor

Chante Britt is nobody's fool—and she's
definitely not standing by her cheating ex-fiancé
and current mayoral candidate, Robert
Montgomery. Too bad he chose to tell the media
otherwise. To escape an onslaught of prying
reporters, Chante flees to her grandmother's
South Carolina beach house.
But when she meets Zach Harrington, she may be
out of the frying pan and into the fire. The man is
arrogant, way too forward—and way too sexy…

Enjoy the following excerpt from
I Heard a Rumor. . .

Chapter 1

Chante Britt filled her favorite pink and green mug with Ethiopian blend coffee, which had been a gift from her best friend and sorority sister, Liza Palmer-Franklin. *That girl knows coffee,* she thought as she inhaled the fragrant aroma. She almost didn't want to pour the creamer into the coffee. She took a sip and realized that it was perfect black. Reaching for the remote to the small TV set mounted over the stove, she sighed as she turned it on. This was her morning routine, and it was getting on her last damned nerve.

Chante was bored, mad, and tired of the purgatory her life had become since her suspension from the law firm she'd worked for, Myrick, Lawson and Walker.

She had been considered a distraction, according to managing partner Taiwon Myrick, because of her relationship with former senatorial candidate Robert Montgomery, who lost his bid for a senate seat after she and Liza exposed the fact that he was a liar and paid for sex with prostitutes. When Chante and Robert had been dating, she'd lobbied for her firm to support his candidacy, which they did. Taiwon liked Robert's pro-business stance on several issues and threw a lot of money his way, even after Chante had expressed her doubts. But as always, Taiwon chose not to listen to Chante. Over the last two years at Myrick, Lawson and Walker, Chante had been working herself ragged to become a partner. But she'd been constantly looked over—despite the fact that she'd delivered over a million dollars in billable hours, boasted a ninety percent winning ratio, and brought in more than a third of the firm's new clients.

Taiwon was from the old-school law community and just didn't believe a woman could be a partner with the firm his family had started. Though she couldn't point to any provable sexual discrimination, she knew it was her gender that had been holding her back at the firm.

So when Jackson Franklin won the senate seat after it was revealed that Robert had been involved with a hooker during the campaign, Taiwon had been happy to blame her for the firm being mixed up in the controversy.

Bastard, she thought as she lifted her head and saw Robert's image on the screen. Chante started to turn the set off. But curiosity got the best of her, so she unmuted the set to hear what he had to say.

"Wonder if he's still out there buying sex," she muttered, then took another sip of her coffee.

"I'm standing here today because of grace and forgiveness," Robert said into the camera. "I made mistakes in my quest to become senator, and I hurt a lot of people. But those people, including the love of my life, have forgiven me. And their forgiveness has given me the courage to throw my hat into the ring to be Charlotte's next mayor."

Chante spit her coffee across the kitchen. Was this man daft? Who was going to support him to be mayor, let alone the city's dogcatcher? And who was the love of his life? Poor woman. She didn't know what kind of mess she was going to be in as the pretend love of Robert Montgomery's life. The only person Robert loved was Robert.

She reached into her robe pocket and pulled out her smartphone to text Liza.

"Last night, as I talked to my future wife, Chante Britt . . ."

"What the . . . !" Chante exclaimed. Forget texting Liza; she was going to have to call her friend and hope that she wasn't interrupting anything going on between the newlyweds.

"This is Liza," her friend said when she answered the phone.

"Robert has lost what's left of his blasted mind," Chante exclaimed. "This fool just . . ."

"Calm down," Liza said. "I'm sure no one is taking him seriously."

Chante's phone beeped. "Hold on, I have another call coming in," she said. Clicking the TALK button, she answered the unknown number.

"Chante Britt."

"Ms. Britt, this is Coleen Jackson. I'm a reporter with News Fourteen. I wanted to ask you a few questions about Robert Montgomery."

Click.

"People were paying attention, Liza," Chante said. "That was a reporter."

"Oh my goodness. While you had me on hold, they showed a clip of his announcement on the news here. He really called you the love of his life. Have you two been seeing each other?"

"Hell no! I haven't spoken to that man since two days after the election, and that was last year."

"I can't believe him. What does he think is going to come of this, and why would he think that you would agree to being . . . ?"

Chante's phone beeped again. She looked at the incoming caller's number and saw it was another unknown one. "I'm guessing that's another reporter," Chante said. "What am I going to do?"

"Issue a statement. I'll write one for you to e-mail to all the media outlets in Charlotte. This will blow over. Let's just take control of the narrative and wait for the next news cycle. Everyone will move on to the next thing and you can get on with your life."

"Thank you, Liza. I'm going to go for my run now."

"Has your suspension been lifted yet?"

"No. And I'm guessing this latest stunt from this asshole is going to give them another reason to keep the suspension going."

"I still think you should start your own firm," Liza said. "You don't need them."

Chante sighed. Part of her agreed with her friend, but there was something about the security of becoming a partner at an established law firm. Maybe she wanted that partnership so that she could prove her mother wrong.

Allison Louise Cooper-Britt had grown up as the ultimate southern belle. She attended South Carolina State College for one reason—to obtain her MRS. That happened when she'd met and married Eli Britt. He'd been the crucial catch: wealthy family, right complexion, and a member of all the right organizations.

When Chante had graduated from college and decided that law school was more important than a husband and a family, her mother wished her failure. Thankfully, her smarts and a few of her father's connections had given her the blueprint for success.

She and her grandmother, Elsie Mae, had a much better relationship than she had with Allison. Probably because they were so much alike. Elsie Mae Cooper had carved out her niche in Charleston, South Carolina, by selling her handwoven baskets to tourists. In 1972, she began adding unique pieces of South Carolina culture to the baskets and opened a gift shop on Folly Beach. Elsie's Gifts and Goodies became one of the beach's most popular tourist attractions.

When Elsie Mae retired from running the shop, she sold it to a historical group while keeping a forty-nine percent stake in the company. The residual income allowed her to travel the world at will. Of course, Allison thought her widowed mother should spend her time in a rocking chair on the front porch. That was not Elsie Mae's style at all, and her world traveling and adventure seeking became a bone of contention between mother and daughter.

Chante wished she had her grandmother's fearless nature. She knew for a fact that Elsie Mae would've started her own firm without giving it a second thought.

Her grandmother wouldn't have taken all the grief she'd subjected herself to for that partnership. Part of her knew she'd be fine if she struck out on her own. She had a huge client base, and she was a proven winner who'd made millions for her clients. But she was afraid. Afraid that if she failed, her mother would lord it over her, just as she'd always done with the fact that she isn't married.

As if that was the only thing she was supposed to do with her life. Rolling her eyes at the ringing phone, Chante hit the IGNORE button on another unknown call, then shut the phone off.

When she received Liza's e-mail with her statement and a list of contacts to send it to, Chante was ready to pound the pavement and Robert's face. Lacing up her sneakers and popping her ear buds in, she opened the front door and was blinded by flashbulbs.

"What the . . . ?"

"Ms. Britt, have you forgiven Robert?"

"When is the wedding?"

"Will Senator and Mrs. Franklin be there? Have all of you kissed and made up after such an ugly election cycle?"

"Get off my doorstep!" Chante exclaimed. When the members of the media took a step back, she thought they had heeded her demand. That was until she saw Robert walking her way. Narrowing her eyes at him, all she could think was that the media had just saved his life.

"Chante, darling, I didn't mean for this to happen," he said with a huge smile on his face. She watched in abject horror as he walked up the steps and stood in her face.

"You son of a . . ."

Robert wrapped his arms around her and attempted to kiss her. Chante kneed him in the family jewels before storming into her house and slamming the door. All she could hope was that the cameras had caught every minute of it. One thing was for certain: she wasn't going to stick around to be harassed by the media or Robert freaking Montgomery!

Zach Harrington downed a mojito as if it was a glass of water while he sat on the white shores of Folly Beach. It felt good to be an anonymous man in the crowd. In South Carolina, he was just a man on the beach. Back in New York, he was the ex-husband of the "Harlem Madame." Just thinking about the moniker the media had given his ex-wife made him cringe. And the circus! Cameras followed him around the city and camped out at his office building and his temporary home.

He couldn't even meet with the Crawfords about a tract of land they wanted to purchase in Manhattan for new office space. He was sure that Solomon and Richmond Crawford wouldn't want to be photographed outside his office after what their family had gone through in the media lately. Solomon and Richmond had discovered that their father, Elliot, had a son— Adrian Bryant—before his death. Adrian had taken the story to the media around the same time that Richmond had been arrested in Los Angeles for solicitation of sex.

Then there had been Richmond's messy divorce. The businessman in Zach knew that any partnership they'd enter into right now would be a disaster. And he hadn't told the Crawfords that he and Adrian had been friends long before the scandal broke.

Just thinking about the media circus and the money it was costing him made him crave something stronger than a sweet rum highball. When he'd filed for divorce from his wife, Natalie, he thought she'd been having an affair. He had no clue that she was running an escort service from their home on Long Island. It had taken three months for him to clear his name and prove to the district attorney that he didn't have anything to do with Natalie's illegal empire.

She'd been clearing about a million dollars a year. At least she was sleazy enough to hide the money in an account that had nothing to do with his business or their personal accounts. Shaking his head, Zach brought himself back to what was in front of him: a beautiful shoreline, women in barely there bikinis, and the blazing southern sun.

Digging his toes into the warm sand, Zach tugged at his Brooklyn Nets ball cap and grinned. For the next seven days or more, he was going to be anyone he wanted to be, without worrying about the glare of the New York media. Just as he was about to close his eyes, his cell phone vibrated in his pocket. Grabbing it, he smiled when he saw it was his assistant, Kia Clarke.

"What's up, Special K?"

"Your final divorce decree just arrived. You are officially unattached."

"Been unattached. I'm just glad the state has approved it," he said. "Have the reporters stopped calling yet?"

Kia sighed. "You haven't heard the latest?"

"I've been listening to ocean waves. Do I even want to know?"

"She claims there's a black book and you know where it is. We've had a few agents stop by the office, but I told them that without a warrant they couldn't come in. And three more clients have dropped us."

Zach muttered curses that caused a few people to give him the side eye. "Why does she keep tarnishing my name?"

"She doesn't want to let you go, and she isn't trying to go down without taking a lot of innocent people with her. I've never liked Ms. Shady Boots, and I told you that from the beginning."

"I wish I'd seen her true colors years ago," he said, then expelled a sigh.

"Tried to warn you, boss. But you were blinded by something else."

"Don't remind me. How's the baby?"

"Still baking. I'm two weeks overdue, and Dave is stressing me out. That's why I came into the office today."

"Please don't give birth in my office," he quipped. "I'm so happy for you and Dave. I wish I could be there to celebrate with you guys."

"Zach, I'm not mad at you for staying away and getting your head together. And why not have some fun while you're out there?"

"That's my plan. When I come back to New York, hopefully this news cycle will be over and I can get back to my business and spoiling my godson."

"Excuse you, I'm having a daughter. So, you better

get some of the southern girly-girl stuff while you're in Charleston."

"I'm bringing football helmets and shoulder pads," he said with a laugh.

"Anyway. Unless anything major happens, the next time you hear from me, I'll be calling with the news of your goddaughter's entrance into the world," Kia said.

When they said good-bye, Zach turned his phone off, leaned back in his lounge chair, and closed his eyes. The warmth of the sun did little to ease the chill he felt creeping up his spine. Even though he'd divorced his criminal wife and had had nothing to do with her sex peddling, his boutique real estate firm was suffering. A couple of clients had taken their business elsewhere, costing him fifteen million dollars. The loss hurt, but his company was strong—for now. If he kept losing the big clients, then he would be hurting, as well as his employees.

Part of him wanted to push Natalie into the Hudson River with a hundred pounds of weights attached to her Louboutins. But he was nonviolent, and he just planned to let everything blow over. He was going to have to diversify, and maybe he would find a great investment down south that would make up for his losses. Down here, he wouldn't be cast as the husband of the "Harlem Madame." He could create a southern branch of his business, buy some cheap land, and turn it into gold. After all, he knew his Midas touch was still intact. At least, he hoped so.

Groaning, Zach decided it was time for another drink and some more girl watching.